A Sahib's Daughter

Disclaimer

Published in the United States
By Tollymore Publishing

Edited by
First Editing

Cover design by Laura Harkness

ISBN-10: 0988865610
ISBN-13: 978-0-9888656-1-7

Website: www.ninaharkness.com

A Sahib's Daughter

Nina Harkness

TOLLYMORE PUBLISHING
2013

Dedication

In loving memory of my father,
Ashwani Wason

CONTENTS

Chapter 1
Sikkim and Darjeeling, 1933-1952

She had been warned but hadn't listened. There was no denying it. Prava had known deep down that he was not to be trusted.
But she went ahead just the same, giving rein to her desires in a
way she never had with Prem, seizing an opportunity that she knew
would never again present itself and indulging a passion that was
as wild as it was short-lived.

Prem had been utterly devastated and disbelieving, though
remaining her staunchest ally until her swelling belly made it
impossible for him to deny. Assuming Prava belonged to him, he'd
held back all those years, respecting her far too much to degrade
her with his lust, holding her, kissing her and containing his desire
till he thought he would explode.

Now she'd slept with another man, making it apparent that
she hadn't felt the same passion for him. He found he could say
nothing, he simply could not speak. He just left town with his hurt
and his love coiled up inside his heart. She must not have wanted
him, and the betrayal made a mockery of his loyalty and his absti-
nence. All he could do was take himself away from her, though
there was no escaping that hollow feeling in the pit of his stomach
that would sneak up on him insidiously, when least expected, a
pain that would grip his entrails. He learned to evade the attacks
by filling up every moment of his time. He started a tire business
just as automobiles were becoming popular. He made a name for
himself and became a philanthropist who supported worthwhile
causes.

What he didn't know and had no means of finding out was
that Prava missed him desperately and experienced the same kind

of pain in her stomach, a pain that had nothing to do with the child inside her. The Sikkimese community frowned on her indiscretion even more than her family did. It was whispered that she had slept with a Bihari. Some said it was a Bengali, a plains person with dark skin. But when Ramona was born, she had a milky complexion and almond eyes just like any other Sikkimese girl's. In fact, she was a beautiful child who matured into a woman of striking appearance with clearly defined features and black hair that swung over her shoulders.

The family rallied and supported Prava in whatever way they were able. When Ramona was ready for school, Prava took her to Kalimpong where nobody knew them. She made it known that Ramona's father had died in a car accident when she was a baby. Ramona attended St. Bernard's Homes, an orphanage and school known for its high quality of education, run by Welsh missionaries. She learned to speak impeccable English, with encouragement from Prava who wanted her daughter to become a school teacher.

Prava worked in a curio shop frequented by tourists visiting the picturesque Himalayan town. After Ramona graduated from school, she went to teachers training college and was offered a job in Darjeeling at St. Jude's, a co-ed boarding school on the outskirts of town. They packed their bags again and moved to Darjeeling where they rented a cottage on a hillside beneath the Mall.

St. Jude's was an impressive school built on extensive grounds. Constructed of gray stone, its turrets, arches, gothic balconies and cloisters reminded Ramona of the medieval castles she'd read about in books. It faced the snow-capped Kanchenjunga Mountains that captured hues of pink, purple and orange at sunrise and sunset. Its students and teachers were an international mixture of nationalities from America, Australia, New Zealand and England.

On the first day of school, the teachers were required to attend a meeting in the dining room. There was a sumptuous tea of butterfly cupcakes, sugar frosted cookies and chicken sandwiches.

"I'm going to get fat working here," whispered Ramona to Sandra Williams, an Anglo-Indian teacher who had grown up in the school. Her mother, Cheryl Williams, was the senior girls' matron.

Sandra giggled. "Impossible! You have a lovely figure. You could never get fat." She looked enviously at Ramona's trim form in her faded blue dress. A male staff member joined them, his plate laden with food. He was stocky with smiling eyes and wore mustard-colored trousers, a brown shirt and a loud green tie.

"Hey, ladies," he spoke with a British accent, "I'm Reverend Bob Jameson. I'm very happy to meet you. And you are?"

"I'm Ramona Roy. This is Sandra Williams."

"Well, I would sure like to get to know you ladies better." He turned to address Ramona. "Maybe we could go into town sometime and catch a movie?"

"Yes, maybe," said Ramona. "That would be lovely. Could you please excuse me for a second? I need to speak to the principal."

Later on, she said to Sandra, the only other woman who seemed to be her age, "I don't find these foreign men attractive at all! Do you?"

Sandra giggled and blushed, "I don't know. Not him, anyway. But he certainly seems to like you."

Bob Jameson and every man in the room! Ramona's hair hung sleek and glossy down her back. Her arched eyebrows framed delicate slanting eyes. Her unassuming air of confidence added to her appeal, with all her emotions transparent and clearly expressed.

Most of the teachers lived in the school, had round-the-clock responsibilities and were devoted to the children in their care. There were missionaries intent on saving souls, women whose hearts had been broken, spinsters incapable of, or not interested in, finding husbands, or widows with nowhere else to go. The school took them all in, giving them jobs where they were respected and appreciated and a place where they felt they belonged.

Ramona didn't yet know what she wanted out of life. As the school term progressed, she felt she had too much happening in her personal life to devote all her energy to activities and students the way the other teachers did. She was glad she lived in town and had a place to escape.

3

Their new home was a stone cottage down a winding laneway so close to the Mall that they could hear the clip clop of the ponies ridden by tourists and school children. A mossy wall ran across the front of the compound, which was entered through a narrow gate kept fastened with a twist of wire. Sweet honeysuckle curled over the gray stone, trailing golden fingers to the pathway below. Wild roses climbed and tumbled over themselves in fragrant disarray, crawling up the cottage's walls and smothering its gable windows. An aged pomegranate tree had woven its knotty branches into the verandah railings as though wishing to enter the house. Its fruit would drop and split open, the red, seedy juices spilling out like gaping wounds.

The cottage had its own unique scent, a combination of mansion floor polish and pine logs. In the wood floored kitchen were a small cooking stove and an open-shelved dresser stacked with dishes, pots and pans. The drawing room was furnished with green wicker chairs with faded embroidered pillows and a bookshelf that housed Prava's collection of women's magazines that went back ten years or more, "Woman," "Woman's Own" and "Homes & Gardens," each magazine reflecting the fashion and trends of its' time. A creaky staircase led to the two bedrooms, each furnished with two narrow wooden beds, a chest of drawers and ancient mirrors.

Prava settled happily into their new life. Her small inheritance and savings, combined with Ramona's salary meant that she didn't have to work any longer. Sometimes, Ramona didn't think this was necessarily a good thing. Prava now had too much time on her hands. She sat on the verandah most of the day, shelling peas, knitting or sipping cups of tea in the sunshine. She quickly made friends with the neighbors and kept a vigilant eye on all their comings and goings.

Her habit of thrift grew worse as she grew older, and her insecurity made her more miserly by the day. She had always deprived Ramona of anything pretty or frivolous so when Ramona received her first paycheck, she rushed to a fabric store in Chowrasta with Sandra in tow. Like any other young woman, she craved pretty things, above all fashionable dresses like the ones other teachers at St. Jude's wore. With Sandra's help, she decided on a length of cotton fabric and called for the tailor who worked at the store. He showed them a selection of Sears's catalogs from which Ramona picked the style of dress he would create. He took her measurements and promised to have it ready in a week. Next they raided the stores for a pair of white shoes and a stylish handbag to match her new dress.

It was a wonderful feeling to have money, especially money she'd earned herself.

"Let's go to Glenarys for tea," she said grandly. Glenarys was one of the fanciest restaurants in town, with real linen table cloths and heavy silverware. Panoramic vistas of the Kanchenjunga Mountains could be seen from the rear. The front windows offered views of the street, perfect for people watching, and were preferred by the locals. The girls opted for a seat by a front window and ordered a pot of tea with lemon tarts and cream horns. The restaurant was empty except for a group of rowdy British men at a table near the bar.

"And what brings you pretty ladies to town?" one of them asked. He was short and balding and had the loudest laugh of them all.

"We're teachers from St. Jude's," said Sandra. "This is my friend Ramona. I'm Sandra."

"Delighted to make your acquaintance," he said. "I'm Geoffrey. Geoffrey Peters. These are my friends Jack, Jimmy and Tony, all tea planters."

Ramona was unaccustomed to the company of young men, especially British ones, and regarded them somewhat disdainfully. They had loud honking voices, laughing raucously among themselves in sharp contrast to their polite, well-mannered attitude to the ladies.

One of the men said something in a low voice to Geoffrey. He turned to Sandra and said,

"Are you, by any chance, going to the dance at the Gymkhana Club next week?"

"We don't know anything about it," replied Sandra, who'd heard about the dances at the Gymkhana Club and always wanted to go to one.

5

"We'd like to invite you ladies along. It's next Saturday at five o'clock. Do come!"

The other men, starved for female company, joined in.

"Please."

"Say yes."

"Save us a dance!"

Ramona and Sandra looked at each other questioningly. Finally, Ramona said,

"Okay. Yes, we'd love to."

"Smashing."

"Cheers!"

"Wonderful," the men chimed in.

Sandra blushed and Ramona giggled. When they called for their bill after the planters left, they were told that the British Sahibs had already settled it.

"Well, look at that!" cried Sandra. "Maybe now you'll start liking foreign men."

"Perhaps, though I don't care for any of them, nice as they are. I'm glad I'll have something to wear," said Ramona, thinking of her new outfit. "I hope my dress will be ready in time."

The following Friday she went excitedly to the tailor. It was Good Friday, a school holiday, the day before the dance. She was told the dress was ready and went into the little dressing room to try it on, hoping it wouldn't need to be altered. It was white cotton with red polka dots, caught in at the waist with a red sash. It had a full skirt that came to just below her knees. Ramona looked at herself in the full-length mirrors, a luxury she didn't have in her bedroom at home. She had never had anything so pretty in all her life. It was a little tight around the bust and more revealing than she'd intended, but there was no denying that it flattered her curves and emphasized her slim waist.

Elated, she rushed home, eager to show the dress to her mother. She put it on, took the shoes out of the box and put them on over her new ankle socks. She regarded her reflection appraisingly in the tiny mirror, placing the white handbag over her elbow. Perfect! She ran out of the room to find Prava.

"Ama, where are you?" she called, twirling her full skirts. Prava appeared in the drawing room and could scarcely recognize the young lady standing before her. Suddenly, all the years of accumulated bitterness and insecurity seemed to surge out of her.

"What's the meaning of this!" she demanded. "Have I scrimped and saved all these years for you to rush out and spend money the minute my back is turned?"

Ramona feared for a moment that her mother was going to strike her.

"Ama, I paid for it all myself," she pleaded, tearfully. "And I give you more than half of what I make."

But Prava was too enraged to hear anything Ramona was saying.

"How dare you do this? Take those things off at once and stay in your room!"

"I will go to my room," cried Ramona, "but only because I choose to be alone. I'm twenty-one years old, and you can't treat me this way."

She stormed upstairs; all pleasure in her new possessions evaporated. This arrangement was not going to work if her mother didn't relinquish some measure of control over her. Perhaps she was too old to be living with her and she should move to the school with Sandra and the other single women. Become like one of them, an old spinster with no life to call her own.

Was this what she really wanted, she wondered? Or was she simply living the life her mother had planned for her? She took off the dress, the shoes and socks and put them away. Prava would not be pleased to see her go to the dance in her new clothes. But she had nothing else to wear, and there was no question of not going. Sandra was looking forward to it too much. And so, until now, had she.

Saturday afternoon finally came around, and Prava couldn't pretend that she didn't know about the dance. Ramona had told her all about it, only omitting mention of the dress in order to surprise her with it. Already regretting her outburst, Prava had been slightly subdued ever since. Apologizing to her daughter would not have crossed her mind, but she tried to make up for it in her own way, cooking Ramona's favorite chicken korma for lunch and offering to do her ironing.

When Sandra arrived in the afternoon with a small overnight bag, Prava took off to a neighbor's house for tea.

"Just leave the front door unlocked when you leave," she told her daughter.

Ramona was relieved not to have to flaunt the dress in front of her. She and Sandra were going to get ready for the dance together. They dressed excitedly in Ramona's room. Sandra had dozens of dresses to choose from, more dresses than occasions in which to wear them. She had chosen yellow chiffon for this Easter Saturday. Her cheeks were flushed in anticipation of the adventure ahead. She secretly hoped Geoffrey would be there, not daring to confide her thoughts to Ramona who did not like British men.

"It's not too revealing, I hope?" asked Ramona, surveying herself anxiously in the tiny mirror.

"Of course not! And you know it looks good on you. Just don't wear it to school, or you'll drive Bob Jameson crazy."

"I won't, don't you worry! Though it was meant to be something I could wear to school."

The Gymkhana Club was only a few minutes away, approached by a winding roadway above the Mall. It was a fresh spring evening with just a hint of chill in the air. A setting sun cast golden rays through branches of the fir and spruce trees that proliferated in the town. Land Rovers and jeeps from the tea plantations drove up noisily, dilapidated taxi cabs deposited local residents and chauffeured automobiles honked and squawked their way past lower caliber vehicles. Many, like the girls, arrived on foot. Suddenly nervous and apprehensive, they hung back wondering if they were crazy to have come.

"Let's go home!" whispered Sandra, "I don't see any of the men." No sooner had she spoken than Geoffrey appeared, smiling broadly.

"You made it!" he said, proud to have pulled off the feat of bringing two pretty young ladies to the dance. "I'm so glad. You both look wonderful!"

He looked different, too, in a dark gray jacket and blue tie. His sparse hair was slicked back neatly, and he wore nice leather shoes, Sandra noted. She liked men who wore good shoes.

He guided the ladies into the crowded ballroom. Ramona gazed in wonder at the revelation of light and movement and sound that engulfed her. Elegant dancers circled the floor to music from a small orchestra on the stage. Ornate mirrors on the walls reflected and multiplied the light from crystal chandeliers more magnificent than anything she'd ever seen. A gilt edged ceiling of celestial blue shimmered above the myriad colors below.

They joined the other men seated around a table, and were handed glasses of punch, something Ramona had never tasted before. It was icy and delicious and made her head spin. Suddenly they were dancing under the chandeliers, circling the room, becoming part of the sparkling reflections. When the music stopped, she walked back to the table, starry-eyed and flushed, and saw that there was someone walking towards her, a man with light brown hair and eyes, tall and somewhat gangly.

"My name is Charles Clarke," he said, holding out his hand and smiling into her eyes. "May I have this dance?"

She gazed up at him, dizzy from the punch, breathless from dancing and blinded by the light of the mirrors. She felt him take her hand and guide her on to the floor. His arm went around her, and they were dancing.

"Who are you?" he asked. "What's your name?"

She smiled up at him, for once not a trace of cynicism in her eyes.

"Just Ramona," she said. "I live close by, and teach at one of the local boarding schools."

"Well, just Ramona," he teased, "You are by far the most beautiful woman in the room."

Speechless and confused, she could think of nothing to say. When the song ended, he held her arm possessively, defying anyone to approach her and take her away from him. She was overwhelmed, mesmerized by his eyes and when the tempo slowed, the beating of his heart against hers. They danced until the music died and the orchestra left the stage.

"I would really like to see you again, just Ramona," Charles said.

"I'd like to see you too." She floated on a cloud to the celestial ceiling above.

And later, reflecting on what he'd said to her and their conversation, she wasn't quite sure it could have been possible, or that she'd heard right, but she had a faint memory of him saying to her, "If I don't marry you, I won't marry anyone!"

She found herself overcome with emotions that were unfamiliar yet exhilarating. She couldn't wait to see him again, to gaze into those eyes and feel his hands on her back.

"Well?" Sandra gave her a dig, "What's up? What are you smiling at? And who was that man you were dancing with all night?"

They had crept into Ramona's room as quietly as they could to avoid waking Prava.

Ramona brushed her hair vigorously. "I don't know the first thing about Charles Clarke, but I think I just met my future husband."

Sandra was speechless. Ramona was obviously more clueless than she'd realized. One dance with a man, and she wanted to marry him! If only life were that simple!

"You're so sweet and funny," she laughed, carefully folding her yellow dress.

"One minute you don't like Englishmen, and the next you're going to marry one! Are you going to see him again? Did he ask you out?"

Ramona looked at Sandra with surprise. "Of course, I'm going to see him again. Don't you believe me? He's the man I'm going to marry."

Sandra didn't know what to say. British Sahibs did not marry local women. It simply didn't happen. Her own mother could attest to that. And she, Sandra, was living proof of the outcome of such unions, belonging nowhere, with a mother exiled for sleeping with a Sahib. Certainly, they made promises and spoke fine words.

They gave a woman a great time, sometimes living with them for years and fathering several children. But when it was time to go home, they would simply return, never to be heard of again, leaving behind women whose lives were devastated. Sometimes, if he had a conscience, the Sahib would set the family up in a house and send them money. But more often than not, the woman would return to her family in disgrace, with her light-skin children and no prospect of ever marrying.

These children were regarded with curiosity their entire lives, especially if they were fair- haired or had fair skin, stigmas they couldn't shake off. Ramona was not oblivious to what went on, Sandra knew that much. The Anglo-Indians evolved from these alliances were commonplace and more sociably accepted since Independence in 1947. She knew Ramona didn't need a history lesson, perhaps more of a reality check. But she didn't have the heart to extinguish the light from her eyes just yet. And there was always a chance she would return to her senses the following day, once the effects of the punch had worn off.

But next morning, Ramona was still exuberant. She prattled excitedly to Prava over breakfast, describing every detail of the night before, leaving Sandra no option but to join in. She, too, had had a wonderful time. Geoffrey was going away for a few weeks but had promised to get in touch when he returned. Well, she wouldn't hold her breath. She'd heard that one before.

"And he's taking me out to lunch," she heard Ramona announce. "He's coming to pick me up at noon."

Sandra noted the intense disapproval of her mother; her emotions held in check no doubt because of her presence. Would she try to forbid the relationship, she wondered? Could she be that heartless, that obtuse?

Sandra left for church while Ramona floated upstairs to her room to dress. Prava went outside to pick mint leaves for chutney, her lips set in a tight line, a chill in her heart. Should she have been more open with Ramona? She had certainly schooled her severely, warning her against lustful strangers, hesitant of going into too much detail for fear of revealing her own past indiscretion. Now she feared alienating her daughter by disapproving of Charles, especially after her outburst over the new dress. Ramona would assume it was because she was still resentful about it.

Upstairs, Ramona started to wonder if she'd been imagining things the night before. Had he really meant that he wanted to marry her, or was it just a joke, something British people said in jest? And did she even want to marry him? Well, she certainly intended to find out.

Charles arrived on time dressed in navy trousers and a gray sweater and looking suddenly unfamiliar to her in daylight. He politely invited Prava to join them for lunch. She desisted, although pleased to be asked. Filled with misgivings, she told them to go and enjoy themselves. She took scant comfort in the knowledge she had instilled in Ramona that the worst thing that could happen to a girl was to become pregnant out of wedlock. She wanted a better life for her daughter than the single state she had suffered. No man had been willing to take her and her daughter on, not that she had ever sought one.

Ramona could scarcely dare to look at Charles now that she was confronted with the reality of him. She wore her old blue flowered dress and her new shoes. Her feet were aching from dancing the night before. She decided not to wear a cardigan, although there was a chill in the air because she didn't have one that quite matched.

"I hope you don't mind walking," he said. He was staying at the Planters Club, a short distance from her home.

"Not at all," said Ramona. "I walk all the time."

She was as striking as he remembered. Pretty wasn't the word for her. It felt good walking beside her. It had been more than six years since his breakup with Sarah. He'd been home once to visit his sister Pauline and had evaded her efforts at matchmaking. He didn't know what he wanted, but it wasn't the kind of woman he met in the drawing rooms of London: safe, predictable and much too domesticated for his wayward way of life. Not that he preferred to live alone. It was damned lonely on the tea estates but better alone than with the wrong woman.

12

Ramona was different. He recognized in her a quality he couldn't quite define, something he had waited for all his life. Like arriving in India and falling in love with it. When he looked into her eyes last night, it confirmed what he'd suspected when he'd first spotted her across the room. Now she met his gaze, and there were no more questions, just the answers he'd always been waiting for.

Could she have a clue what he was thinking, he wondered, as they walked in the crisp sunshine? Did she have any idea what an unconventional chap he was? There was a chance she just wanted a lunch date, a pleasant Sunday outing. All he had to offer her was a lonely life in tea. She was a teacher and had her whole career ahead of her. But when she turned and faced him, her emotions transparent across her face, he knew with certainty he had to have her, that she was destined to be his wife and that somehow the fates had ordained that he come to this far-off country to find her.

Two weeks after the dance at the Gymkhana Club, Sandra Williams was in the middle of teaching a math class when the peon arrived with a message for her scribbled by the school secretary. A Mr. Geoffrey Peters had telephoned. He wanted to take her to see "From Here to Eternity," showing that night at the Capital Theatre.

Chapter 2
India, England 1946

Charles disembarked from the *S.S. Adventurer* at the India Gate Dock in Bombay, little knowing that his status was about to change from Charles Clarke, Esq., of Hertfordshire, England, to that of a British Sahib with the power to issue orders, command respect and demand obedience from native Indians with no justification other than his white skin.

Around him, bewildered and sea-legged fellow passengers thronged the gangway, unsure whether to grab their hats, their belongings or the shaky handrail. People waiting on shore searched for loved ones, welcoming them with shrieks and embraces as they emerged. With apprehension, Charles scoured the melee of greeters, not knowing what to expect. At last, he spotted a placard with his name across it brandished by a man in a white chauffeur's uniform. At the sight of Charles, he smiled and raised his hand in a salute.

"Salaam, Sahib! Welcome to India!"

He explained that he would drive Charles to a hotel for the night and return in the morning to take him to the station where he would board the train to Calcutta.

They waited for his luggage, in stifling heat, amid the inevitable pandemonium caused by the arrival of passenger ships to the port. Frenzied porters in red tunics and black turbans appeared with the luggage they had collected from the cabins and were following passengers to their vehicles outside. Charles was amazed to see his cabin trunk appear beside him as if by magic. The trunk contained, among other necessities, his dinner jacket, walking boots, khaki pants, malaria tablets and solar topee hat, items considered necessary by his sister Pauline for the lengthy sea journey and his first weeks in India. The rest of his belongings were being freighted to him by the East India Shipping Company.

Once outside the docks, he was conveyed in a dilapidated Ford Austin through busy streets that teemed with people, vehicles and creatures of every size, color and description: automobiles with horns barking, tongas drawn by mangy horses, bicycles with their bells tinkling and rickshaws hauled by lithe-bodied men shouting at people to get out of their way.

Lining the streets he saw shops packed with exotic merchandise: brightly colored garments, brass statues, terra cotta urns and ivory figurines. Food stalls displayed pyramids of spices, bulging gunny sacks of grain, and baskets of fruits and vegetables that overflowed onto the footpath. He passed boulevards flanked by white colonnaded buildings, elaborate red brick mansions and ornate temples in eastern architectural styles. Rising above, as far as the eye could see, were minarets, ramparts and gilt-edged copper domes defining the city's skyline.

Charles stared spellbound out the window. He had no idea what adventures awaited, but his excitement and anticipation were a welcome respite from the months of heartache he'd recently endured. Sarah had married someone else. After all their years together, she had left him for Howard Russell. Charles had been about to propose to her but somehow, the time was never right, and he couldn't seem to summon up the words that would have bound her to him forever. While she was visiting her aunt in Surrey, he had even gone so far as to choose a ring, a sapphire with diamonds on either side. But she had returned to Hertfordshire a different woman, aloof and unapproachable. Finally, in her mother's drawing room, white-faced and trembling, she told him it was all over between them and that she was marrying someone else.

"Please don't be angry with me," she pleaded. "You know I'll miss you terribly."

It wasn't that she didn't love him. She just had her future to consider. She couldn't spend any more time waiting for him. And he had to admit it was true that they had made no promises to each other, except for what had been implied.

He later heard that Howard had a magnificent house in Hadley Wood. His father owned a printing company that would be passed down to him. It was already providing Sarah with the little luxuries that Charles couldn't possible afford on his salary as an insurance adjuster.

Sarah had been his best friend, besides the woman he assumed would be his wife. What had prevented him from taking the next step? How could he contemplate a future without her? He was certain she was feeling the same heartache. It was impossible that she did not. He missed their sojourns into London, their Sundays spent at Hyde Park Corner, the museums and their favorite tea shop near Regent's Park. He was lost without her. He felt confined in his tiny, terraced house in Friern Barnet which he shared with his sister, Pauline, and would walk disconsolately for hours in the hills surrounding Barnet or through dismal neighborhood streets.

He had light brown hair and eyes and, although tall and somewhat gangling, showed promise of becoming handsome as he matured, though he obviously wasn't handsome enough for Sarah.

Pauline felt unable to reach out and help her heartbroken brother. If he would only open up and express his feelings, she knew he would feel better. But he didn't know how to deal with his feeling of loss, and she just couldn't find the words to alleviate his distress.

He commuted daily to his insurance office at Kings Cross, waiting on the platform for trains that ran with endless regularity, rather like the pattern of his own humdrum life. He realized suddenly that marriage to Sarah would entail a life time of commuting just like this, with the added responsibility of her welfare. Was that how he really wanted to spend his life? Was it perhaps the real reason for his hesitating to propose?

Flipping through the classifieds in the *Guardian* on the train home one evening, he'd seen the advertisement for a tea planter's position in India. All that were required, it said, were patience, fortitude and the guts to withstand the difficult conditions there year after year. He felt a surging excitement as he read the words. India! He was fascinated by the idea of living in the colonies. He had always wanted to travel, explore and seek adventure…and here was the opportunity to do so, just when he most needed it!

He realized he had Pauline to consider. She shared the home they'd grown up in. Their mother died of pneumonia in 1936, ten years ago. After she died, their father took to going directly to the pub from his office in Highbury, returning home later and later, until one night he didn't come home at all. He vanished from their lives, and they never heard from him again, though on one occasion years later, Pauline thought she had spotted him at Oxford Street Station, drunk and shouting obscenities to a group of women.

Pauline was twenty-seven and seemed unlikely ever to marry. She had taken care of Charles who was only fourteen when their mother died, giving up her dreams of college. She now worked as a nurse at the Friern Barnet Mental Asylum close to their house. It was a dismal institution in a walled compound behind metal gates. People grew accustomed to the sight of "escapees" strolling along High Street in their dressing gowns, harmless inmates who returned in time for tea and a token reprimand from asylum staff.

Pauline was committed to her job and never complained about its unreasonable demands on her time and her goodwill. She had met a man named Sean Bartholomew, who was Irish and a chauffeur for a Jewish family in Hendon. He would sometimes pick her up in the family's shiny Rolls Royce, causing her to giggle and wonder what the neighbors were saying. There was a delicate balance to their friendship, which any hint of romance might have toppled. They were on easy terms that neither saw any reason to change.

On the day Sean left the family's employment, he purchased a navy blue Bentley automobile in order to pursue his dream of starting his own chauffeuring company. Brimming with excitement, he inveigled his way through the asylum gates in the limousine and drove up to the front door just as Pauline was finishing her shift. He asked the startled receptionist to tell Pauline that he had come to pick her up and to please look out the front window. Pauline laughed with embarrassment when she saw Sean standing beside the splendid car and waving to her. The inmates and staff got wind of what was happening and shouted and waved to Sean from the windows. With delight, they watched as he opened the car door for a blushing Pauline and whisked her away through the gates.

Charles arrived home from work one day to find the letter he had been waiting for. It was from the Dooars Tea Company. He ran upstairs to his bedroom and opened it filled with trepidation, scarcely able to take in its contents. They were offering him the job! He was the successful candidate! Pauline was downstairs cooking dinner. She was still in her scrubs, her hair pinned back. He didn't know how to break the news to her and wished he had confided in her sooner to prepare her for the shock.

"Who's the letter from, Charlie?" she asked, as he entered the kitchen, envelope in hand.

"It's about a job," he said, buttering a piece of bread apprehensively. "A job I applied for a while ago. I never thought I'd be successful."

"I didn't realize you were looking for a new job. Aren't you a dark horse! Where is it?"

"Well, the thing is, with breaking up with Sarah and everything; I thought it might be a good idea to get away for a bit. Then I saw this job in the paper and thought I'd give it a go, never really thinking...."

"Well, go on," she said, fascinated.

"The thing is... it's in India, in the tea plantations. Would you be very upset if I were to accept it and leave you?" He looked at her questioningly.

"India!" she cried. "Isn't that a surprise? I'm not sure...but, yes, of course, of course, you should accept. It's the kind of thing you've always wanted to do."

"You're sure now?"

"Course I am!" she said, not able to comprehend the magnitude of what he was suggesting. "Long as you let me come visit."

"Course, I will. I would love that. Thanks, Sis. I'm positive this is the right step for me."

And it was only a few weeks later that he boarded the *Adventurer* for the three-month voyage to Bombay. Now the battered Ford Austin was dashing headlong toward the Queen Victoria Hotel from where he would take the Great Peninsular Railway to Calcutta on the second leg of his journey to the tea plantation in the Dooars.

Chapter 3
Dooars, 1946

The remote region known as the Dooars was nestled in the foothills between the low-lying Ganges plain and the towering Himalayan Mountains on the northern border of India. With its undulating hillsides and summer rains, the conditions were perfect for the cultivation of tea, not perhaps with the high aroma of Darjeeling tea, but with a larger yield that compensated for any deficiency in flavor.

Although the newspaper advertisement and the executives in London who had interviewed Charles stipulated that the successful candidate required 'patience, fortitude and guts' to endure the difficult conditions year after year, there was compensation for the loneliness and seclusion of life on the tea estates. Pioneering planters saw no reason why they should not make themselves comfortable and enjoy what local benefits were available to them.

There was money to be made in tea, and planters were given every incentive to remain loyal. If they were dismissed, it was usually for insubordination or drink. Land was cheap and plentiful, labor even more so. They were housed in airy bungalows with expansive grounds and retinues of servants to maintain them. But the loneliness could be soul destroying and wasn't for the faint of heart. Suicide by planters unable to endure the isolation was not uncommon. The life called for a certain level of endurance. India demanded it, the isolated plantations even more so.

Charles woke to unfamiliar and unrelenting bird song from outside his window. He dozed on and off, exhausted from his travels. He vaguely recalled a bumpy ride on narrow roads in the dark the night before and the estate manager's driver taking him to his bungalow.

"Sahib e-sleep," he was instructed, in broken English. "Eat and e-sleep. Burra Sahib coming tomorrow."

He remembered a long soak in the tub, ridding himself of several days' soot and grime from the steam locomotive that had hissed and puffed its way across the vast country. His dinner of fish cakes, peas and mashed potatoes served by the night watchman was followed by a blissful night's sleep in a bed covered with a white mosquito net.

He saw that a tray had been placed on a wicker stool beside his bed and that someone was pouring him a cup of tea.

"Salaam, Sahib. Chai," said the man, saluting and placing the cup on the bedside table. Then he pulled the curtains open and left. A groggy Charles sipped the tea, which was strong and delicious.

"Probably freshly manufactured as well as freshly brewed," he thought to himself. He wondered what time it was. Feeling a little more alert, he walked over to the French windows that opened into a verandah skirting the front of the house. He stepped outside the room and was greeted by the astonishing sight of a garden with an abundance of flowers, shrubs and trees that were strange and foreign to his untrained eye. Surrounding the compound, as far as he could see, were low bushes with satin leaves which he assumed were tea. Fragile trees interspersed between the bushes cast down puddles of shade.

In the distance, he saw forested hills with a canopy of blue sky above them. The only sounds were the birds that had woken him and the clatter of dishes in the house. He went inside to wash and dress and suddenly realized that he was starving.

As Charles emerged from his room, the bearer appeared again and pointed him to a wicker table on the verandah for a breakfast of porridge, scrambled eggs and toast. Just as he was finishing his breakfast, Charles heard the sound of a vehicle approaching. One of the gardeners opened the gate, and the jeep he had ridden in the night before swept up the driveway scrunching on the gravel. A burly man with red hair jumped out and came up the steps.

"Hallo, hallo, hallo! Charles, welcome to Ranikot!"

They shook hands. Charles recognized by his accent that the man was a Scot.

"How d'you do? It's Greg, isn't it?"

"Greg Moorhead. Very pleased to meet you. I hope you found everything to your satisfaction. Do you have everything you need?"

"Absolutely," said Charles. "I had no idea what to expect, but it's been wonderful so far."

"Splendid," said Greg. "I'm relieved to hear that, to say the least! This place isn't everyone's cup of tea. Pardon the pun."

Charles offered him breakfast.

"Thank you, no, I've already eaten. Must get back to the factory. Are you up to it? Splendid. Don't forget your topee. The sun can be lethal."

"I'll try to find it. I'm still somewhat disorganized." He went to his room and rummaged for his hat. In a trail of dust, they set off in the jeep.

"Every tea plantation stretches for hundreds of acres, with a manager in charge, and one, maybe two assistants, the office staff, known as baboos, and a large labor force, sometimes in the thousands, to pick and process the tea," Greg shouted over the engine.

When they arrived at the factory, the first thing that struck Charles was the aroma of fresh tea. Greg explained that raw green leaf delivered from the plantation was laid out on racks in tractors, ready to be fermented, rolled and dried. The manufacturing process transformed the leaf into coarse, black grain, rich and pungent, as it came off the drying belts. The tea would be boxed in plywood chests and shipped to auction houses in Calcutta and London.

Charles was shown his office, a tiny room off a narrow corridor. In it was a desk piled with files, a wooden chair and an ancient filing cabinet. Everything was covered with a film of tea dust. A small window overlooked the dingy flowerbeds outside. The room was humble and basic, but to Charles, remembering the fourth-floor cubicle in London where he used to spend his days, it was heaven.

23

"Sorry, there's a lot of paperwork waiting for you, but not all of it's urgent," said Greg. "And paperwork is only a small part of your job. The majority of your time will be spent on the estate, checking the machinery and making sure things are completed on time. You'll drive the jeep when I'm not using it."

"I'll have to learn how," said Charles. "I didn't have a car in England."

"Not a problem, old chap," said Greg. "We'll have you running around in no time at all."

This was getting better and better! He didn't have to spend his days pushing paper any more. He would be outdoors exploring these wonderful surroundings.

His first real opportunity to explore his bungalow came at lunch time. Greg showed him a rickety bicycle he could use until he had learned to drive and bought his own vehicle. He pedaled the half mile or so to his house which was an elevated structure with white walls and a green corrugated tin roof. No sooner had he ascended the flight of steps than his bearer, as though reading his mind appeared with a chilled lime drink.

On either side of the living room were bedrooms with adjoining bathrooms. The rooms were adequately, if sparsely, furnished. In each bathroom was a claw-foot bath tub and ancient, vitreous china sinks. Hot water was supplied from a boiler in the outhouse kitchen. Charles noted that his trunk had been unpacked and his clothing neatly hung in the wardrobe. Would he ever have to do anything for himself? He had never been more pampered in his life!

Both bedrooms and the living room opened to the front verandah where Charles guessed he would be spending most of his time. The wicker dining table and chairs, on which his breakfast had been served that morning, was at one end and a pair of planters' chaise lounges, made of wicker and teak, at the other.

The kitchen was a short distance from the house. There he met the cook, who wore a threadbare vest and sarong and was sweating profusely in the heat given off by the Aga range. Apart from a dilapidated sink and a small, mesh cupboard, there was little else in the room. Food was stored in the pantry at the back of the house, which was just as well, given the intense heat of the kitchen.

Lunch was an Indian curry, a dish he had first tasted on the train. Fragrant and spicy, it had been served in metal bowls with a dollop of rice on the side. Here it was served in white porcelain china on the polished mahogany dining table. Charles communicated with the servants in nods, gestures and the occasional word, realizing that he would quickly have to learn Hindi.

After lunch, he pedaled back to the factory feeling the full force of the afternoon sun bearing down on him. He stopped, fascinated, to watch coolie women picking tea. They were dressed in gaudy costumes with blouses that revealed bare, brown midriffs and scrawny breasts. Their earrings, nose rings, bangles and anklets clinked and jingled as they moved. They swiftly and skillfully picked leaves off the tops of the bushes, chattering and singing as they worked.

He heard the cry of a child and saw in a shady clearing an improvised "crèche" where babies lay in wicker baskets. Small children scampered and played around them. His mind went back to the women in the office at Kings Cross. They, too, wore jewelry to work, although nothing nearly as flamboyant as these women were wearing. In London they were not permitted to sing and chatter as they worked and most certainly didn't have their babies and children close by.

In the afternoon Greg drove Charles around the plantation.

"We have a workforce of about twelve-hundred, so it's important to take charge and make a show of strength. Any sign of indecision is seen as weakness. Some workers are rather tough to deal with, and it is getting more difficult these days with laborers making increased demands. They're not as unsophisticated as they used to be, which the Dooars Tea Company is notoriously slow to recognize."

"Look between those trees." He pointed to a section of jungle. "A tiger was spotted there last week. Normally, they avoid humans as much as we avoid them, but occasionally they get hungry. And once you have a man-eater on your hands, you're in serious trouble."

"Are they protected in any way, the tigers, I mean?"

"Not nearly enough. They are widely hunted for their skins and for various medical remedies. It's the same with elephants. Such a tragedy! We used to have to carry a weapon any time we were in, or close to, the jungle, which is no longer the case. Do you have a gun?"

"I don't...yet," said Charles. "But I understand there are opportunities to hunt in these parts."

"Absolutely. We hunt wild boar and deer mostly, which are not endangered in any way, and also wood pigeon, pheasant and duck. If you're interested, you're welcome to join me on shikar. I have to warn you, though. It can be grueling out there in the jungle what with the heat and mosquitoes."

"Count me in," said Charles. "It's just one of the reasons I wanted to come to India."

"By the way, my wife asked if you would like to come to dinner tonight, nothing fancy, just a chance to become acquainted."

"Thanks very much. I'd be delighted," replied Charles.

"I'll send the driver to pick you up around seven. Casual dress is fine. We're pretty informal around here."

When he bicycled to his bungalow later that afternoon, he was served tea with hot buttered toast and jam. After tea, he realized that his bearer was asking him for money for provisions.

"Rupees, Sahib. Stores," said Jetha, his bearer. "Bazaar."

"Yes, of course," said Charles. He reached for his wallet. "How much?"

He had no idea of the value of money in this country or what it would cost to feed himself. He held out ten rupees. Jetha stared in disbelief, holding up his palm as if to stop him. Charles wondered if it was too little, until he saw Jetha hold up five fingers. Five rupees? He figured that was less than a shilling. What could one buy with a shilling? He had been wondering where his groceries came from and was planning to ask Greg about it later. He gestured that he would not be needing dinner that evening and went to his bedroom to bathe and change. He badly needed to cool off and freshen up after a day in the heat. He shaved and changed into khaki trousers and a white shirt hoping that this was the correct interpretation of "casual."

A thicket of lychee trees and a giant bougainvillea bush concealed the Burra Bungalow from the road. As Charles stepped out of the jeep Greg came down the steps to greet him.

"Good to see you. Welcome to our home away from home! This is my wife, Lorna. Darling, meet Charles."

Lorna stretched out her hand. Sophisticated and self-assured, her blond hair was impeccably styled. She wore red lipstick and a navy blue dress that showed off her white shoulders. She was probably in her mid-twenties and might have been prettier had it not been for her thin lips.

"Scotch okay for you?" asked Greg. "You don't mind if we sit outside for a bit?"

"Wonderful," replied Charles, who had never been much of a drinker except for the occasional glass of ale or lager at the Pig and Whistle in Barnet High Street.

"You have a beautiful home," he said, looking around appreciatively. He'd thought his bungalow was attractive, but this place was magnificent. The scent of roses wafted up from the garden beneath the verandah. Palm trees that bordered the expanse of lawn were silhouetted against a golden sky.

After cocktails, they went inside for dinner. They sat at one end of a long table served by bearers in white jackets and maroon caps, moving soundlessly in and out of the room. They were served tomato soup followed by an excellent chicken casserole and sherry trifle for dessert.

"This is delicious," said Charles, appreciatively. "Did your cook prepare it?"

"I have to admit that I seldom cook anymore," smiled Lorna. "Occasionally, I'll bake a cake or a batch of biscuits, but it's pretty hot back in the kitchen."

"I don't think I'll ever get used to being waited on," Charles said. "I'm afraid I shall become quite spoiled living here."

"You'd better believe it," said Greg. "When Memsahibs return to England after a lifetime in tea, they find themselves at a total loss without servants to do everything for them."

"It's even harder for the Sahibs having no one to give orders to after being in charge of a workforce of thousands," said Lorna. "I worry that Greg might have to resort to ordering me around." She laughed. "The only consolation is that planters usually retire with their fortunes made. It's easy to save money when there's so little to spend it on."

"And it would take a lot of money in Britain to replace the lifestyle we've been accustomed to," said Greg. "Don't forget that, darling," he teased his wife, "just enjoy it while you can."

Chapter 4
Dooars, 1959-1963

It was half past five. If the car didn't start soon, they would have to abandon the whole idea. They had risen before dawn to make the three-hour drive up the mountain to Darjeeling. A jeep could have made the same journey in less than three hours, but Charles was only an assistant manager and did not have access to the company jeep for personal business. In fact, many cars were able to make it in less than three hours. But the Clarke's gray Ford V8 was no ordinary car.

It was an unreliable and temperamental old guzzler, prone to over-heating and breaking down just when it was most inconvenient. Today, it wouldn't even start. Kala the Nepalese driver bent over the engine furiously, muttering something about the choke. Kala looked forward to their trips up the mountains. Usually, he didn't even have to drive as Charles preferred to drive himself and was only taken along because the car was so unreliable.

Once they arrived in Darjeeling, they would park on the street below the Planters Club. Kala would sit and gossip all day with the other planters' drivers. Charles would give him a rupee for his lunch. He would spend it on a hot meal of momos and soup followed by biris and betel hut from the paan shop tucked in the hillside beneath Keventers Cafe. Kala chewed paan constantly. Strong and bitter, it warmed his insides, staining his teeth a treacherous shade of red.

He gave the car a final crank while Charles pumped the accelerator. For a moment, they thought the engine had caught, but it only spluttered and died for what seemed like the hundredth time that morning. The sun had risen steadily, drying the dew on the lawn that sloped down to the bamboo thicket bordering the compound. Sparrows fluttered in the mango trees, Ramona's chickens squawked and fussed in the kitchen garden. In the distance, the wail of the electric siren summoned the plantation laborers to work, signaling that it was six o'clock.

Didi, the Nepalese ayah, was in the house with the baby. Ramona had spotted Ram, the pani wallah, arriving. He was disappointed to see the car in the driveway, having anticipated a quiet day with plenty of opportunity to play with his catapult. She remembered that the cook and the bearer had the day off. Was there even anything to eat in the fridge? They had been planning to stock up on provisions in Darjeeling.

In the back seat, Samira was asleep on the coats and sweaters that only emerged for these trips or on rare, chilly winter evenings. She would be bemused to find herself in the car when she woke up and not in Darjeeling as promised. She had been born at the Planters Nursing Home there four years ago, followed by Mark two years later. Warm and flushed, she was oblivious to the tempers beginning to fray. Ramona, not the most patient of people, and eager to escape the monotony of the tea garden, was struggling to control her temper.

By this time, two gardeners, assisted by Ram and Kala, with much ado and heated discussion, were pushing the car, which still refused to start. Finally, Charles emerged from the driver's seat mopping his brow and said to Ramona.

"Looks like we're not going to make it today. I'm sorry, darling. We'll have to give up the idea. Perhaps we can try again next week."

He knew how much she looked forward to these trips, not just because of Prava, but because it meant she could visit shops and restaurants and be among people.

Samira awoke dazzled by the sunlight and puzzled to find herself alone in the car. She stuck her head out of the window and shouted,

"Daddy, Daddy! Let me out!"

"I'm coming, darling," Charles laughed, lifting her out of the back seat. "Our silly old car wouldn't start today, so we'll have to go see Grandma another time. Let's go find Mummy."

They walked into the house, and Ramona reappeared on the verandah with Mark in her arms, looking hot and disheveled in her Darjeeling clothing.

"To think we sat in the car all that time scarcely daring to breathe," she said, indignantly.

"And look at us in these warm clothes," said Charles. "You have to see the funny side of it."

"Well, I might, but our bacon certainly won't," Ramona told him, "It's just eggs for breakfast, I'm afraid."

"Why don't we go for a whole weekend sometime soon?

"Don't make promises you can't keep," said Ramona. "I've got a better idea. How about getting a new car, one that actually goes?"

"What? And get rid of the Silly Old Car?" Charles bantered, using Samira's nickname for the Ford.

"Perhaps we could buy a proper car," suggested Ramona, smiling, "an Indian one that starts first time?"

"I agree," said Charles, sarcastically. "If we're quick and put our names down immediately, we could have a new car in as little as five years."

That was true. The waiting list for new vehicles was endless. Ramona groaned. "Perhaps the Silly Old Car isn't so bad after all."

"Perhaps not," agreed Charles. "All she needs is a little tender loving care."

Ramona stepped into the verandah where breakfast had been laid out on a yellow and white checkered tablecloth. In the garden below, Ramchand was watering the flowers, but his attention was elsewhere. She could hear sounds coming from the lawn on the other side of the house and wondered what was going on. She walked the length of the verandah to investigate and could scarcely believe her eyes. The children were running on the grass, shrieking with excitement, with three tiny animals in pursuit. They didn't look like puppies or kittens, she thought, and then she gasped. They were leopard cubs! She ran down the steps toward them.

Samira saw her and screamed, "Mummy, Mummy, come and see!"

Nina Harkness

The cubs were adorable, only a few days old, covered in downy fur and playful as kittens.

"Be careful, darling," she said to Mark, who was trying to lift one of them by its tail. "Where on earth did they come from?"

Just then she noticed an old Nepalese man crouched in the shade by the bungalow. He rose and saluted.

"Where did you get these animals?" she asked, in Nepalese. "Where have you come from?"

Before he could answer, Charles, home for breakfast, appeared.

"Why, Gurung, what are you doing here?" he spoke in Hindi, not having mastered Nepalese.

"Salaam, Sahib. I bring these to show your babas," Gurung said, in English. "I think they like." He had walked three miles to do this.

"That's very kind of you, but where did you find them?"

"The mother she die, Sahib. My friend find cubs. Mother shot in number six area, Sahib. She practically dead." Gurung was proud of his mastery of English, which he'd acquired during his days as a Gurkha in Burma.

"What the hell do you mean, 'practically dead'?" asked Charles in sudden panic. An injured leopard could limp around for days, striking terror in the villagers and putting lives in danger.

"Is she dead or isn't she?"

"Oh, yes, Sahib. She dead, practically dead. One day or two maybe." He held his nose to demonstrate.

"Thank heavens for that. The question is who shot her?"

He turned to Ramona who was as taken with the cubs as the children. "And what's going to happen to these little blighters?"

"Can we keep them, Daddy?" cried Samira. "Please?"

"I wish we could, sweetheart, but they grow into the most ferocious creatures. Let's get the camera, so you can show Rachel pictures of them when she comes this summer."

Ramona ran indoors to fetch the camera and a tip for Gurung. It was touching that he had come such a long way just to show the cubs to the children.

32

Meanwhile, Charles was heading toward the garage. The area of the plantation Gurung was referring to too close for comfort. He wanted to be certain the leopard was as dead as he claimed. The children posed for their pictures with Gurung and the cubs. They would be excited about this for weeks.

"I'd better go and check things out," Charles said to Ramona. "I'll be back for breakfast in a bit."

"Jetha!" he called up to the house. "Bring my gun! Hop in, Gurung."

The cubs were safely ensconced in a cloth bag on Gurung's lap.

"Good-bye, little leopards," said the children, sadly.

Gurung's faced glowed with excitement and a sense of importance. He had been photographed with the children by the Memsahib, she had given him a very generous tip, and now he was in the front seat of the Sahib's beautiful car, being driven by him through the estate for all to see!

In their excitement and concern for the cubs, the children could barely eat breakfast. Ramona spent the morning reassuring them that they would be looked after by the nice man and that the animals were not excessively sad over the death of their mother. In the end, Mark agreed that the cubs had seemed quite cheerful "and smiling."

Life on the plantations seemed to resist the development taking place elsewhere in the country. To Ramona, the news bulletins on the BBC World Service and All India Radio may as well have been from another planet. The rebirth since Independence was slow to permeate the remote plantations in the Dooars. The effects of self-rule were barely felt here. Now and then, violence broke out on the labor lines, and there was the occasional skirmish between laborers and management, even when management was increasingly represented by new Indian Sahibs. All of which created in Ramona feelings of despair. Ironically, the tea labor force, rebelling against taking orders from white Sahibs, was often just as affronted by orders from fellow Indians.

She was undecided about this new breed of Sahib. She sometimes resented the attitude of the young Indian planters, freshly graduated from St. Xavier's or St. Columbus, ready to defy old patterns of existence in what they considered one of India's backwaters. On the other hand, she was proud of their assertiveness and youthful determination, without which Independence would not have been possible.

And here she was married to a British Sahib, one of the remaining few, and mother to children who were both English and Indian. Samira had inherited Charles' color, his light brown hair and eyes and his pale skin, yet her features were Ramona's. Mark on the other hand, had Ramona's black hair, but his features were those of Charles. Ramona had often gazed at her babies in wonder, marveling that they could be hers, her beautiful children with names chosen by their grandmother.

She thought back to her whirlwind romance and courtship with Charles. Everyone had been skeptical of his intentions, especially her mother and Sandra, warning her to take it slow and be careful. But how could she be? The weekends when Charles came to visit couldn't come soon enough. They were crazy about each other.

"Marry me now!" he urged, unable to return to the solitary existence he'd led since he left home. He couldn't bear to be without her. But they had to wait till the end of the school year to marry in a small civil ceremony attended by Prava, Bob Jameson, Sandra, Geoffrey and Sandra's mother, Cheryl.

Ramona sighed as she wandered among the roses in the fragrant dusk. When summer came her amaryllis lilies, sweet sultans, oleanders and maidenhair fern would be battered by the heat and monsoon rains. There were days when she spoke to no one but the servants. The house was silent after the children left home, first Samira and then Mark. Life could be unbearable for women who couldn't adapt to the isolation, despite their efforts to recreate 'home' in the alien landscape.

Ramona had discovered a passion for her garden, to the delight and relief of Ramchand, the young gardener who regarded the landscaped acre as his personal property. Memsahibs would come and Memsahibs would go, but he, Ramchand, would remain, just as his uncle, Bijoy, did before him. This was the Chota Bungalow, and he knew it was only a matter of time before Charles was either promoted to Burra Sahib and the Burra Bungalow, or else transferred to another plantation. His biggest fear was that a Sahib or Memsahib would curtail his annual supply of seeds from Calcutta.

He had once visited the annual flower show at the club with his uncle to assist with the Burra Bungalow entries. He had never been more inspired or amazed by the sights he saw that day, displays of fruit and vegetables and fabulous flower arrangements! The scent of flowers and vegetables inside the club and in the tent outside was intoxicating. Beautiful Memsahibs arrived with strange wonderful bouquets, and little girls in colorful dresses made sweet posies that were entered in a contest of their own. He couldn't stop talking about the sights he'd seen. Ramchand's dream was to enter a flower show and win First Prize and a red medallion, or even be "Highly Commended."

When Ramona, not realizing any of this, showed an interest in his flower beds and vegetable patch, it awakened his dreams of glory. She ordered seeds for flowers and vegetables he'd never planted before, corn flowers, pansies, geraniums, Brussels sprouts and celery. She designed new flowers beds and asked Charles to let them have a second gardener. Life had never been better. Ramchand became Ramona's devoted slave.

In the golden twilight, Ramona saw the electric lights being switched on in the house and realized that Jetha had arrived for his evening shift. Charles would be home from the factory soon, and the best part of the day would begin. She heard the jeep arrive at the gate and ran over to meet Charles and Greg.

"Hello, Charles. Greg, how are you?"

"Just fine thanks, Ramona," said Greg. "And how much longer is it now?"

Ramona knew he was referring to the children's half-term holidays, knowing how she counted the hours until their return. . Rachel, his own daughter, was at boarding school in England, pining for her pony and the familiarity of Ranikot. Rachel's time with them during her summer holidays and occasionally at Christmas, was brief and precious.

"Two days, Greg. But it'll seem like two weeks," Ramona said.

"I must remember to send Raja for Sammy to ride while she's here. He could do with the exercise."

"Thanks so much. She'll be thrilled."

"Well, I'd best be off. By the way, Charles, don't, whatever you do, forget to ask the mechanics to take a look at the Sirocco tomorrow. We don't want her playing up with the superintendant coming next week."

"Will do," said Charles "Thanks for the lift."

He put his arm around Ramona as they stood and waved good-bye. Greg and Lorna Moorhead were from Aberdeen and had lived in Ranikot for seven years. Greg's 'Pukka Sahib' attitude and abrupt manner could sometimes cause offence, but after a few scotch and sodas he would mellow and entertain everyone with a seemingly endless supply of jokes. Lorna, the more conventional of the two, would be driven to despair. The couple had always been supportive of Charles and welcomed Ramona with open arms. Ramona and Lorna had become pregnant within months of each other.

"I could do with a hot bath," said Charles, as they walked toward the house. "What's for dinner, by the way?"

"Mutton cutlets with mint sauce. But dessert's a surprise."

Dessert was always a "secret" in the Clarke household, especially when the children were home. The cook was sworn to secrecy and took great delight in keeping Sammy and Mark in suspense over their favorite part of the meal.

"Oh, go on."

"Absolutely not. Actually, I can't even remember," said Ramona. "And before I forget, we're almost out of coal."

"Write me a chit."

"Do I have to?"

"Then don't blame me if I forget."

"How does Greg put up with you?"

"With difficulty, I imagine. Anyway, unlike you, he had no choice in the matter."

"Now you tell me."

They smiled at each other, very much in love.

Chapter 5
Dooars, 1964

"Mummy, wake up, Mummy." Mark stood patiently beside the side of the bed, clutching his toy monkey. Ramona stirred and woke to see Mark's anxious eyes and quivering lower lip.

"What is it, darling? Did the elephants wake you?" The trumpeting of elephants could often be heard from the jungle beyond the labor lines, loud and discordant and especially terrifying in the middle of the night.

He shook his head and she saw that he had taken his pajama bottoms off and realized that he had wet the bed again. She sighed, reaching over to pick him up and cuddling him to her. His body was cold and damp, and he clung to her for warmth. She decided to send for the doctor baboo in the morning even though it was Diwali. Her heart ached at having to send them to boarding school so young. When Samira first returned from school, she was tongue-tied and couldn't speak to either parent for two whole days, even though she had yearned for them and asked her matron every day if this was the day her mummy was coming to fetch her. She had buried her face in Ramona's arm, hungry for her comfort, but unable to say anything.

At school, they were each permitted one toy. Samira fell asleep sobbing each night, clutching Maryanne, her doll. When the ayahs smacked her for crying, she would bury her head in the pillow, so they wouldn't hear her sobs. The pain in her heart for her mother constricted her chest and sometimes wouldn't allow her to breathe. She was small for her age and taunted by the bigger, tougher girls. When they raced up the four flights of stairs to their dorm, she couldn't keep up with them and would cling to the banisters gasping for breath.

While Samira grew increasingly shy and withdrawn, Mark became more sensitive and vulnerable. His eyes would fill with tears at the slightest provocation, and he sucked his thumb to the bone. Ramona was driven to distraction. But there was no alternative short of home-schooling the children.

Samira came to her mother's bed for cuddles and morning tea and knew at once that Mark had had an "accident" when she found him there asleep. Charles had left for the factory. She leapt onto the bed on the other side of her mother.

"If I had three children, one of you would have to sit on top of me," smiled Ramona. She hugged her tightly, happy that Samira had come to see her, sensing the child's gradual withdrawal. But Samira did not like to be hugged or kissed for long. Ramona released her and said,

"It's Diwali, so we have a busy day today."

"Yay, Diwali!" Samira cried. "Will there be fireworks?"

"Of course, and sweets and lots of little lights."

"Can I have sparklers, please, please?"

"If you're really good."

"I'll be good," promised Samira, happily.

"The doctor baboo's coming today but not to see you, so don't worry."

Whenever the doctor baboo arrived to give the children vaccinations or injections, Samira would run away and hide. She would tear round and round the bungalow, and Ramona would send Ram or Didi to catch her. Kicking and screaming, Ramona, Didi and the hapless doctor would have to hold her down.

After breakfast, Ramona supervised the placing of little oil lamps along the verandah and down the front steps. Gifts of sweetmeats and dried fruit had been arriving daily from their vendors. Later in the morning, after the doctor baboo left promising to send his latest bedwetting remedy, Ramona and the children went to Mal Bazaar to buy fireworks and provisions. Mark was wearing the soldier suit Ramona had ordered for his birthday because he never stopped talking about being a soldier when he grew up. This was inspired by the military convoys during the war with China. They had to wait for the interminable military vehicles to pass and would stare apprehensively at the soldiers with their rifles sitting in the back of the trucks. Mark decided that he wanted to be one of them, a brave soldier with his own rifle.

He had his toy rifle over his shoulder and clutched his toy monkey which went everywhere with him. Samira wore her red pinafore frock with little blue boats on it. She liked it because the front had a big pocket with slots for each hand. Her hair flowed down her back with the weight and luster of Ramona's black tresses. At school, her hair was tightly braided each day by the school ayahs. If she wriggled or fidgeted, they would smack her across the back of her head till her eyes welled with tears, but she never told anyone. All the little girls suffered the same fate.

Kala parked the car beside a row of shops in Mal Bazaar. It wasn't much of a town, just a smattering of makeshift buildings and a petrol station that had sprung up beside the thoroughfare. Trucks and buses sped past, blasting their horns at the disorderly cyclists and pedestrians who were oblivious to any sense of urgency. As soon as the old Ford V8 was parked, it was accosted by peddlers and beggars. Although initially appalled and dismayed by the sight of them, Ramona and the children had grown inured to the beggars' disfigurements, tossing coins into their tin cups. Peddlers thrust cheap plastic playthings, water balloons, grotesque dolls, flutes and rubber bouncing balls under their noses. Sometimes, Ramona would humor the children with the purchase of some shoddy toy that would be in pieces within the hour.

Decrepit cows with protruding ribs scrounged scraps discarded by the roadside tea shops and vegetable stalls. Mangy pariah dogs scuffled and scratched in the dusty laneways. It was almost as though all the business of the day was conducted on the streets and sidewalks. A dentist set up his practice, cross-legged on a coir mat, subjecting his patients to an assortment of instruments with little regard for hygiene or the pain he was inflicting. Hunkered close by was a man selling knives displayed on a piece of fabric with his sharpening tools beside them.

The children paused to watch, enthralled, a monkey man with his distinctive rattling drum and cast of three monkeys, a mother, father and baby. The monkeys danced and performed a hilarious wedding ceremony where the female in a red veil pursued the male with her baby in tow. Mark giggled as the monkeys ran around collecting coins from the spectators in their tiny humanlike hands.

When they arrived at the shop where Ramona bought her dry provisions, the owner, seeing the children, announced that he had Coca-Cola. He sat cross-legged on a white, padded platform in the middle of the store, presiding over the piles of grain. There was a smell of turmeric and gunny sacks. One of the associates handed chilled bottles of Coca-Cola to the children, while another weighed Ramona's order under her watchful eye. Samira guzzled hers down in a few seconds, gasping as the bubbles went up her nose. She watched covertly as Mark sipped at his, knowing that he could never finish the bottle.

"Tell her to stop watching me," he whined to his mother. He knew what Samira was waiting for and was determined to finish the Coca-Cola to the last drop.

"I'm not!" Samira protested.

"There's no hurry, darling," said Ramona. She paid for the food, and the packages were placed in a basket in ready for the coolie to transport to the car. They all waited and watched as Mark struggled to finish as much of the Coke as he could, a brave soldier with a rifle over his shoulder and monkey under his arm. The pressure was too much for him. All pleasure in the drink dissipated and with lower lip quivering, he conceded defeat.

"I don't like it," he lied, feebly, holding out the bottle to his mother. What was left of the Coke was handed to Samira, who seized it triumphantly and gulped it down.

That night, the children had to wait until after dinner before Charles would allow them to play with the fireworks. The house looked beautiful with the electric lights switched off, lit only by the flickering oil lamps. Samira and Mark ran into the garden, a safe distance from the house and watched in fascination as Charles and Jetha let off Catherine wheels, fountains and rockets. They were given sparklers and tore around the garden shrieking and waving them in circles until they fizzled out.

In the distance, the laborers beat their drums, a sound that reverberated through the plantation until the early hours every night during the Diwali season. The throbbing of the drums became louder and louder until they realized it came from just outside the compound. A group of laborers stood by the gate waiting to be invited in.

"Jetha, let the coolies in," Charles said, in Hindi.

Ramona and the children retreated up the steps to the verandah, while Charles went to greet the visitors, several men and women obviously in a state of inebriation. They had come to dance for the Sahib and his family, they said. Samira shivered in fear, seeing the whites of their eyes roll in the light of the oil lamps. The women, whose eyes were heavily lined with kohl, wore coral and gold necklets and earrings that were so heavy that their lobes were grotesquely stretched. Mark ran into the house and clung to Didi in terror.

The dancers formed three rows one behind the other with their arms around each other's waists and chanted loudly to the beat of the drums. They ran forward with their heads facing the ground and then backwards with faces to the sky, back and forth, back and forth in a terrifying and never-ending dance. Finally, unable to take any more, Ramona signaled to Charles to make them stop.

"Shabash! Shabash!" Charles praised them, not wanting to cause offence. He presented the leader with the bottle of rum Jetha had fetched from the liquor cabinet. It was accepted joyfully, and the group made their way out of the compound, laughing and talking as they vanished into the dark.

Samira had run indoors for fear of being put on display. Sometimes, the coolies asked to look at the children up close, fascinated by their light skin and eyes.

"Can they possibly be real?" they asked each other in wonder, gazing at the children who were so different from theirs. Ramona

43

would smile and indulge them, but Samira would pout, hating the attention, and Mark's eyes would well up.

"They just want to look at you. They've never seen children like you before," said Ramona, who identified with their curiosity. "Try to be nice."

Samira and Mark were stealing peas in the vegetable garden. Ramona and Charles were taking their afternoon nap, and Ramchand had gone home for lunch. Didi didn't know where they were and was too hot to care. There was nothing as delicious as fresh peas, but they were bad for their tummies, and they weren't allowed to pick them. There were rows of cauliflower, cabbage, carrots and beetroot. The peas and tomatoes were in the back corner, supported by canes. There was also a pineapple grove, but the children didn't like to play there because the fronds were prickly and scratched their legs.

Samira announced to Mark that she knew how to make babies. A girl in her class, Nilofer Sharma, had told her.

"You don't!" said Mark in disbelief, although quite liking the idea of having one.

"I do so! It's easy. She said a boy and a girl just have to rub their bottoms against each other, and they'll have a baby."

"But where would it come from?" he asked.

"I don't know. It just appears like magic. That's what she said. Shall we try it?"

"I don't know." He grew wary. "What would we do with a baby?"

"We could play with it, of course. Didi would feed it and take it out in the pram. It'll be fun! Now stand behind me and rub your bottom against mine."

They stood back-to-back in the vegetable garden and rubbed their bottoms together. Even to their innocent minds, there seemed to be something illicit about the business of making babies. They stepped apart and waited, looking all around.

"I don't see one," said Mark.

"Maybe we have to wait a little while."

"Are you sure you got it right?" he asked, suspiciously, not knowing whether to be relieved or disappointed. "Maybe we should ask Mummy."

"No, silly. I heard her tell Daddy she doesn't want any more babies. Let's come back later and check. I know! Let's go catch tadpoles!"

They sped off to their new adventure, any thought of babies already forgotten.

Chapter 6
Dooars, 1966-1968

"Daddy, look at my report card," Mark ran up to him, as he arrived home for lunch. "I got an A in sums."

While there was no doubt in his mind that he loved his children, Charles, whose own father was a dim memory, and someone who'd had little or nothing to do with his offspring, had no role model to emulate in his relationship with them. He did not feel a strong connection with either child and showed a cursory interest in their activities apart from a vague sense of obligation to be something of a disciplinarian.

"Well done, son. I'll look at it in a minute." He was hot and tired and preferred to read the newspaper. Ramona gave him a dark look. She wanted the children to do well in school and pored over their reports with intense interest. Samira's teacher had said that she was doing better in class but "tends to think she knows everything." Mark's teacher said that he needed to be more assertive and participate in class discussion.

She read fairy tales to the children, filling their minds with vivid impressions of princesses, knights and wicked stepmothers which combined to build impressions in the children's minds that were completely unrelated to actual life. Ramona found it tedious to bathe or dress the children. Didi had always done those things except when they were babies. Prava had sent Didi to them by bus from Darjeeling shortly after Samira was born. It was Didi who took them for long walks to the river in the afternoons, pushed them on the swing in the garden and put them to bed at night. She could not read to the children but told stories about Tibetan warriors, ferocious yetis and yaks. She taught them to sing the Nepalese songs that she sang them to sleep with each night.

There was a small, shallow swimming pool in the compound of the Burra Bungalow that Greg said they were welcome to use whenever they liked. One day, Samira refused to step into the pool, seeing the reflection of the sky in it. She was somehow convinced that she would sink into the depths of the sky reflected in the pool. Didi had coaxed and cajoled her, demonstrating the shallowness of the pool by stepping in it and disturbing the reflection. But even with her feet planted firmly on the bottom, Samira had not been able to fully comprehend why she didn't sink to the depths reflected in the water, as high as the clouds in the sky.

Didi had little privacy when the children were home from school. They were full of curiosity about her. She took her meals squatting on a low stool in the dingy kitchen, holding her plate in one hand while she ate with the other. The children sat beside her, watching her eat with their mouths watering. She made the food look so delicious. She ate with her fingers, deftly rolling the rice into little balls, popping them into her mouth followed by a quick bite into a green chili. She never scattered salt over her food but put it in a heap on one side of the plate. Occasionally, she fed morsels of rice into their open, bird-like mouths. Ramona would have been horrified had she known.

Samira spotted Didi on the swing in the back garden one afternoon when she was supposed to be taking a nap. Jetha was pushing the swing, and they were both laughing. There was something familiar about the way he touched her that disturbed Samira although she did not understand why. Jetha had a wife and two daughters. She knew because Ramona gave him Samira's old clothes.

Samira had learned to keep her thoughts and observations to herself because she always got into trouble if she divulged them to anybody. Mark could not be trusted to keep a secret. Ramona would scold Samira and tell her to mind her own business. Charles would let her speak and say, "Yes, dear. Now run along." It was obvious that he hadn't listened to a word she said.

꒰ᴥ꒱

"What did you do, Samira?" Mark called through the locked door of the box room. When they were naughty they were struck with a hairbrush or a hanger, whichever was handiest. But when they were really bad, Daddy dragged them, kicking and screaming to the dark, scary box room and laid them on one of the shelves. Then the door would be locked.

"N...n...othing," sobbed Samira, "I don't know what I did."

Mark understood. It was sometimes hard to fathom adults. It was no use appealing to Mummy. She always took Daddy's side. Nor to Didi, either. She just whispered to them to be good children and scuttled away to the back verandah lest she incur the Sahib's and Memsahib's wrath.

Mark had been in the box room and knew its horrors. He was close to tears.

"Shall I get Mummy?" he asked. "Don't cry, Sammy."

Ramona suddenly appeared and swooped down on him.

"Leave her alone! Go to Didi, Mark Theodore!" she said.

But for once he was brave, like the soldier he so wanted to be.

"Let her out! Let her out!" he shouted, his heart aching for his sister. He glared at his mother with tears in his eyes, ready to take off in case Daddy appeared, and he was locked up as well.

Ramona opened the box room door and released the sobbing Samira. Her face was blotchy with tears. "Go wash your face and brush your hair," she said. "It's time for lunch." Samira ran to the bathroom and looked at her red eyes in the mirror. The tepid water from the tap soothed her skin as she rinsed her face, but inside her a feeling of resentment festered.

The Chalsa Polo Club was comprised of a large, square building, six grass tennis courts, a children's playground and a small lawn. It had a white, corrugated tin roof like most of the planters' bungalows. When it rained, the sound of the rain on the roof was deafening. And during the monsoons, it rained almost every day. The compound was straddled by a nine-hole golf course, bordered by the Murti River. It was years since polo had been played on what was now the first fairway.

The club was accessed through a low verandah that jutted out onto the lawn. Inside the clubhouse was a ballroom with a stage, card room, two squash courts, a billiard room, library and bar. Over the years, the ballroom floor echoed with the patter of children's feet, the sound of chairs dragged across it on movie nights and the reverberation of dancing feet. A portrait of Queen Elizabeth took pride of place over the mantelpiece, and pictures of other royals were displayed under the glass tops of the cocktail tables. An ancient piano cowered in a corner, its ivory keys yellowed and split with age and decades of pounding fingers. Within its secret recesses reposed sweet memories of melodies from long ago.

Like most planter households, the Clarkes looked forward to "club days." They travelled in the cantankerous Ford V8, laden with two sets of golf clubs, changes of clothes and the sandwich and cake tins containing their tea. As they drove, Mark was singing his version of a Hindi film song in a thin, high-pitched voice that rose in a wailing crescendo.

"Dil katta dekho, Dil katta dekho,
Oh Dilly Walla, Oh Dilly Walla."

Higher and higher he went, repeating the words over and over, assured of a captive audience.

"Shut up! You're singing it all wrong," said Samira, holding her hands over her ears.

"Why don't you sing 'Muffin Man'?" suggested Charles.

"Or 'Ten Green Bottles'?" said Ramona.

"Or not sing at all!" Samira cried.

Mark burst into tears.

"I don't want to sing those old songs. I just want to sing 'Dill katta dekho," he howled.

"Okay, darling, you just sing whatever you want to sing," Ramona said, for the sake of peace. So the singing resumed for the rest of the trip, with no one daring to comment.

All the children adored Uncle Anil. Any time he visited, he brought them Cadbury's Fruit and Nut Chocolate bars. The children were excited because they had been invited to his house for Chinese food. They didn't get invited out to dinner often. Samira wore a yellow dress that stuck out all around her and asked Didi to put her hair up in a pony tail.

"Not too high in the back, though," she instructed. Didi brushed the tangles out of her hair. "Wait! Stop!" cried Samira. She spoke in Hindi. "I saw a curl! Didi, I saw a curl in my hair, and you brushed it away!"

"No, baba. There was no curl."

Nor would there ever be. Her hair was straight and glossy down her back, too sleek and stubborn for even a hint of a curl. She didn't see how it swung as she moved and how it gleamed in the sunlight. All she knew was that her hair had no curl and was too slippery to withstand pretty ribbons, grips or bows.

Anil swung them high in the air when they arrived at his bungalow.

"Again!" squealed Mark. "Again, Uncle Anil."

"Sammy! What a pretty yellow frock!" he stood back in mock amazement.

"But look, Uncle Anil, my petticoat's even prettier." She lifted her frock in front to show him.

"Really, Samira! Put your dress down. That's not ladylike," Ramona said, crossly.

A lady they'd never met hurried down the steps to meet them. Charles and Ramona shook hands with her, and Anil said to the children,

"Say hello to Aunty Sheila."

"But where is Aunty Gita?" asked Mark in bewilderment. "I wanted to see Aunty Gita."

There was an awkward silence. Anil cleared his throat awkwardly.

"Aunty Gita went away, now Aunty Sheila lives here."

"Run along and play, children," said Charles.

It was dark, and they couldn't go outside. There was nothing for her and Mark to do while the grown-ups had their drinks in the drawing room. They drank their orange squash in the verandah, and Samira excused herself to go to the bathroom. She loved to see other people's bathrooms and how she looked in their mirrors. She did not like the way she looked tonight, and the pony tail hurt her head. It was too tight. She untied the yellow ribbon Didi had tied on so tightly it made her eyes bulge, and pulled off the band underneath. That felt much better. But she still wasn't comfortable. Her can-can petticoat was prickly and scratched her legs. It was very pretty with layers of white lace and little satin bows but very uncomfortable, nevertheless. She slipped it off and stepped out of it, rubbing her legs in relief.

Just then, Ramona called them to dinner, and she ran to the dining room to join the adults. In the car on the way home, Mark persisted in wanting to know why Uncle Anil had a new Aunty.

"But why did Aunty Gita go away?" he wanted to know. "I liked Aunty Gita."

"Yes, you've established that," said Charles. "May I ask why, exactly?"

"Well, she had…." he hesitated, blushing.

"She had what?" Ramona prompted.

"Big bosoms!" cried Samira triumphantly, smirking at Mark.

"No! Stop it." He was embarrassed at being caught out.

"Mummy, tell her to shut up!" He glared at his sister.

"He said shut up!" cried Samira.

"Samira, behave. Mark, you know you're not allowed to say 'shut up.' And Gita left because she had to go somewhere else," said Ramona.

"Mummy, you won't ever have to go somewhere else, will you?" he asked, anxiously.

"No, darling, I never will ever go anywhere else," she promised.

In the morning, the telephone rang just as they were finishing breakfast.

"Sheila Memsahib," Jetha announced.

"I'll get it," said Ramona.

"Hello, Sheila. Yes. This is Ramona." She spoke into the phone. "Thanks so much for a lovely dinner. Oh? Really, she is so careless!"

Sheila informed her that Samira had left her can-can petticoat and her yellow ribbon in the guest bathroom.

"I also wanted to let you know that I'm leaving Anil," Sheila said. "I'm going back to Calcutta on the next flight."

Charles groaned when Ramona told him.

"Oh, no! We all know what that means. There's going to be yet another 'Aunty' for us to explain to Mark!"

Samira's bedroom was the dressing room off Mark's room. Although it was much smaller than Mark's and not really a bedroom at all, she was happy with it because she had been allowed to choose the lilac paint and peacock bedspread. The children's rooms led off the drawing room so when there were parties, the sound of laughing and dancing kept them awake.

Recently, however, Samira found herself unable to sleep because of Charles' shouting. It would start about an hour after she had gone to bed. She would hide her head under the covers, blocking her ears. Why was he shouting at Mother? How could he go on and on like that? What could she have done that was so terrible? Samira would scrutinize her parents the following morning. Ramona seemed calm and unruffled. Charles was his normal self. It was most baffling and went on for many weeks until one night the shouting woke Mark.

Without hesitating, he jumped out of bed and opened the drawing room door. From her bedroom, Samira could see him go in. The shouting instantly stopped. She jumped out of bed and followed him, in curiosity and fear. Ramona and Charles were sitting with their drinks, unperturbed.

"What's the matter, darling?" Ramona held out her arms to Mark, and he ran up to sit beside her.

53

"Why is Daddy yelling at you?" he asked. He looked accusingly at Charles.

"Goodness, children, Daddy's not shouting at me," said Ramona, laughing.

"But I heard him. He's been doing it for weeks," said Samira, who had followed Mark into the room.

"I was just telling her things I'm angry about," Charles explained. "I'm not angry with Mummy. There are things in the factory that have been worrying me, and I'm upset with the company. That's all."

"Oh," breathed Samira. So he had been shouting to her and not at her all this time! What a relief.

"Now, off to bed with you. I'll try to make less noise from now on," said Charles, briskly.

Chapter 7
Dooars, 1969-1971

"If you see Caroline, run!" Rachel Moorhead told Samira as soon as the Clarke family arrived at the club. It was December, and Rachel was home for a whole month. They hugged and kissed, happy to see each other, but evidently Rachel had other, more pressing issues on her mind. Ramona and Charles were already striding off in the direction of the golf course, followed by their caddies. Mark was kicking a football with some younger boys.

"But why?" asked Samira, trying to keep up with Rachel, who was running around the side of the clubhouse.

"Coz, I hate her, that's why. Come on!" She said this as she spotted Caroline who had grown tremendously during the past year and who did not seem at all interested in pursuing the indignant Rachel.

"Why? What did she do?" asked Samira, wondering what Caroline could have done to upset Rachel in such a short time. Although Rachel and Caroline had their differences, the three girls had enjoyed good times together over the years. They needed each other in a place where company of any kind was scarce, especially company of their own age.

"Just look at her!" said Rachel in disgust. "That dress…those shoes…and," she whispered in Samira's ear as though the words were too awful to be uttered out loud, "she's wearing a bra!"

"Oh-h," stammered Samira. "How can you be so sure?"

"Because she told me, of course," Rachel said, scornfully. "Just as soon as she saw me."

Samira looked at Rachel, whom she had not seen for almost a year, and gulped. There was no way of saying this without seeming terribly disloyal, but there was no escaping the fact. She might as well get it out in the open.

"I'm sorry, Rach," she said nervously, as though confessing to some awful crime. "But I'm… er…I'm wearing a bra, too. My mother said I had to."

Actually, Samira had been delighted to wear a bra, and there was no debating the fact that she was well ready for one. Rachel glared at her, speechless for a moment, and then stormed, half in tears,

"It's not fair! It's just not fair! You're both all grown up. Nothing will ever be the same again."

Samira, going through the same process of adjustment, knew exactly what she was talking about and burst into tears, too.

"I'm not. I promise. It's still the same old me."

"I don't ever want to grow up and be an old woman," Rachel wailed. "I want everything to stay the same!"

The girls put their arms around each other and sobbed for their lost childhood. It was not easy, having to part for long periods and then being expected to take up exactly where they had left off. The last time they were together, they were climbing trees and riding bicycles, both of which seemed like childish activities now. Suddenly, they were one of the older girls. They didn't want to join in the children's games any more. The adults were busy playing tennis, golf or cards. What was one supposed to do with oneself when one was thirteen years old?

Samira, looking at Rachel, was also aware for the first time of inexplicable differences between them, differences she had never noticed before that were far more intangible than the difference of not wearing a bra. It was not about appearance or maturity but something about attitude. Something she could not quite pinpoint yet in her thirteen-year-old mind.

"I know," she said, "Let's go to the ladies room. Caroline won't find us there." Although they both knew that Caroline was not trying to find them.

Rachel continued the charade. "Okay. Race you!"

The girls sped off noisily, their burden of maturity momentarily forgotten.

They loved the elegant ladies room and would sit and whisper and giggle endlessly on the pink chaise lounge to the annoyance of the ladies who wanted to gossip and powder their noses in private. The room was very grand in their eyes. There were pink silk curtains in the windows and across each of the changing cubicles and pink floral upholstery on the wicker chairs. They sat and viewed themselves from all angles in the three mirrors on the pretty, white dressing table in the center of the room and played with the gilt brushes and cotton-wool balls, pretending to powder their noses, speaking in society ladies' voices until it was time for afternoon tea.

They wanted to sit with the adults at the table on the verandah, not on a rug on the grass with the children. Ramona looked sternly at Samira.

"Please, Mother," Rachel begged Lorna. "We're not children anymore."

"And besides," she added, "Caroline is sitting at the adult table."

"Oh, all right." said Lorna, smiling at Ramona. "as long as you both promise to behave like grown-ups."

Everyone had brought homemade offerings for tea. There were cucumber and chicken sandwiches, chocolate éclairs, meringues, shortbread and cake. Rachel and Samira were on their best behavior, balancing their cups of tea and mindful of not talking with their mouths full, under Ramona's watchful eye. Rachel was sipping her tea with one finger in the air when suddenly her cup slipped and she spilled tea all over herself. She gasped in horror, and Samira stifled a giggle. Suddenly, they were both giggling and snorting so uncontrollably that they had to leave the table and scamper back to the ladies room.

"Oh, no!" cried Samira, wiping away tears of mirth. "We are going to be in so much trouble!"

"Did you see your mother's face?" Rachel was convulsed with laughter as she tried to dry her dress with a towel.

"They'll never allow us to sit with the grown-ups again!"

"And do we really care?" Rachel asked.

"What do you think they'll do to us?" said Samira. She was a safe distance from the box room.

Fortunately for the girls, most of the adults had seen the funny side of the situation, and Anita Dutt had come to their rescue, sensing their predicament.

"Don't be too hard on Samira," she said to Ramona. "She's at a difficult age. The girls are too old to sit outside with the children. They'll learn soon enough."

Lorna smiled across the table at Greg. They saw so little of Rachel that it was impossible to be too hard on her. When they first took her home to Aberdeen when she was three, she had shocked their relations by not being able to speak English, having spent so much time with her ayah and the servants.

After tea, everyone moved indoors, the men heading straight to the bar or to the billiard tables. Some of the ladies retreated to the card room to play bridge, while others went to the library to stock up on books for the following week. When the girls emerged furtively a little later, they were surprised when Charles offered to buy them both cokes, and no one seemed annoyed. Growing up was confusing.

During the journey home that night, Samira asked Charles when they planned to go 'home' to England.

"I don't want to go right now, of course, Daddy, but maybe after Rachel leaves?"

Opportunities for 'home leave' had come and gone over the years. Charles showed no inclination to return to England. He preferred to spend his vacations on safari with the men, hunting wild boar and deer, while Ramona visited Prava in Darjeeling with the children. One year, they visited the Taj Mahal and the Red Fort in Agra, and they frequently went to Calcutta.

Eventually, it was accepted that Charles had no intention of going back, although trips to Britain among both Britishers and Indians were prized.

"You really should go," Ramona's friends would urge her. "even if only for the shopping! My, the shops over there! You simply can't imagine how huge they are, even bigger than your bungalow. Some of them are five stories. Oxford Street is almost an entire mile of department stores, on both sides of the street. You should make Charles take you at least once."

But Ramona had no desire to go. She would smile and say,

"England is much too cold for me. The journey is too long. But someday, we'll send Samira, when she's old enough, and Mark, too. They can make up their own minds about where they want to live." She said it almost as though it didn't matter what they decided, though in her heart she hoped they would stay in India, close to her and Charles as they grew older.

They were both brought up with the knowledge that when they were older they would go to England. They would visit Aunt Pauline in Hertfordshire and see the sights of London. The prospect loomed like a giant milestone in their lives. Samira would weave intricate fantasies in her mind about an England with drizzly gray streets, falling snow and narrow, squashed-up houses. She was not quite sure what she would do when she got there, but somewhere in her dreams would be a fresh-faced English gentleman and herself, richly dressed like the lady on the Quality Street Chocolate tins.

Now, Samira at thirteen was already asking about going 'home.' Charles glanced at Ramona,

"Sammy, this is our home. You can go when you're a little older, if you do well in school."

Ramona sighed. They were already setting stipulations. But she knew they'd been relatively fortunate. She and Charles had been able to sidestep most of the problems that stemmed from "mixed" marriages.

"Mummy, what are we?" the question came suddenly from Mark, sitting beside Samira in the backseat.

"What do you mean?" asked Charles.

"Are we Indian or English?"

"We're both, silly," said Charles. "You know that."

"Then why haven't we been to England?" Samira asked.

"Well, I don't want to go to England," announced Mark. He was parroting what he'd heard his mother say a hundred times.

"I don't want to go," mimicked Samira, giving him a shove.

"Stop it." He glared at her as the car sped home on the deserted road. She had stopped fighting him with her fists, realizing with a shock that he was suddenly bigger and stronger than she.

"You'll both go there when you grow up," said Ramona. "Then there'll be no more questions."

A few days later, Mark ran into the house in great excitement.

"The Pathans are here! Mum, where are you? The Pathans are here."

Samira and Ramona ran to the verandah. The Pathans travelled all the way from Kashmir selling hand-loomed carpets, embroidered linens and furs. The children regarded them with a mixture of fear and curiosity. Their stature was further enhanced by their enormous puggaries that crisscrossed on their heads and were finished off with tails at the back. They wore intricately woven shirts and soft, embroidered shoes that ended in a curved point. Mark sniggered when he saw the shoes that were like the ones worn by the Air India Maharaja mascot. Ramona glared at him and called for Jetha to bring nimboo pani for the visitors.

She tried to tell them that she really wasn't interested in a carpet or a fur, but they persisted in unrolling carpet after carpet across the verandah, deaf to her protests. They unfolded dozens of tablecloths, cushion covers and napkins. Then they started to unpack the furs: gorgeous coats, hats and stoles in mink, fox and rabbit.

"You please try," Ramona was encouraged to try on a mink coat.

"Oh, my," she said. It was soft and luxurious and much too warm for the climate.

"Mummy, you look beautiful!" cried Samira. "Buy it, buy it."

"Gracious, no. It's much too expensive."

"Not expensive, madam," insisted the Pathan. "I make very good price."

It was no coincidence that they had timed their visit for just before the Burra Sahib came home. Charles arrived right on cue and came up the steps.

"Goodness, what's going on?"

"Daddy, it's the Pathans," explained Mark, as though Charles hadn't guessed already.

"What a lot of stuff," he commented. "What's the guess we're going to have to buy something?"

"Sahib, we come very far from Kashmir. You please buy?"

"I feel it would be only right," agreed Ramona. She had her eye on a luscious, brown fox stole that did wonders for her coloring. And Charles who never showed any interest in household matters suddenly took a fancy to a large carpet. Much heated haggling and drama followed as Ramona bargained with the vendors. There would have been no pleasure in the purchase unless she felt an unbelievable bargain had been struck.

"We have made absolutely no profit, Sahib. No profit," the Pathans lied as they reloaded their van.

The Clarke household excitedly unrolled their new, blue wool carpet in the drawing room. And much later, Ramona posed provocatively for Charles in their bedroom in her fabulous new fox fur and nothing else.

Every time Samira returned home from boarding school, she seemed to withdraw further into herself. She read voraciously, lying in her room, or on the swing bed in the verandah. It was not that she didn't like school. She thrived in the company of her contemporaries. It was adjusting to life in the real world that she had problems with. She, rather than Mark, took part in all the school plays, sang in the choir and was among the top students in her class. Mark escaped the pressure to perform and excel that landed on Samira's shoulders. His winning ways allowed him to evade responsibility and get away with things that she was punished for.

While she was sensitive to any form of criticism, comments made by her mother seemed to affect her most. She started to distance herself almost as a means of self-protection. She felt socially inept, always saying the wrong thing. She became distrustful of her ability to express herself, especially in the company of adults. Ironically, her insecurity was interpreted as aloofness.

"Samira doesn't know how to talk," Ramona told people, which was essentially true. But those remarks were humiliating and caused her to retreat further into her shell.

"Is that what you're going to wear, Sammy?" Ramona said when she showed up in a pair of stylish new slacks, ready to go to the club one Saturday. "You should see yourself from behind."

Mortified, Samira ran out of the room without a word and looked at herself anxiously in the mirror. Yes, she was huge. There was no question about that. She changed into one of her old dresses and returned to the verandah.

"Why did you change?" asked Ramona. "There's no need to be so sensitive."

Yes, she was too sensitive. Whatever she did was wrong. But she didn't know how to be better, no matter how hard she tried. Samira felt the knot inside her tighten. Her mood and self-confidence shaken, she didn't feel like going out any longer. But she didn't want to incur Ramona's wrath, so she climbed into the car, massive and ungainly.

Charles' promotion to Burra Sahib necessitated the Clarke family's moving from the Chota to the Burra Bungalow, previously occupied by Greg and Lorna Moorhead. So what would normally have been an occasion for celebration was bittersweet for the families who had spent so many happy years together. Despite their huge pay rise and elevated status, Charles and Ramona mourned the loss of good friends and neighbors.

The Moorheads were not the only ones leaving. British Tea Companies were hiring local managers who were proving to be as capable, if not more so, than their British predecessors. They spoke the language and instinctively understood the culture of the labor force. They were also far cheaper to maintain. There were no expensive flights to and from the United Kingdom and greatly reduced re-location and medical costs.

The person who was most apprehensive about the Clarkes' move was Ramchand. He knew that Jetha the bearer, Kala the driver, Mohammed, the Muslim cook and, of course, Didi, were all moving with the family to the Burra Bungalow. He would never find another Memsahib like Ramona. She had cooperated with him in every way, allowing him all the fertilizer and seeds he needed. She had understood that it was not his fault when the entire rose garden was attacked by red spiders. And although she had ranted and raged when they lost a section of lawn when he inadvertently mistook weed killer for fertilizer, she accepted his inability to read the English writing on the packaging. He would have done anything for her. He was going to greatly miss her and the babas. Nothing would have made him happier than moving to the Burra Bungalow and working with Mohan, the head gardener there. It was hurtful that they had not even considered taking him along. Each day, he went to work hoping to be called by the Memsahib and be told that he was going with them.

His house, where he lived with his wife Usha, was in a cluster of weather-beaten, thatched huts made of bamboo and clay. It was always cool and dark inside their home because of the bamboo thicket in the back yard that shielded it from the sun. Fronds of an old banana tree obscured the house from the laneway that led to the water pump. He went home to Usha every evening and gloomily told her that he had not heard anything that day. But she didn't need to be told. She could gauge his mood by the way he dragged his feet and bowed his head. The day of the move was rapidly approaching, and he moped about the garden, wondering what the new assistant manager would be like.

Finally, one afternoon when he was supposed to be at work, Usha heard Ramchand's footsteps racing up the path. She ran to meet him and saw him joyfully waving a piece of paper. The Memsahib had finally called for him. He was going to the Burra Bungalow with the Memsahib! And not as under-gardener, they wanted him to be their head gardener! His black eyes shone, and Usha caught her breath with happiness for him. The reason they had not said anything to him before, he told her, was because they knew that Mohan was thinking of leaving, and they wanted to be sure first. He was the happiest man in the world.

Nina Harkness

She didn't tell him that she had bled all day. He hadn't even known that she had missed her last two periods. She had waited to tell him till she was absolutely sure, not wanting to disappoint him with another miscarriage. Now, they would have to start all over again. She was much younger than he was, but the pressure on her to produce a child was intense, both from his family and hers. But tonight they would celebrate. They would visit their families and share the good news. No one needed to know that there was bad news as well. She would keep that to herself.

Chapter 8
Dooars, 1977

Lying on the grass, Samira gazed at the sunset sky that shone a brilliant orange behind the branches of the giant Poinciana tree. Indian colors, she thought to herself, reveling in the feeling of peace the garden gave her: the gaudy ochre hues of mangoes, gold-Mohr blossoms, marigolds and saffron. The shriek of cicadas from secret recesses in the trees blended into the ringing twilight silence. Silhouettes of a hundred starlings streaked across the mango saffron sky. In the jacaranda tree, a flock of orioles assembled for their evening chorus.

Throngs of plantations workers trudged home in the tired dusk, trailing long shadows that leapt and jiggled on the dusty pathway behind them. Like their owners, the shadows balanced earthenware pitchers on their heads, trundled thin bicycles or tugged lagging children by the hand.

Mark was often restless these days. He had been consumed with a sudden burst of energy as the temperature cooled, after his lethargy in the heat of the afternoon. He was on vacation from his university in Calcutta. Samira was home from college, a graduate at long last.

"Sammy, where are you? I know you're out there," he called.

"Go away!" she said, wishing he'd leave her in peace. "What d'you want?"

"Let's play hide-and-seek. I'm bored!" He ran toward the shrubbery, challenging her over his shoulder to join him in their childhood game. Samira laughed, humoring him, wondering if they would always behave like children when they were together. They played the familiar game with old expertise, reverting to well-known hiding places, running sure-footedly in the deepening shadows and screaming with laughter when discovered. Suddenly, the blast of a motorcycle driving up the gravel driveway shattered the tranquility of the evening.

"Who's that?" asked Samira, seeing a young man sauntering over to them, somewhat peeved at having their game interrupted.

"It's Ravi," said Mark. "Ravi Anand. He's the new assistant manager at Baghrapur."

Baghrapur was the neighboring estate on the other side of the Murti River. It was a large, isolated plantation, bordered by the river to the west and a forbidding expanse of jungle to the north. Many years ago when they were young children, the plantation manager had been attacked by a rogue elephant that ran amok, crashing through the villagers' houses and destroying their precious vegetable patches. On hearing about it from the breathless messenger, the manager had leapt into his jeep and rushed to the scene. He discovered the tusker with one of the laborers borne aloft in his trunk, about to batter him to death, impervious to the showering of rocks by the frenzied villagers. The Scottish planter had aimed his rifle right into the eye of the elephant, saving the man's life. Since that day, he was affectionately known to the planters' children as "Uncle Elephant."

Ravi approached Mark and Samira. He was of medium height, with wavy hair that reached his collar. Samira could discern even through the half light that his eyes were vivid green. He had clear-cut features with defined eyebrows and walked with a confidence that was a near swagger, qualities almost guaranteed to bring out the worst in Samira's insecurities.

"Ravi," called Mark. "How are you, man? Come and meet my sister Samira."

"Samira," he emphasized her name. "I'm very pleased to meet you. What a pretty name."

Obviously a bit of a smoothie, Samira decided, and most likely a product of St. Columbus or one of the other fancy Delhi universities. He'd be lucky if he lasted two seconds in tea.

"Pleased to meet you, Ravi," she countered, resisting the urge to emphasize his name they way he had hers. "Welcome to the Dooars."

"And where have you been hiding?" he asked.

"I just graduated from college in Darjeeling."

"Look," said Mark, still in the throes of their game." It's getting dark. We were in the middle of hide-and-seek, Ravi. Rather juvenile, I know, but it's one of the things people who don't have television do to amuse themselves. Will you join us?"

"Sure," said Ravi, somewhat taken aback.

"Good. Samira, you're 'it.' Come on Ravi, let's go hide."

Samira wondered how old he was, counting to the obligatory twenty. Probably only slightly older than herself, she guessed, if this happened to be his first job.

"Ready or not, I'm coming," she shouted, running off to search for them in the shadows. The garden rang with shouts of laughter. Ravi was "it," and then it was Mark's turn. Samira, breathless from running, and searching for somewhere to hide, crawled behind a clump of flowering jasmine. She gave a start when she realized that Ravi was already there. She giggled and was about to tiptoe away when he pulled her down beside him.

"Sshhh!" he whispered. They could hear Mark counting out loud at the far side of the garden.

"I knew Mark had a sister, but I wasn't expecting one so pretty," he said softly. She saw that his eyes were fringed with black lashes. The scent of jasmine hung heavy in the soft air. He placed his hand under her chin and looked deep into her eyes. Samira gazed back, overcome with surprise and light-headed with the cloying scent. His hands stroked her hair in flowing movements that extended down to her chest, with a gentle pressure against her breasts. Or was she imagining it?

"Do you realize how lovely you are?" he murmured.

In a state of confusion mingled with a rush of sexual excitement, Samira was speechless. Was she mistaken, or had he really been that forward? She jumped to her feet trying to hide her discomfiture. Thankfully, Mark appeared at that moment, a little surprised at finding the two together. Samira mumbled something about being tired and wanting to go back indoors. Inexplicably, it seemed to Mark, Ravi announced that he was leaving, too.

"But you just got here. Why so soon?" he asked in bewilderment. Normally, Ravi lingered during these visits, hoping for an invitation to dinner, postponing the return to the solitude of his bachelor bungalow.

"I have to make some phone calls."

"See you at the club on Sunday?" Mark persisted.

"Of course. Say good-bye to Samira for me." He leapt on the red motorcycle and disappeared. The roar of the motorcycle's engine could be heard long after the pinprick of light from the tail light vanished from sight.

Samira retreated furtively to the swing bed in a corner of the verandah, hoping to be left undisturbed until she'd collected her thoughts. She knew that Charles and Ramona would be relaxing in the drawing room before dinner. But Mark knew her only too well and found her almost at once.

"What was all that about?" he demanded. "What made you take off so suddenly?"

"Sorry, Mark. I'm... not good with new people. I didn't mean to be rude."

"You need to give people a chance," he said, "not judge them so quickly. He's not a bad chap, and a damn good tennis player. Just what the club needs."

"I'll do my best," she mumbled. "People like that always manage to make me feel insignificant."

He knew that it took time for her to feel relaxed around new people. She had grown up with an acute consciousness of not "belonging" and had developed a defense mechanism to protect herself from being hurt. Her self-confidence had developed during her time in college, but Mark knew that being at home didn't always bring out the best in her.

"I really like him and am sure you'll get to like him, too," he said, as they went inside to join their parents for dinner.

The Clarkes were late arriving at the Club on Sunday. Samira regarded the prospect of seeing Ravi again with a mixture of anticipation and dread. She was excited to meet friends she hadn't seen since her return, realizing how few of the old-timers remained. By the time she made it to the tennis courts, Mark and Ravi were in a game of singles. She joined the spectators on the wicker chairs courtside waiting for a game. Ravi was an accomplished player. Mark was right about that. She had to admit he looked very good in his tennis whites.

"My, who's that handsome man?" she heard one of the women asking.

"That's Ravi Anand," said Anita Dutt. "He's the new assistant manager at Baghrapur."

"Oh, is he married?" she heard the other woman ask.

"No, no. Not yet. But I'm sure he will be soon."

"Samira, you should grab him," said Anita. "Look how cute he is."

"I don't want to get married yet," said Samira, blushing.

"What rubbish!" said Anita. "You're a college graduate. It's high time you got married."

"Sammy, come and play mixed doubles with us," Mark called from the court, to Samira's relief, putting an end to the conversation. "Pia will be our fourth."

He insisted on teaming her with Ravi, and she resigned herself to the fact that it was inevitable that they'd be seeing a lot of each other.

"Hi, Sammy, how are you?" he called, with a little too much familiarity, she thought, already using her nickname. "Which side of the court do you prefer?"

"Hello, Ravi," she replied, coolly. "Shall I take the forehand side?" She knew her forehand was her strong point.

"No problem."

He spun his racquet to see who would play first, and after allowing the ladies a brief warm up, the set started. Charles always said you could get to know someone better on the tennis court in five minutes than you otherwise could in five years. Samira quickly discovered that it was impossible not to like Ravi. He had a knack for genuinely enjoying himself and connecting with everyone around him. He was confident without being cocky. Mark would have been the first to sense that and would certainly not have developed a friendship with him if he were.

69

Ravi had never met anyone quite like Samira, accustomed as he was to the highly tuned culture of the girls in Delhi. She had none of their sophistication, running around the court in her short, frilly skirt, intent only on winning. It was difficult to gauge exactly how she was to be handled. It was clear that she would not be pursuing him, which was something of a novelty to him. He regarded her reserve as a challenge to be penetrated and knew that his normal mode of conquest would be ineffectual against her.

The son of a successful doctor in Delhi, he had grown up with all the benefits of a pampered middle-class child. He was educated at St. Martin's Academy and St. Columbus College and had planned to go into advertising. He had a certain innate creativity and artistic flair. But things had come too easily to him, and he grew bored. He felt suffocated by the familiarity of the city. Funnily enough, the notion of working as a tea planter had arisen after a game of tennis at his club when he was dismantled by an excellent player who turned out to be a tea planter from Assam. They sat over a beer at the bar afterwards, and the idea of becoming a planter captured Ravi's imagination. It was only a matter of time before he left the stifling city for the soft air of the Dooars.

If what he wanted was a change, Baghrapur most certainly provided that. He enjoyed the feeling of space and independence from his large, extended family. He reveled in the freedom of his own bungalow and a staff to take care of his needs. True, he missed his friends, but it didn't take him long to get to know people at the club. He quickly learned what was expected from him at the factory. He knew instinctively how to address the workers and command their respect.

Ravi had always had a weakness for the ladies. In Delhi, there was always some obliging female fluttering around him in her salwar kameez. He had fallen in love a few times, but in the end found the girls too sweet, too cloying. He felt he needed some resistance from a woman to sustain his interest, but his green eyes and charm made him irresistible, even to the most cynical of women. He had never met anyone like Samira, and the fact that she appeared completely oblivious to his charms captivated him. Marriages were still often arranged in his circles, and he knew that his female relatives were on the lookout for a suitable match for him. He was only twenty-four. There was no hurry to marry, but there was no doubt that he was a catch, even now that he was far away in the gardens.

After playing and freshening up, they joined the others in the verandah of the clubhouse where afternoon tea was being served. In golf slacks and tee shirt, Ramona was at the head of the long table.

"Hello, my dear," she said to Anita. "Did you bring your famous samosas today?"

Anita was another old-timer, an Indian woman accustomed to British ways, having to re-adapt to a more Indian culture. She had strong, dark eyebrows, eyes that she outlined with a sweep of black eyeliner and chins that wriggled and jiggled when she laughed, which was most of the time. Her flesh bulged under her cropped blouse that revealed her ample midriff. She wore a blue and mustard sari that she used to wipe the sweat off her face.

"Of course, I did, Ramona! I brought enough for everybody, I hope."

There were also contributions of pakoras, gulab jamuns and sandesh. The days of macaroons, meringues and cucumber sandwiches were over.

"Have you met the new chap from Delhi?" Anita continued, dipping her samosa in mango chutney. "I saw Samira playing tennis with him today. Very handsome, no?"

"Yes, I've met him. He's very handsome," agreed Ramona, who knew exactly what Anita was getting at.

Charles sat at the other end of the table with the young people. Samira looked around, happy to be home and increasingly comfortable in company. Ravi was easy and relaxed and already seemed to know everyone. Maybe she'd been too quick to judge him. And it wasn't as though there were many young people around.

At lunch time the following day, they heard the phone ring in the drawing room. Jetha ran to answer it and returned, addressing Samira.

"Missy Baba, Ravi Sahib telephone kia."

Mystified, she went to the telephone. Mark looked surprised.

"Hello, beautiful," Ravi's voice said. "How are you? I was wondering if you'd like to take a spin on my bike this evening."

"Hello, Ravi," she said, surprised. "Gracious, I've never been on a motorcycle before."

"Well, that's not a reason. You can trust me. I'll be very careful not to break you."

Samira had to laugh. "Oh, all right. It sounds like fun."

"What did he say?" asked Mark, jealously. Ravi was supposed to be his friend, not hers.

"He wants to take me for a ride on his motorcycle this evening."

"That's nice," said Charles, absently. "Where is he taking you?"

"That's not the point," said Mark. "The point is why is he taking her and not me?"

"Stop it, Mark," said Ramona. "It's none of your business."

"Thank you, Mother," said Samira, glaring at Mark. "Sometimes, people want to see me, not you, believe it or not."

"Now, you two, you're not children anymore," Ramona interjected.

"Coming, dear?" Charles held out Ramona's chair for her to rise. "Time for my nap."

"Typical," thought Samira. "He always takes off at the slightest sign of confrontation."

Her indignation with Ravi had evaporated, and she was suddenly glad of an opportunity to get away from her family, even if only for a few hours. Mark had a lot of growing up to do. It was time he realized that the men who came by were not always there to see him. Meanwhile, she was excited about her date and digested the implications of Ravi's phone call. A young man wanted to see her and had asked her out. She actually had a date! He would be here in a few hours.

She ran to her room and searched through her wardrobe for something to wear. What did one wear on a motorcycle? After the comments her mother made about her new trousers, she hesitated to wear them. But it really wouldn't do to wear a dress or a pair of shorts. Maybe she should stop considering the opinion of her mother? She found the red trousers and tried them on with a white, halter-necked blouse. She swung around and regarded herself from behind. She filled out the pants nicely. She decided that she would wear them and that they actually looked quite cute. Red trousers for a ride on Ravi's red motorcycle! By the time he arrived, her outfit had been complimented with red lipstick and a red-and-white striped headscarf to protect her hair from the wind.

When she heard him arrive, she ran down the steps to meet him, excited, a little nervous and beset with her usual insecurity.

"Phew!" he said when he saw her. "You look like a movie star!" He looked into her eyes, happy to see her. Samira smiled and felt herself relax.

"Really? Thank you!"

"Yes, really. Are you ready? Hop on and hold on to me."

Mark watched them stealthily from the verandah above. Feeling slighted, he didn't come down to greet Ravi. From the corner of her eye, Samira was aware he was lurking in the shadows. She settled into the motorcycle's seat and placed her hands on Ravi's shoulders. With a roar and a lurch, they were off. It was an exhilarating moment.

They didn't talk much. It was too loud. She wondered where he was taking her. Not that it mattered. She enjoyed the sensation of speed and being so close to him. She wasn't nervous at all about being alone with him or being on the bike. He maneuvered it with great skill, and she felt no qualms about trusting him.

She saw that they were going in the direction of Mal Bazaar. When they arrived in the town, he turned off the highway and went down a road she'd never been on before. They stopped near a lake with an ancient shrine beside it, festooned with marigold garlands. A magnificent banyan tree spread its branches offering dense shade by the green water.

"What a pretty spot!" said Samira, jumping off the motorcycle. "I've never been here before."

"I'm glad you like it."

People walked around the lake enjoying the cool of evening, laying offerings on the shrine or resting in the shade of the tree. They were curious about the glamorous young couple, the foreign lady in red trousers, and the green-eyed man. Children stopped to gawk at them, and a few young men made lewd comments about Samira. Others gathered around to admire the shiny red motorcycle. Ravi sensed Samira's discomfort.

"Maybe we should leave. I'm sorry."

"It's not your fault. It's just the way things are around here."

They had no option but to go back to Ranikot. As they pulled away, Ravi placed his hand over her hand resting on his shoulder. In the dying light, it seemed natural for her to rest her cheek against his back. He drew her hand around his waist, and she moved closer, both arms around him.

"Stay a while," she urged, when they got back to her bungalow. "Have a drink with us."

The family was on the verandah in the twilight.

"Well, how was it?" they asked.

"Did you fall off?"

"Did he go too fast?"

Ravi and Samira laughed. He took a seat beside Mark and sensing that he was feeling left out, made an effort to mollify him, which didn't go unnoticed by Samira. She discovered that she was beginning to like him a lot. He didn't take much persuading to stay for dinner. Mark regained his good humor, and they arranged to play tennis next club day.

As Ravi took his leave after dinner, Samira accompanied him outside to have a few moments alone with him.

"I had a wonderful time," she said.

"I'd like to do it again, if you would. I'll find somewhere better for us to go next time."

She laughed. "I'd love to. And it doesn't really matter where we go."

He drew her to him and put his arms around her waist. "Am I allowed to kiss you now?"

She felt herself blushing and at a loss for words. He took her silence for consent. His lips found hers, and he kissed her softly and gently.

"It would be easy to love you," he whispered. "And I think that maybe I do."

Then he was gone, and she lingered in the garden under the big, round moon pasted against the purple sky. She needed time to collect her thoughts and cool her flushed cheeks, still feeling the tingle of his kiss on her mouth.

Chapter 9
Dooars, 1977

It was the day of the Annual Flower Show at the club. Ramona had been preparing her exhibits for weeks. Ramchand had thought of nothing else for months. He refused to trust the other gardeners with watering his prize plants or applying fertilizer. Each day, he zealously studied the skies for rain. Too much rain and his fragile flowers would be destroyed, too little and his vegetables would shrivel and die.

He was the only gardener who knew the exact level and angle of pruning required to ensure a healthy re-growth. Everything needed to be planned to the last detail. He didn't want his prize specimens maturing too early or too late. One of the cauliflowers in his vegetable garden was colossal, a prizewinner for sure. But it would be past its prime by the day of the flower show. It would just have to be sent to the kitchen to be eaten by the Sahibs. What a waste!

At this time of year, he begrudged having to part with his produce. He wanted to have as much of a selection as possible for the big day. Normally, he took pride in preparing the daily baskets of fruit, vegetables and flowers and delivering them to the Memsahib. The smile on her face was thanks enough for him, even if she didn't always make a comment.

The morning of the flower show Ramchand woke at the crack of dawn and tiptoed out of bed trying not to disturb Usha. There was much to be done. He rushed to the bungalow, hoping the Memsahib wouldn't be late. In the house, Ramona sipped her morning tea, sitting up in bed. Charles had roused her before leaving for the factory, so she would have plenty of time to spend with Ramchand selecting their exhibits. Meanwhile, Samira awoke with a tingle of excitement running down her spine. Today was the day of the flower show, and Ravi had invited her to go with him. She wanted plenty of time to wash her hair, do her nails and experiment with the new makeup she'd bought to make herself look pretty.

Ramona threw on an old pair of slacks and went to find Ramchand. The garden was a flurry of activity. All the gardeners had been summoned early to help with the preparations. Kala had fetched the factory's pickup truck and was waiting to transport the plants to the club. She found Ramchand crouched over the cabbages.

"Salaam, Memsahib." He rose to his feet and touched his hand to his forehead. They walked up and down the rows of vegetables and selected the plumpest, ripest and most impressive produce. Then they moved to the flower beds, instructing the gardeners on what blooms to pick and how to best arrange them for the journey.

It was mid-morning before the truck was loaded. Kala would drive to the club with Ramchand beside him in the passenger seat. It was a perfect day. There was plenty of cloud cover but no smell of rain. Ramona was to follow in the car with Mark after lunch. Kala would drive the car back to the bungalow to get Charles, who wasn't going until late afternoon. Kala would drive the truck back at the end of the day. Samira didn't need a lift. She was going on the motorcycle with Ravi and in all probability would return with him.

Ramchand was in his element, issuing orders to the other gardeners as though he was a Sahib. He didn't care about losing popularity with his helpers. It was the result that mattered. He wanted to make sure all his exhibits were clearly identified with the labels he had been given by one of the organizers. He kept an eagle eye on them to make sure no one with lesser exhibits switched his labels. When she arrived with all the other Memsahibs, his Memsahib would prepare her entry for the Ladies' Flower Arrangement using the flowers she had chosen. People were coming from all over the Dooars to participate. He had made his selection of flowers for his Gardeners Bouquet and knew exactly how he was going to arrange it.

Back in the bungalow Samira was still experimenting with her makeup and trying to decide on an outfit. Ramona and Mark had left after lunch. She couldn't go in a tennis skirt or shorts or one of her evening dresses. She had already worn her red slacks. All her dresses were old and tired. Why hadn't she thought to order something new? She badly needed to go to Darjeeling to shop. She searched frantically in her wardrobe and spotted an old purple dress she'd never worn because it had never fit her properly. She was running out of time.

She tried it on in desperation, struggling with the zipper. It wasn't too bad, a trifle short maybe. Or was it a little tight? She decided it would have to do and grabbed a pair of white sandals. They were filthy. The only other pair that looked decent was a pair of high-heeled black pumps with pointy toes, not something she would normally wear during the day. She heard the unmistakable sound of Ravi's motorcycle. Well, at least her hair and her face looked good. She had spent a lot of time making sure of that. She rummaged around, found a chiffon scarf that Ramona didn't want because it made her look too severe and ran down the steps to Ravi.

He whistled when he saw her.

"You look incredible! That's some dress."

"Do you think it looks okay?" As usual she was anxious.

"It's more than okay. It's beautiful. Now come here."

He kissed her on the mouth softly and looked into her eyes. Shaking, she tied the scarf around her hair and climbed behind him.

They looked everywhere for Ramona and Mark when they arrived. The flower show was in full swing, and everyone was there. Ravi walked with his arm around Samira. Ramona was just putting the finishing touches to her flower arrangement when she spotted them. A look of horror crossed her face. Samira had been rushing up to her and stopped dead in her tracks when she saw her.

"What's wrong, Mum?" she asked.

"Come with me," she said to Samira, marching her into the ladies' room. Ravi looked puzzled. Samira mouthed the words for him to wait.

"Where did you get that dress?" she demanded. "And why are you wearing those shoes?"

"It's… it's an old dress I never liked. The garden tailor made it," she stammered. "And my white shoes were scuffed, so I had to wear these. I didn't have anything else. Do I look awful?"

The look of distress on her face awakened an old memory in Ramona. She remembered Prava castigating her for the clothes she'd bought with her first paycheck and how it had made her feel. She had sworn to herself that day she would never treat her daughter the same way. And why exactly was she upset with Samira? She didn't look at all bad, just more adult than she'd ever seen her, especially because of the way she'd made up her face. Actually, she looked amazing, even though the dress was much more adult than what she normally wore. And the high heels seemed to accentuate how adult and, well, sexy, she looked.

"No you don't look bad at all. You look lovely. I was just surprised, that's all. I'm sorry. Now go and find Ravi."

"Thanks, Mum." Samira was genuinely surprised by her quick about turn. "Good luck with your arrangement."

She ran to find Ravi, not quite sure what to think and found him, not surprisingly, at the bar with Mark.

"Wow-ee!" exclaimed Mark when he saw his sister. "Nice dress!"

"Hi, sweetheart," Ravi murmured in her ear. "You look delicious."

"Give me one second, please," said Samira. She had dressed and run out of the house in such a hurry. She had to find out why everyone was reacting to her this way.

"Samira, is that you?"

It was Anita Dutt, large as life. She sniggered at Samira, looking her up and down.

"Ah, yes. I saw you with Ravi. I understand." She gave her a knowing look.

"You look very sexy. I'm sure he'll go for you," she shouted after Samira, as she ran to the ladies' room for the second time that afternoon. In the full-length mirror, she saw a woman in classy, high-heeled shoes, immaculate makeup and perfect hair, wearing a dress molded to her curves.

"Ohhh," she said to the woman. Was that really her? Tall, grown-up and sophisticated.

"Hi, Sammy. Gracious. Look at you. Aren't you all grown-up!" said a woman walking in.

"Hello, madam….why, Sammy, I didn't recognize you!" someone else said, as she walked across the ballroom. She was elated and confident knowing for once that she looked sensational. She went to find Ravi so that she could spend every moment of her newly found sensational-ness with him.

Then she ran into Charles.

"Hi, Daddy," she purred. He stared at the stylish, young woman, speechless.

"Sammy? Is it you?" He genuinely wasn't altogether certain.

"Daddy!" she said. "Of course it's me."

"Yes, dear, I know. You look very nice. Now where's Mummy?" he hurried away, at a loss for words.

Ramchand and the other gardeners were waiting outside the marquee while the judges went through the exhibits. No one was allowed inside until the judging was over. The suspense was unbearable. In the clubhouse, the Memsahibs were waiting, trying to hide their impatience. Memsahibs were not known for their patience at the best of times. Finally, the judges emerged, and the ladies thronged in, followed by the planters and then their gardeners after a respectable period of time. Ramchand frantically looked around. He hoped for a "Highly Commended" rosette, at least one to take home to Usha.

In all the commotion, he saw Ramona beckoning and pointing to his "Gardener's Bouquet." It was a combination of scarlet and purple blooms, roses, pansies, violets and trails of morning glory against a background of palm fronds. The rosette attached to it did not say "Highly Commended." He didn't understand why Ramona and all the others were congratulating him and thumping him on the back. "Best in Show" it said on the large red rosette. That must be good judging by everyone's response. His English was not that good.

It was Ravi who understood his confusion and translated for him. He whispered in his ear, so no one else would realize he didn't know what it meant. Ramchand stood gazing at the rosette with tears in his eyes. He had the best exhibit in the show! He, Ramchand! His eyes met Ramona's, and she smiled at him warmly. Mark came over and hugged him. Charles shook his hand and said,

"Shabash, Mali. Shabash."

A beautiful young lady seized his hand. In a haze, he realized that it was Samira, his Missy Baba, who was excited for him.

And as if that was not enough, there were other awards, First Prize for his Ena Harkness Roses, Third Prize for his gooseberries and there it was, the coveted "Highly Commended" rosette for his display of Sweet William. What more could a man ask for? He cared nothing for the wads of cash that accompanied the gardeners' awards. He couldn't wait to get home and tell Usha.

He and Kala were the last to leave. There were many other exhibitors loading their vehicles, and they had to wait their turn. He tucked a red rose and a few strawberries away for his wife. She had likely spent the day alone waiting for his return. He knew Ramona wouldn't mind. Back at the bungalow, he unloaded the truck, exhausted. It had been a long day, long, but possibly the best day of his life.

He took the short walk to the labor lines and walked up the path to his home under the banana trees. The house was lit and filled with people. Baffled, he walked in holding his rosettes, the red rose and the strawberries. Had they already heard about his success? For the second time that night, he saw things in a blur and didn't fully understand. And for the second time that night, he heard news that he had been waiting a lifetime to hear. Usha ran up to him smiling joyfully. It had nothing to do with his rosettes, his red rose or his wads of cash. With eyes brimming over with tears, Usha broke the news to him that she was beyond her first trimester for the first time. She was with child!

Over the following months, Ravi, Samira and Mark fell into a routine that worked for all three of them. Mark acknowledged that

the couple wanted a certain amount of alone time, which he was happy to accommodate as long as they included him in some of their activities. They played tennis as often as they could, though it was not tennis season and the courts were often water-logged. It seemed that it was always either too hot or too wet. There were only so many destinations to drive to on the motor bike. Samira refused to include Ravi's bungalow as a viable destination, no matter how hard he tried to persuade her otherwise. It was not so much that she didn't trust him, as much as she knew she could not to be relied on to resist him.

She finally accepted a dinner invitation to his house with Mark as chaperone. It was a hot, muggy night. Bright, yellow stars lit their way from the car to the verandah in the moth-infested air. There wasn't much information about Ravi to be gleaned from his bungalow. It was furnished by the company, and he had few personal effects. There was a picture of his parents on the mantelpiece, a distinguished-looking couple looking sideways away from the camera in a typical studio pose. Samira noted that Ravi had inherited his father's green eyes and his mother's chiseled features. There were no books, as he was not a reader, but there were interesting pictures on the wall and brass sculptures on the mantelpiece.

Samira walked over to study them, commenting,

"My, what an interesting collection of statues!"

Ravi watched her quizzically and laughed to see her blush when she realized that it was a set of Kama Sutra figurines in various sexual poses, most of them requiring a high degree of gymnastic prowess.

"Ohhh!" she was embarrassed by her faux pas. "I didn't realize what they were."

"Sorry, baby, this is a bachelor pad."

Mark had seen the figures many times and was memorizing the poses for future reference. He wondered whether Ravi and Samira had made love. It was obvious that Samira had never been here before. And there was nowhere else they could have possibly done it. Or was there? He was going back to college soon, and they would have plenty of opportunity to do whatever they liked. Not that he thought Samira would necessarily allow Ravi to have his way. She was too much of, well, not a prude, but she was too smart to be taken advantage of. One thing was clear. Ravi was smitten by her.

In some ways, he couldn't wait to go back to college. At least there were plenty of young ladies there. His college mates always came back full of stories about their sexual adventures. He hated to admit that he was a virgin. There wasn't a single girl remotely in his age group to be seen for miles.

Ravi's bearer came in with their drinks, Kingfisher beer for the men and Ruby wine for Sammy. There were also peanuts and hot gram.

"Well, it's nice to get away from the old folks once in a while," said Mark.

"They're probably enjoying the break from us as much as we are from them," laughed Samira.

She and Mark had never done this before. It had always been the family that was invited out to dinner or went on trips. This was fun, something new and exciting and part of being an adult. She looked towards Ravi's bedroom. If she took one of her bathroom investigations, would he direct her towards his room or the guest room? Well, she was going to find out.

"Ravi, where's the bathroom?" she asked.

"Come this way." He leapt up gallantly and showed her into one of the bedrooms off the drawing room. She could see at once that it was the guest bedroom.

"The bathroom's through there," he said. "I hope you'll find everything you need."

She walked in, bolted the door and looked around. There were pink towels on the towel rail and pink soaps, shampoo and bubble bath. As though he were expecting a woman guest! Were these for her or did he have a penchant for pink? She noted that everything was new and unopened. Should she say something? She walked out to rejoin the men.

"Nice bathroom," she grinned.

"I tried to find everything you'd need," said Ravi. "I hope I didn't miss anything."

So it had been for her. That was really nice of him. Or was it that he'd been hoping to…well, if he had he would have put it all in his bathroom. Right? What would she do if…or when…he tried to make love to her? She knew that it was only a matter of time. Did she want to? The answer was obvious. She did! But that didn't mean she would. Even after all these months, she wasn't altogether sure she trusted him.

Suddenly, the phone rang. The sound echoed through the sparsely furnished room. Ravi rushed to his desk and grabbed it.

"Yes, hello, Papa. How are you? I'm fine. How's Mama? Good, good. I see. I don't think so. No. Well, let me think about it. I'll call you back soon. Love to Mama. Bye."

He replaced the receiver, somewhat flustered. It was obviously a trunk call from Delhi, which perhaps explained his brevity.

"Sorry. That was my father. Family matters, nothing urgent. Let's have dinner! I hope you're hungry."

He went to the back of the house and ordered the bearer to serve dinner. Afterwards they played cards late into the night, then drove home and crept about the house and into their beds like mischievous children.

Chapter 10
Northern Ireland, 1943-1971

Justin Laird grew up in Newcastle in County Down, one of the five counties of Northern Ireland. His father, Edward, owned a bakery shop on the promenade. Irene, his mother, helped run the shop in the mornings after Justin and his brother Adrian went to school. Edward started the ovens up early so that a fresh batch of soda and wheaten farls would be ready for his first customers at eight o'clock.

By the time Irene arrived to help prepare the scones, potato bread and doughnuts, the smell of freshly baked farls was already wafting down the street. She was a stocky, full-bosomed woman who had married late in life. She was Edward's second wife. His first wife had left him for a young jockey from Kilkenny, leaving him to rear the two boys, who were three and six. Irene's family owned a farm in County Armagh. The oldest of seven, she assumed that she had been left "on the shelf" when she was still single at thirty-five. She worked as a hairdresser in Newry, in one of the side streets facing a parking lot in an unfashionable part of the dingy market town.

Newry was close to the southern border, and its residents were well situated to participate in cross-border trade. Farmers sold their produce to the highest bidder, which would be largely determined by the value of the Irish punt against the British pound. People would buy their petrol, groceries and other necessities in either the North or the South, depending on which was cheaper at the time.

During a period when goods were cheaper in the South, a customer walked into the salon where Irene worked from the parking lot across the street. He was badly in need of a haircut. He was at pains to explain that he was not normally a frequenter of these unisex salons, as though there was something illicit about them, but had a very important meeting to attend in Dundalk, for which he needed a haircut.

Irene had appeared from the back of the salon and threw a cape over his shoulders. She was soon tut-tutting about the state of his hair. Edward, a well-built, clean-shaven business man, was not accustomed to feeling intimidated or to having his hair cut by a woman. He was unprepared for the feeling of helplessness he experienced in the hands of Irene. But yes, he trusted her judgment implicitly, he told her, enjoying the pleasant sensation of her gigantic assets pushing against his shoulder. He agreed that he wanted a style that was professional and distinguished. At that moment, there was nothing he wouldn't have done just to gain her approval.

So she snipped away, promising him that he would be pleased with the result. When she spun him around to look in the mirror, he was aghast to see that she had cut off his prized comb-over, and that he now looked like exactly what he was, a balding, middle-aged man, with no comforting lock of hair to conceal the naked patch on his head. Feeling exposed and vulnerable, he rushed out of the salon to his meeting in Dundalk, where he succeeded in closing the sale of his petrol station in Belfast.

He discovered to his intense surprise that Irene had been right. People started to take him more seriously. There was no more of that giggling behind his back that he had tried so hard to ignore. Also, luck seemed to go his way. Not only did the sale of his petrol station in Belfast go smoothly, he was also successful in acquiring a small bakery shop in Newcastle for next to nothing. Every time anyone complimented him on his hair, he thought of Irene. He also found that he could not forget the sensation of her breasts pushing against his back. So it was perhaps not completely by chance the next time he was driving through Newry that he happened to stop at the Snip It and Set It salon. He told the receptionist that he needed a cut and asked for Irene.

He had timed it for just before five o'clock, so he could invite her to join him for a drink after work. He took her to the very grand Manor Hotel where he ordered gin and tonics. They sat at a table by the window in the bar. With auburn hair and a freckled face, she was by no means an attractive woman, yet her ample proportions and flamboyant style of dress gave her a certain presence. She had a hearty laugh and launched into her second gin and tonic with gusto. Because it was going so well, he asked for a table in the dining room and bought her dinner.

He didn't have time to waste. He wanted someone who would keep house, care for his boys and keep him warm at night. Not only did she excite him sexually, something his thin, beautiful wife had failed to do, she didn't seem to be in the least bit deterred by the fact that he had two young children who needed to be taken care of. She had no illusions as to her marriageability. But as the days passed, they developed a passion for each other that took them both by surprise. They went to her family's farm where she introduced him around proudly, and it emerged that in addition to her other attributes, she also knew how to bake.

Adrian was nearly seven years old and Justin still three when they first met Irene after the civil wedding ceremony in Downpatrick Town Hall. She gathered the boys into her arms and rustled up something for them to eat, her remedy for every situation in life. Adrian still remembered his mother and bristled at the thought of her having left on account of some insufficiency on his part. He grew sullen and insecure, never revealing his memories of his mother to anyone. Justin grew up oblivious to the fact that Irene was not his real mother. Adrian continued to maintain a certain distance from Irene, which she could never quite permeate, with the result that she lavished all her pent-up motherliness on Justin.

They bought a large house perched on a cliff overlooking the sea in Newcastle, in the lea of the Mourne Mountains. It turned out that Irene had a penchant for grandeur, something that Edward was only too happy to indulge. The house was renovated to satisfy her newly established standards and filled with expensive antique furniture and paintings. Of course, Edward being the businessman that he was made sure that they never paid retail for anything. Consequently, they gave the impression of being much more affluent than they really were.

Irene worked conscientiously at the bakery and at rearing the boys. It seemed that her blessings were never ending when the years passed, even when it emerged that she was unable to conceive.

"You see, I already have a family," she said to Edward. "I have my two sons, which were given to me by the Lord before I knew I could never have children of my own."

The bakery flourished as the boys grew up. Adrian went to university in Leeds where he studied engineering. He was considered to be the brains of the family. Justin was the clumsy one who lagged behind in class and who couldn't be relied on to carry out the simplest chore. Anything he was asked to do, he did so badly Edward would say it was easier to just do it himself.

"That fool son of mine can't even mow the lawn," he complained to Irene.

But Justin was smart enough to know that if he did a job badly enough he would get out of ever having to do it again. So while Adrian proudly cut the grass in perfect stripes, Justin sat in the house and ate scones with Irene. While Adrian suffered in miserable digs in England, Justin stayed home, his meals cooked and his laundry done by his mother. When this became too cloying and restrictive even for him, he applied for a job in the Sirocco Plant in Belfast where he practiced the engineering Adrian was still studying. There he heard about how their air conditioning and drying machinery were shipped to many destinations across the world, including the tea plantations in India.

He rented a red-brick, terraced house on the Holywood Road in Belfast, convenient to where he worked. He had been reared a Methodist, attending church every week. Like the majority of the population, however, he couldn't identify with the bigotry that was rampant in the country. The sectarian violence was perpetuated by a surprisingly small percentage and festered only in certain neighborhoods. Unlike Adrian, he didn't want to escape the troubles by simply crossing the water to the mainland. He felt a certain stigma against his countrymen any time he visited England. So when the opportunity arose at work to conduct inspections and supervise new installations in India, he jumped at it. He had been seeing a young lady, Lorraine McIlroy, who worked at the Harland and Wolff Shipyard, but did not feel a strong sense of commitment to her.

She was tiny, delicate and soft-spoken. He had never seen her without her high heels, nail polish and lipstick, not even when they got together at weekends and visited the zoo or one of the stately homes near Belfast. She had shoulder-length auburn hair and never looked anything short of immaculate. They had great times together. She made him laugh and had unlimited energy. He thought of her as his little bird, colorful like a robin or a canary, with skinny legs, tiny feet and large, hazel eyes. She pecked at her food like a bird and spoke in high-pitched, reedy tones.

"But what about us?" she said to him, with wide eyes when he broke the news that he was going to India.

"Ach, I'll be back before you know it," he said. "It's only for a few months. I'll write to you every day."

He knew he couldn't expect her to wait for him, but this was something he felt had to do. It was his opportunity to see the world, advance his career and escape the province.

His mother was equally upset.

"Why India?" she cried. "Go to France or Spain like everyone else!"

"Ma, it's business," he said. "Not a vacation."

She was petrified at the thought of his travelling somewhere so alien and far away. And dirty! She hated anywhere or anything strange and foreign. Heaven knows what diseases he might catch. She couldn't sleep from worry. But he was adamant. He took all the vaccinations they said he needed and had to apply for a passport. He had never been overseas.

"Ma, I'll need my birth certificate," he said, over the phone. "I'll pick it up this weekend." There was silence on the line.

"You there?" he said. "Did you hear what I said?"

"Yes, dear." She spoke faintly. "Cheerio."

She was taking it badly. But surely she wouldn't stand in his way? He took Lorraine home for the weekend with him, separate rooms, of course. Edward tried to tell Justin to come without her, saying there was something important they needed to discuss. But Justin wanted to compensate for leaving Lorraine for so long. He didn't want to upset her further by not spending the weekend with her. They arrived in Newcastle in time for lunch on Saturday, a feast of chicken soup, pork chops with homemade apple sauce and mashed potatoes.

Both Edward and Irene were subdued over lunch.

"Everything okay?" Justin asked. Surely they were taking things too far. Adrian had left home right after his A Levels at eighteen and never come back apart from the occasional visit.

"Your Da would like to talk to you after lunch," said Irene. "You can sit in the dining room."

They were eating lunch in the kitchen. The dining room was reserved for Christmas dinner and sometimes not even that. It was too perfect to be eaten in. The cherry table gleamed, and the matching sideboard was laden with Irene's collection of silver which she polished every fortnight.

Lorraine and Irene went into the lounge to watch "Crossroads" on television.

"What is it, Da?" asked Justin, genuinely worried now.

"It's about your birth certificate," said Edward, uneasily.

"What about it? Is it lost? It's no big deal if it is, you know?"

"No, it's not lost. I have it here. There's something we haven't told you son."

"What? Am I adopted or something? Everyone says I look exactly like you."

"No, you're not adopted...exactly. It's that your Ma, well, she's not really your mother. Now, she's terrified of what you might do."

"What! You're joking! How can she not be my mother?" Justin was shocked. "I mean, usually it's the other way round."

"Your real mother walked out on you and Adrian when you were three years old. He was old enough to remember her."

"But he never said anything to me!" Justin said.

"He said he started to a few times. But you didn't seem to understand. And you were always so fond of Irene."

So Irene had showered him with love even though she wasn't really his mother! And now she was afraid what effect the news might have on him.

"Well, she's still my mother. It doesn't change anything as far as I'm concerned," he said.

"Is that so?" said his father, greatly relieved. "We just didn't know how you might react."

Not normally demonstrative, the two men embraced, and Justin went to the lounge and put his arms around Irene.

"Really, Ma, did you think I'd just go off you or something?"

"I didn't know what to think. We thought you'd be angry. Now I don't know whether to laugh or cry! Bygorra!" She wept tears of relief.

"Well, I'm a bit angry, so I am. You should a told me sooner."

Lorraine was puzzled, not knowing what was going on. Justin filled her in briefly and Edward said,

"Well, I think I need a stiff drink after all that. What d'you say, Ma?"

"For sure!" she agreed. "You have something, too, Lorraine."

Justin saw in the birth certificate later that his real mother's name was Doreen McVeigh. He had no curiosity about her and no desire to look for someone who had deserted him when he was only a baby.

Chapter 11
Northern Ireland
1971-1972

Justin flew by B.O.A.C. from Heathrow to Bombay and then on a dilapidated India Airways Dakota to Bangalore in southern India. He visited a number of tea plantations in the Nilgiri Hills before flying to Calcutta and taking a train to the cotton mills outside the city to inspect their Sirocco equipment. Then he flew to Jorhat to make the necessary repairs and recommendations regarding the machinery in the plantations of Assam.

There he encountered a fellow countryman, Tom Davidson, manager of Yong Tung Tea Estate. As there were no hotels, planters were required to provide board and lodging for visiting agents and engineers for a small fee remitted by the tea companies. Tom and Martha, his wife, were from Hillsborough and hadn't been back in six years. Both were hungry for news of home. She instructed her cook to prepare shepherd's pie and chips for their visitor.

"Alas, I have no Smithwicks or Guinness to offer you," Tom said, mournfully. "We'll have to make do with the local brew."

"So, Justin," he said later, puffing on his after-dinner cigarette in the fresh air of the verandah. "How do you like India? Bit of a change from Belfast, eh?"

"It certainly is," Justin agreed. "But I feel like a change is just what I need. Fact is I almost wish I didn't have to go back. The lifestyle here suits a fellow like me."

"Interesting you should say that," Tom said. "If you really mean it, I know there's a position in a nearby garden waiting to be filled. It's for assistant manager. With your experience, it shouldn't be too long before you get your billet."

Justin was silent, deep in thought. Things were moving almost too quickly. But the thought of staying here, away from the trouble-stricken city and escaping the dismal Belfast winters, was appealing.

"I have to admit I'm interested," he said. "really interested. But how do I go about applying?"

"Leave it to me, my friend. I'll say a few words in the right ears. You're perfect for the job."

Justin could scarcely sleep that night as he mulled things over in his mind. Irene would be heartbroken, of that there was no doubt. But he had to live his own life, and this was what he wanted to do. Then there was Lorraine to consider. He was surprised how much he missed her. But she would never fit in here. She was too fragile. Or was she? Under all that lipstick and powder was a resilience that he felt he had underestimated. It could get awful lonely here for a chap on his own. His mind churned all night long.

He made his farewells in the morning and visited the next plantations on his list. He flew back to Belfast and received a phone call from Jefferson Brothers the very next week. They wanted him to fly to their offices in London for an interview. Tom Davidson's recommendation and his experience with Sirocco and the fact that he had visited a tea plantation made him an ideal candidate. He received a job offer in the mail a few days later, requiring him to report for duty in one months' time.

This time, it was his turn to visit his parents filled with trepidation. He wanted to tell them two things. One was that he was going to accept the job in India, and the other was that he intended to propose to Lorraine. He didn't know if she would accept, but he felt that his happiness would be complete if she went with him. He recognized that he was acting impulsively, but it was his way. He wasn't one to overthink things and talk himself out of them.

His next step was to approach Lorraine's father and ask for her hand in marriage, still with no knowledge as to whether or not she wanted to marry him. She had missed him and was delighted to see him back, but he didn't know if it went any deeper than that. Toby, her father, was skeptical. She had a good job in the shipyard.

Why would she want to go all the way to India? But wasn't going to stand in the way of his daughter's happiness, and if that's what she wanted, then he was welcome to her. He had plenty more daughters to contend with, heaven alone knew.

Justin went to Rea's Jewelers near the city hall in Belfast and bought an engagement ring, a diamond surrounded by rubies. Then he took Lorraine to their favorite spot beside the River Lagan and on bended knee, asked her to be his wife. He was going to India to be a tea planter and wanted her to go with him. But he would understand if it was not for her and if he was not the man she wanted to spend her life with.

"I'm shocked," she cried, her high-pitched voice rising. "Good Lord! What a surprise! You want me to go to India with you?"

"It's very far away, and things will seem strange and foreign," Justin explained. He wanted to be honest with her. "Yet in many ways, it will be an easy life for you and certainly very different from anything in Northern Ireland."

She was overcome. This was certainly unexpected. But she had missed him while he was gone. She knew she loved him, even though he didn't make it sound too romantic. Had he even said he loved her? Yet it was romantic, in a strange sort of way, going to a strange, exotic country and starting an exciting new life. It would be an adventure, and yes, she was happy, very happy, she said, to accept his proposal. He threw his arms around her. He had been so afraid she was going to say no. Somehow, he needed to have her beside him as he embarked on the biggest adventure of his life.

They had a lot to accomplish in a very short time. Both had to submit notice to their places of work, he to Sirocco and she to Harland & Wolff. They had a wedding to organize, a journey to plan and their new life in India to prepare for. Once Irene got over the disappointment of Justin's leaving, she entered wholeheartedly into preparations for the wedding and for India. The list of items they needed was interminable. Lorraine wanted to take all her clothes and shoes. There were linens to pack, crockery and cutlery, medication, pictures, ornaments and kitchenware. They had a mountain of possessions that needed to be shipped.

The wedding was at the city hall in Belfast. It was a simple, civil ceremony followed by breakfast at the Malone House Hotel. Lorraine arrived in an ivory dress that came to just below her knees and fitted her tiny form like a glove. She teetered in high-heeled satin shoes with little bows on the toes. She was like a china doll that would shatter if dropped, a child permitted to dress in woman's clothing. Her veil was a concoction of satin and lace that perched on her head like a butterfly. Her pale skin was accentuated by a very red lipstick and her dark, nervous eyes. She clung to Justin's arm as if her legs could not support her.

Justin and Adrian, faces scrubbed and pale, wore dark gray suits. Adrian was recently divorced but had already met someone else. To Irene's relief, she was not at the wedding. It was difficult enough having to cope with Lorraine's large family. At least they were Protestant, she said to herself. It made everything so much simpler, especially when the young ones came along.

Irene was resplendent in her mink stole that she'd found on sale at Robinson and Cleaver, unfortunately too late for Adrian's wedding. Unable to resist a bargain, she'd bought it knowing it was only a matter of time before another mink-wearing opportunity would come along. This was not the large wedding she would have liked for Justin, but she knew the photographs would be displayed on her mantelpiece for years to come next to the photograph of Adrian's wedding. Should that be taken down now they were divorced, she wondered.

She had an irrepressible desire to impress Lorraine's family. It simply would not have done for her to have been outshone by the mother of the bride. Bernadette was an older version of her daughter, skeletal with ashy-gray skin from years of smoking and frizzy bronze hair.

"Brassy," thought Irene, "probably colored at a cheap salon or even at home." She would never have allowed a customer to walk out with those metallic tones.

Edward stood tall beside Irene in his three-piece navy suit. Now that Justin was going so far away, he wondered if he should have gone easier on his younger son, given him more respect. Obviously, he had done well at Howden Sirocco and had easily secured the tea planter's position. Other fathers encouraged their sons to enter the family business, but Edward had always made it clear that he wanted to cash in on the business as part of his retirement. Newcastle had blossomed into a thriving tourist destination, far from the troubles in Belfast and Armagh. Maybe it was time to think about putting it up for sale. And he had been feeling those pains down his arm. He knew people who went "on the sick" and were paid benefits by the British government for the rest of their lives.

Justin felt a new protectiveness towards his wife when they were married. While not consciously aware of it, he needed the presence of a woman in his life, someone to replace Irene. He was getting the best of both worlds, setting off on his bold adventures with his beautiful, young wife on his arm.

As for Lorraine, she was besotted by her new husband. When he left for India without her, she blamed herself for not doing more to keep him. What was a girl supposed to do? Give in sexually and risk being branded a slut, or save herself and lose her man to someone else who would? She had already decided to give in to him sexually when he proposed to her out of the blue.

From what he said, life in the tea plantations was lonely, and she would miss her family and friends. But how could she be lonely with him at her side? She didn't need anyone but him. And she wouldn't have to work in the secretarial pool at the shipyard any longer. She was going to be a married woman who didn't have to support herself and would live in a house with servants who did everything for her!

Justin and Lorraine would not have time for a honeymoon. They had too much to do. They had to finish packing and sort out which items to ship and which to take with them. All things considered, Lorraine could not be unhappy about not having a proper honeymoon.

"Sure, the trip itself will be a honeymoon, darling. This is all so exciting."

"It is, surely. Are you going to the doctor for your vaccinations this morning?" Justin felt warm towards his undemanding wife.

"Yes. My ma's coming with me. We have some shopping to do afterwards."

"Now, make sure you get yourself some comfortable things to wear. It's very different out there, you know that."

"You've told me a hundred times. You're my wee dote, and I love you." She put her arms around his neck and kissed him on both cheeks. She was the happiest girl in the world.

She had researched books on India in the library in Belfast, scrutinizing pictures of hunting scenes, fearsome warriors, tigers, elephants and ladies in elegant dresses being fanned by native boys, all suggesting to her idyllic romance. Who needed a honeymoon when such luxury awaited them?

Chapter 12
Assam, India, 1972

No amount of research could have prepared Lorraine for the shock of arriving in India and experiencing its bizarre sights, massive population and unrelenting heat! Everywhere, there were mosquitoes and insects that made her skin crawl. She screamed when huge, brown lizards appeared out of nowhere and ran up the walls.

"Darling, they're only tick-ticks! They're completely harmless," said Justin, finding himself in the tenuous position of having to justify his decision to move to the country and to explain away its abundant faults. The servants, who seemed alien and foreboding, made her nervous.

"Are you going to leave me alone with all these outlandish men?" she said, panicked as Justin prepared to go to work on his first day.

"Lolly, I can't stay here with you, and you know you can't come with me. You'll be perfectly safe. They're not going to attack you."

She locked herself in her room after he left. She curled up on the bed under the mosquito net, jumping at every sound. When someone knocked on the door, she cowered under the sheet and shouted at them to go away. She was still there when Justin returned home at lunch time.

"You silly goose! You can't stay in here forever," he said, hugging her. She clung to him, delighted to have him returned to her, safe and sound.

"Tom and Martha have invited us to dinner tonight," he said. "They're the couple from Hillsborough I told you about. Won't that be nice?"

"It'll be nice to meet a woman from back home," said Lorraine. "Although I'm sure they'll be very grand and sophisticated."

But the prospect of the outing gave her something to look forward to and prepare for in the recesses of her bedroom. She unpacked her dresses and hung them up in one of the wardrobes. She arranged her bottles of perfume and makeup jars on the dressing table and laid out her shoes. It was reassuring to be surrounded by pretty, familiar things. She had lots of new dresses and hoped one of them would be good enough for dinner tonight.

She took a long soak in the tub and began to relax. She washed her hair and wrapping herself in her dressing gown, ventured onto the verandah to dry it in the sunshine. The bearer prepared a tea tray and brought it out to her. He was gracious and polite, and Lorraine began to feel slightly ashamed.

"Er...thank you, bearer," she said, in her fluting voice. He had brought a plate of ginger biscuits with the tea. It was very nice sitting in the sunshine and having food and drink served to her. When her hair dried, she put it in rollers, painted her toenails and looked in her wardrobe.

When Justin came home hot and sweaty from the factory, he found her in the drawing room, wearing a frothy pink dress, white, high-heeled shoes and a pearl necklace.

"Now, isn't that a picture?" he said, relieved to see her smiling again. "I have the prettiest wee wife in the world!"

"Do I look okay?" she asked twirling her skirt.

"You look wonderful. Now, I'd better go and get cleaned up, and we'll have a drink before we leave."

Fifteen minutes later, he emerged in gray trousers and a pale blue shirt.

"We have the use of the garden jeep for a couple of weeks. After that, they expect us to use our own transportation. We'll need to look around for a car of some sort. Maybe Tom will be able to help us find one."

Driving through the silence of the black jungle to the neighboring tea garden was a new and frightening experience for Lorraine, after the extensive research she'd done on the wildlife and warfare in the country. Although it was only seven, it was already dark. The glare of the head lamps cut through the darkness on the road before them. The garden roads were two narrow strips of dirt with grass growing in the middle. They passed no one on the way. It was reassuring to see the lights of the Davidsons' bungalow. Tom and Martha were already at the top of the steps to meet them.

"Lorraine, how nice to meet you. Aren't you the pretty one? Congratulations, Justin. We're delighted you got the job. It's good to see you again." Martha embraced them warmly.

"I can't thank you enough for your recommendation," said Justin.

Tom kissed Lorraine's cheek and said, "Welcome to Assam. I hope you'll be very happy here."

Lorraine was still jet-lagged and exhausted from the journey. The humidity sapped her energy. Moths hovered around the lights on the verandah, and mosquitoes were attacking her unbitten skin. Tom and Martha weren't in the least bit grand, in fact, quite the opposite. There was not a trace of makeup on Martha's face, and she flopped around in a pair of comfortable open-toed sandals and wore a simple dress.

"Let's go inside, or you'll be eaten alive," she said. "How gorgeous you look! My, what a beautiful dress! Is this what they're wearing in Belfast these days? We are so out of it here. All my clothes are made by the garden tailor. Look at her wee shoes, Tom, and her adorable purse!" Lorraine couldn't help but feel warmed by Martha's genuine friendliness.

Justin was delighted by the effect his new wife was having and hoped that she and Martha would become friends. They passed a very pleasant evening. Tom said he would put Justin in touch with someone who was selling a car. He also succeeded in persuading him to take up golf and thought he knew of someone who wanted to get rid of his clubs.

"Of course, Lorraine should also take up golf," Martha said. "And tennis, too." They surveyed Lorraine dubiously. She looked like a china doll that should be on display in a glass cabinet. She was surely too frail and delicate to brandish tennis racquets and golf clubs. But Lorraine was full of surprises. She had apparently spent her teenage summers at a caravan site in Portrush playing golf.

"And also darts and pool," she confessed, somewhat shame-facedly. "But I'm very rusty. I haven't played in years, not since I started working."

"Well, you're one up on me there," said Justin. "Though I did play tennis in Newcastle, the few times it wasn't raining. We had a group that played on Wednesday nights and Sunday mornings. I might even have packed my racquet. Our luggage hasn't arrived yet."

"I've played a little tennis, too," said Lorraine. "But on grass courts that really weren't very good."

"Well, that's all we have here," said Tom. "There are four courts at the club. I hope you'll both come on Sunday. I'll see if I can find a set of golf clubs for you, Justin." Obviously, he hadn't quite taken it in that it was Lorraine who was the golfer.

The couple took their leave feeling greatly encouraged about life in tea.

"You were wonderful!" said Justin, taking Lorraine's hand. "And I hope you're going to enjoy the golf here as much as you did in Portrush."

"Oh, I'm really not sure I'll play. I was only a kid, and I don't want to make a fool of myself."

"Why don't we just play together to start with?" suggested Justin. "That would be fun, wouldn't it?"

"Darling, that would be lovely," said Lorraine, willing to do anything that would keep her husband beside her in this alien land.

The following morning, Justin was woken by screams from the bathroom. He jumped out of bed to see what was wrong and was horrified to see Lorraine pointing at a large yellow and brown snake curled around the base of the toilet. He grabbed her and shut the door. Then he ran to the back of the house shouting for the servants.

The bearer was confused at first but quickly understood there was something in the bathroom. He looked inside, unperturbed and shut the door again. He went to fetch one of the walking sticks on the umbrella stand and went into the bathroom brandishing it with both hands. Justin watched in horror as he manipulated the snake around the stick and took it out the back door of the bathroom. One of the gardeners killed the snake quickly and painlessly with a curved swathing knife. The bearer walked back into the house to replace the stick in the umbrella stand. He indicated to Justin that someone must have left the back door open.

"It was me! I opened it last night to let some air in. Jesus. I don't think I can bear this." Lorraine was aghast.

Justin was shaken, too. A snake in the house! That was a little hard to take. Was it dangerous, he wondered? What if it had attacked Lorraine? He would have to get some advice from Gordon Mills, his manager, or from Tom. He just couldn't afford to take any chances. He hated to leave Lorraine after what had happened, but he had no choice.

"I'm sorry, Lolly, but I have to go to work. I'll try to get home a little earlier at lunch time."

Lorraine had the jitters and didn't feel safe anywhere in the house once again. What if there were other snakes curled up elsewhere? She didn't want to be left alone but couldn't very well keep company with any of the servants, could she? Suddenly, they didn't feel as threatening as they had before. They were actually very polite, and she began to realize that they were human beings just as she and Justin were. She found a notebook and pen, went into the back verandah and summoned the bearer.

She decided that she was going to learn their language and that he was going to teach her, starting now. She pointed to herself and said,

"Lorraine Memsahib. You?" she pointed at him.

He was of medium height, probably in his thirties, with a pleasant demeanor. He already knew a little English and seemed to realize that she wanted to learn to communicate with him. He pointed at himself,

"Rama, bearer." He was proud of his title.

The lesson continued, with Lorraine taking notes. "Eidher ow" means "Come." "Jow" means "Go." They progressed from words to phrases, Lorraine trying to think of all the things she would need to say from day-to-day. Finally, she was able to indicate that she wanted the house searched for snakes and that the doors were to be kept firmly closed at all times. When Justin came home for lunch, he was relieved to find her with her notebook and pen, looking cool and collected.

"Are you feeling a little better, darling?" he asked, kissing her neck.

"I think so," she replied. "I had the entire house searched in case there were any other snakes lurking in corners."

"I take it they didn't find any?"

"I sincerely hope not. Are you hungry, darling?"

"Starving."

"Good." She called to the bearer in her high-pitched voice. "Ramu, khana liaw!"

Justin looked at her in admiration. "You're a wonder! You never cease to amaze me. I'm a very lucky man to have you as my wife."

"And don't you ever forget it!" she said.

That afternoon, they went out to do some serious shopping. First, they went to look at the car that Tom had recommended. It was a blue and white, two-door Standard Herald that Lorraine fell instantly in love with. The young planter who was selling it had a wife and three children and needed a bigger vehicle. After some heated discussion, they agreed on a price, and the car was theirs. Their driver drove home in the garden jeep leaving Justin and Lorraine to continue on in the Herald.

Their next stop was another plantation, also at Tom's recommendation. There they purchased a set of used golf clubs from a planter who was retiring. He wanted to get rid of most of his household items, and they found a few things that they had not thought to ship. They also bought a pair of Wilson Tennis racquets and an old typewriter. They loaded up the little car and drove home elated with their spoils.

"You were robbed on the car but stole the racquets and clubs," Tom told them later. "Don't ever pay for anything major again without consulting me, not for a while, anyway." He revealed to Justin that the snake was most likely a viper with a deadly poisonous bite.

Everything was strange and new to the young couple. Lorraine continued to learn Hindi with assistance from Martha and Ramu. She made copious efforts, poring over her notebook and practicing her pronunciation. Later that week, she told Ramu what groceries she wanted from the local market. She thought it would be nice to have chicken for Sunday dinner.

"I was horrified when he returned home with a live chicken," she told Martha the next day. "But didn't know enough Hindi to tell him we wanted to eat chicken, not rear them."

Martha and Tom laughed.

"You have a lot to learn, Lorraine," said Tom. "That's how chicken is sold in these parts! Don't worry, the cook will slaughter it. Just don't get too attached to the bird before you eat it!"

Chapter 13
Assam, India 1974

Justin and Lorraine became popular members of the club, especially when it became apparent that Lorraine was quite the athlete. She had a charismatic personality that people warmed to, and Justin had a difficult time keeping up with her in her social interactions, as well as on the golf course and the tennis court. She became quite the social belle with her wardrobe of stylish gowns and shoes. Months went by, and they both learned to adapt to the new lifestyle. It was undeniably lonely at times. They missed home but found themselves increasingly involved in the closely woven community.

There was one vital component missing that would have made their happiness complete. More than anything, they wanted to start a family of their own. But month after month went by and Lorraine was unable to conceive.

"Hardly surprising with those tiny hips of hers," Irene said to Edward, after receiving a letter from Justin saying that, no, Lorraine was not pregnant yet.

"I think I might suggest to Justin that maybe it's time they ran some tests."

The opportunity arose when Justin had to fly to Calcutta on business. They made an appointment with a specialist there, and Lorraine accompanied him on the trip. Despite the circumstances of her visit, it was wonderful to be in a city again. Calcutta was very different from Belfast, but after Jorhat, the shops and restaurants and hotels seemed extremely exciting.

They were put up by the company in the magnificent Grand Hotel and enjoyed eating at the fashionable restaurants on Park Street. They went to Mocambos, where they had delicious European food and danced to the strains of a sultry crooner accompanied by a four-piece jazz band. They had a fabulous tea at Flurys, and Lorraine went on a shopping spree at Newmarket, a shoppers' paradise where shoes, clothing, jewelry, curios and just about everything under the sun could be acquired. She loved the shoes made by Chinese craftsmen and added several pairs to her collection.

On their last day in the city, they went to the food hall for provisions to take back with them. A tantalizing aroma of new bread came from Nahoums' Bakery. The floral hall was redolent with the scent of roses, geranium, dahlias, marigolds, chrysanthemums and carnations. Vegetable stalls were laden with mountains of produce. Exotic species of fish wriggling on slabs of ice fascinated Lorraine, but she averted her eyes hastily from grotesque animal carcasses dangling from hooks in the meat market.

Brightly dressed housewives flitted from store to store followed by coolies balancing baskets with their purchases on their heads. It was difficult for Justin and Lorraine to restrain themselves, but there was only so much they could take back on the plane. They made do with bacon, sausages, sticks of barley sugar and a lump of cheese.

"Let's come back soon," said Lorraine, relishing the energy of the city despite having spent two mornings at Woodlands Nursing Home undergoing tests. Now, all they could do was wait for the results. They tried to avoid the subject on their little vacation. There was nothing to be gained by dwelling on it, although the subject weighed heavily on their minds.

Two weeks later a bulky envelope arrived, addressed to Lorraine. Justin brought it home with the rest of the mail at lunch time.

"You open it, darling," Lorraine said, faintly. "I can't bear to look."

He tore the envelope open and tried to decipher its contents. "It seems that everything is normal," he said. "They say you're in perfect health and can see no reason why you shouldn't get pregnant. They suggest...." his voice trailed off. "They're recommending that maybe I should be checked out."

Not in his wildest dreams had he ever imagined that the problem could lie with him. The notion was inconceivable. Surely all they needed was to be patient to give it a little more time.

"You?" gasped Lorraine. "Surely not?"

How could this be happening to them? They were both young and athletic, and their sex life was more than healthy.

"Let's give it a rest for a while," Justin suggested. "We have plenty of time. I can't go back to Calcutta right now. Besides the Golf Championships are coming up. We should focus on getting ourselves ready. You have a real chance of winning."

"You're right, darling," agreed Lorraine, though she wondered if she'd be able to summon up any interest in participating. All she could think of was the child she so badly wanted. She had assumed responsibility for not being able to conceive. The fact that the problem might lie with Justin only made the situation worse and more final.

"Come home," Irene urged Justin, in response to his letter. She knew there could be nothing wrong with Justin. They just needed to run some proper tests on Lorraine. God only knew what the level of health care was in that country.

"Come home for a while. It will do you both good to get away from that place."

Secretly, she hoped that coming back might entice them to stay. Adrian had remarried in England and didn't want children. He was too busying partying with his young wife, who definitely didn't want babies. She was still a baby herself. And Irene worried terribly about Edward's health. The bakery shop was up for sale, but there were no buyers. Every time there was a bomb or sectarian shooting on the news, their hearts sank. The economy fluctuated according to the level of violence.

Actually, Justin was due home leave in a few months. He would have served three years in tea and was entitled to a paid trip home with his wife. It seemed like a good idea to have themselves examined in Belfast. The city had some of the best hospitals in the world, thanks to the troubles.

So in a matter of weeks, Justin and Lorraine landed at Aldergrove Airport, met by both of their families. Lorraine was amazed by how pale everyone looked. She burst into tears when she saw her mother who had aged tremendously in the three years since she'd last seen her. Her hair's brassy tones had subsided into dirty streaks of gray, and her skin sagged like that of a much older woman from all the years of smoking. Toby and Edward had both lost a little hair, and Edward had gained weight. Only Irene looked better than ever, resplendent in a green mohair coat and freshly set hair.

Lorraine gasped at the blast of cold air that hit them as they stepped outside the terminal. They'd forgotten how it felt to be cold. Despite the dismal sky and the bleak countryside, it was very good indeed to be home. They had six weeks to reconnect with family and friends. They planned to split their time between both families and perhaps visit Donegal for a few days. But first, they needed to go to the Royal Victoria Hospital in Belfast.

The next morning, they went to the hospital for their scheduled appointments, regarding the foreboding façade of the Royal Victoria Hospital with feelings of dread. Lorraine clung to Justin's arm. The lingering hospital smell sank to the pit of her stomach. They walked through long, echoing corridors, and she waited shivering with cold and fear, while Justin was whisked away by one of the nurses. She felt she would never be warm again. Scruffy men in anoraks and dirty sneakers and women in ugly, comfortable shoes patiently waited beside her. Her feet froze in her high-heeled pumps despite the stockings she was wearing for the first time in years. Finally, her name was called. She panicked momentarily, wishing Justin was with her. But, almost as if to compensate for the hospital's austerity, the nurses teemed with kindness and goodwill.

"Now just you follow me, dearie. Go you behind that curtain and put this on, with the opening at the back." She was handed a hospital gown. She gave blood and urine and had her blood pressure taken. There was another long wait to see the doctor, who was gruff and unsympathetic.

Finally, the ordeal was over, and she was reunited with a pale, subdued Justin. This was his first hospital experience. They couldn't wait to get away from the cold dankness of the hospital. In Calcutta, it had been totally different. There Lorraine was a Memsahib, and the hospital was for the privileged, with all the facilities and comforts of a luxury hotel.

Once in the bracing air outside, they found they were starving and dived into a pub for some lunch.

"I think the occasion calls for a drink. I need something to steady my nerves. What d'you say?" said Lorraine.

"I absolutely agree," said Justin, who needed a drink like never before in his life. They ordered sausage rolls, the first they'd had in years. They were hot and delicious, just as they remembered them. They both started to feel better and decided that a second round of drinks was in order.

They were at Edward and Irene's house in Newcastle a few days later when the phone rang. Edward was home from the bakery, and they were about to cook dinner. It was the urologist who asked to speak to Justin.

"We have a full report out to you in the mail," he said, "but I thought I'd call you as it's a Friday. I'm afraid the news isn't good."

"I see," said Justin, his heart sinking. "What is it?"

"The problem is not with Lorraine. It's with you. It's a very unusual condition, and there are no symptoms. Some men produce abnormal antibodies against their own sperm. The antibodies attack the sperm on the way to the egg, preventing fertilization."

"In other words?"

"In other words…permanent infertility. I am truly sorry."

"But surely, there must be some treatment, some kind of remedy?" Justin struggled to digest the implications of what the doctor was saying.

"I will do some further research. Believe me, if there is anything that can be done, I will do it. And if you and your wife require counseling of any kind, I'll gladly arrange it."

"Thank you kindly," said Justin. "And thanks for taking the trouble to call me."

It was obvious to Lorraine, Edward and Irene that the news was not good from the tone of Justin's voice in the hallway. They waited silently as he entered the room and sat on the sofa beside Lorraine.

"That was the doctor," he said. "It seems the problem lies with me, something to do with my sperm preventing fertilization."

There was shocked silence.

"Well, at least now that they know what the problem is, so you can get treated for it," said Edward.

"Apparently, it's something that can't be treated," Justin said. "It's my fault we can't have a baby, Lorraine. It's me, not you."

Irene started to weep. "Now, don't be carrying on like that."

Lorraine clung to Justin's hand, weak with disappointment, but filled with sympathy for her husband.

"It's okay," she said, struggling to keep her voice steady. "It's not a question of fault. At least we know now. So we can't have a baby. It's not the end of the world."

Justin was filled with gratitude toward her. She never failed to amaze him. He knew, more than anyone, how much she wanted a family and how children would transform their lonely existence in Assam.

"We can consider adoption or maybe focus on other things," she continued. "Now, did I hear anyone mention a hot Scotch? There's got to be a few advantages in not being pregnant!"

"Aye, you certainly did." Edward jumped up, always happy to oblige where alcohol was concerned.

Irene was still struggling to come to terms with the realization that there were to be no grandchildren in her future. Not from Justin at any rate. But despite her intense disappointment, she appreciated Lorraine's stoicism. Many women would have been bitter and resentful in her situation.

"I'll go and get dinner started," she said. "Now, you just sit here, the both of you. You're not to do a thing except comfort each another."

She followed Ed into the kitchen. He was heating the water for the scotch.

"Let them alone a while," she said to him. "Give them their drinks and come and help me with dinner, if you would."

In the other room, Justin stared at the fire trying to digest the implications of the news. Of course, adoption had always been an option in the back of their minds, but it wasn't something they had ever discussed. That would have been like admitting defeat.

"How can I make it up to you?" he said to his wife.

"Ach, don't you go being a martyr," she smiled. "The problem could just as easily have lain with me. We are a unit. It doesn't matter where the fault lies. Surprisingly enough, I feel a sense of relief. At least we know where we stand now. We can get on with our lives. And maybe start to enjoy our holiday a little."

They spent their days playing golf, tennis and visiting favorite haunts. They drove through Strangford, taking the car ferry across the lough to Portaferry. They had lunch at the Portaferry Inn and continued on to Mount Stewart, a stately home surrounded by spectacular gardens. They travelled up the Antrim Coast, with its cliffs that plunged into the North Sea, to visit the Giants' Causeway.

Lorraine spent time with her family in Belfast, enjoying shopping sprees with her mother and sisters and just being able to sit in coffee shops and cafes. Justin helped his father in the bakery, which he noted had become run down and badly in need of modernization. He hired roofers to patch leaks in the roof and builders to make structural repairs. Irene picked out some paint, and they painted the building pale yellow with green trim. The final touch was a new green sign with "Irene's Home Bakery" in gold lettering.

Edward was overcome with emotion when he saw how it had all taken shape. Despite his aches and pains, he could not conceive of closing his business. The renovations gave him fresh impetus and renewed hope that perhaps he might find a buyer soon.

Chapter 14
Assam, India 1975

All too soon, it was time to return to the tea plantation. Lorraine appeared to have put the idea of adopting a child out of her mind. She plunged into the wives' social round of coffee mornings, lunches and mahjong and even learned to play bridge. In the heat of the afternoon, she began to write stories on the old typewriter they'd bought.

Justin meanwhile threw himself into his job. He was eager to be promoted to manager. He knew he was impatient with the workers and that it was sometimes difficult to handle the emerging labor force, which was more exacting in its demands than the old-school laborers prior to Independence. There was talk of forming a union. As Justin knew from the troubles in Northern Ireland, it only took a few insurgents to stir up far-reaching rebellions.

That year, the Planters Annual General Meeting had been delayed due to renovations at the Assam Golf and Polo Club. Instead of its usual January date, it was postponed to March and then July, the height of the monsoon season. Consequently, the golf and tennis tournaments that usually coincided with the event had to be cancelled. It would simply be too hot and wet. Even if it didn't rain, the golf course and tennis courts would be water-logged. All the same, it was an occasion everyone looked forward to. Besides the mandatory meetings, there would be fabulous lunches and dinners all weekend, culminating in the Annual Planters Ball.

Lorraine was disappointed that there were to be no tournaments. Her golf handicap was down in the teens, and her tennis game was better than ever before. To compensate, a number of people arranged to go to the nearby Brahmaputra Safari Park on the day following the Annual General Meeting, and Lorraine and Justin decided to join them.

They made the two- hour drive to the Assam Golf and Polo Club in lashing rain. They were being put up for the weekend at one of the plantations near the club. Although it was only a three-day trip, it required a great deal of preparation. Lorraine had to make sure they had everything they needed for two days and two nights of meetings and dinners. She had to pack a ball gown with coordinating shoes and accessories and a dinner jacket and tie for Justin. They also needed outfits for the safari, where they would ride on elephants and in open jeeps. After the servants loaded up the little Standard Herald, there was barely enough room for Lorraine and Justin.

"Just as well there's no golf," said Justin. "Or we would have needed a bigger car."

There were planters from all over Assam at the meeting. Wives and children came along for the social part of the weekend. Lorraine got together with Martha and some of the ladies in the card room, and the days passed quickly for them while the men participated in the business of the day.

On the last evening, it was time for the long awaited ball. A band all the way from Shillong provided the music. Lorraine wore a halter-necked gown of red velvet that she discovered in a boutique on the Lisburn Road in Belfast during their visit home. Justin whistled when he saw her and kissed her bare back.

"As usual, you will be the belle of the ball, but I'll be the man lucky enough to bring you home."

"I'm the lucky one," laughed Lorraine. "You look marvelous in your white dinner jacket."

"Make sure you save me a few dances," joked Justin, as they entered the club where the ball was in full swing.

It was a glorious occasion. Red and white streamers festooned the pillars beside the ballroom. Exquisite floral arrangements surrounded tall, red candlesticks on the tables, spread with white linen tablecloths. A feast had been organized by the local planters' wives whose cooks tried to outdo one another with their lavish and sumptuous preparations. The wine flowed, the music swelled, and the dancers rocked the floor till dawn.

"Thank you for bringing me to this place, darling," Lorraine murmured to her husband as they spun around the floor for the last dance. "I have never been so happy in all my life, despite... despite everything."

She seldom alluded to the one shadow that marred their lives.

"And as I keep saying, you are a truly wonderful woman, and you never cease to amaze me," he said, tenderly.

Lorraine glowed with happiness, gazing into her husband's eyes – she who had the ability to display her love easily in spoken and unspoken words and looks. Justin thought she had never looked more beautiful.

They managed to snatch a few hours of sleep before leaving for the Brahmaputra Safari Park before dawn. The park was a refuge for wild life whose habitats were increasingly becoming eroded. The mighty Brahmaputra River ran down its eastern border. It cut a swath through the state of Assam and was its life blood and source of much of its water and energy. It was a mile wide in parts, and no bridge could span it.

Lorraine groaned when Justin woke her.

"Was this really a good idea? My feet are killing me."

"It'll be worth it," said Justin. "If we're really lucky we'll see a tiger and lots of rhinos."

"I have a hangover. I need some more sleep!"

She pulled the covers over her head. Justin rolled over and tussled with her, mouthing into her neck, "I'm a big scary tiger, and I'm going to eat you all up!"

She shrieked as his body covered hers and his mouth found her lips. Suddenly, they were mad for each other. He reached under the sheets for her naked breasts. She gasped with pleasure as he entered her urgently and passionately.

"Say you love me," she whispered into his chest a few seconds later.

"I love you, sweetheart," he said, propping himself up on his elbow and looking into her eyes. "You are my adorable little wife, and I promise to always do everything in my power to make you happy."

"You don't have to do anything to make me happy," she said, kissing his shoulder, "except be yourself and make love to me every morning and every night."

"You're incorrigible!" he laughed. "Now, get your sweet bottom out of bed, or there'll be no safari for us today."

They arrived in the nick of time just as the group was setting off and had to run to the last elephant and clamber on to the howdah. Prodded by the mahout, it rose in ungainly fashion on to its four legs and plodded steadily behind the other elephants in single file towards the forest. The sky was dark with monsoon clouds. A low fog cloaked the jungle. They were showered by droplets of dew that slid off the rustling leaves above them. The ground squelched and sucked under the elephants' lumbering feet. It was silent except for the hiss and mutter of insects, the wail of a distant parakeet and the flutter of feathers in branches overhead.

They were cautioned to be quiet. Wild animals were easily scared away. The elephants proceeded steadily with a swoosh, swoosh, swoosh through the forest in the damp morning air.

"Sshhh!" hissed the mahout, riding between the ears of their elephant. He pointed to the right. "Bagh."

"Tiger," whispered Lorraine, though it was a word everyone knew.

In fear and excitement, they scoured the undergrowth till they spotted only a few feet away a pair of huge, startled eyes that stared back at them for an infinitesimal second. His privacy invaded, the beast turned his back on them and disappeared into the shadows. There was an awed hush among the humans, thrilled and terrified at the sighting.

The mahout told them they were fortunate as this was the first tiger he'd seen in almost six months. With each passing year, the number of wild animals declined. The convoy continued through the forest and saw a family of deer and a pair of wild boars before coming to a clearing where there were three open-topped Land Rovers waiting.

They climbed off the elephants and into the weather-beaten vehicles for the rest of their tour. They rattled through the forest for a few miles before approaching a stretch of lowland where large numbers of rhino were drinking from the swamp. Hearing the sound, the more timid of the animals took to their heels and fled while others approached the convoy angrily. The drivers baited the rhino, inciting them to batter the vehicles with their horns. Seeing the ferocious beasts so close, the women screamed in terror, and the men laughed with excitement, fearful that they might be speared by the deadly horns. Finally, one by one, the animals were outrun, and the vehicles arrived at the river bank where they came to a standstill. Elated but somewhat shaken after the bumpy ride, the group was directed to a pathway that ran through the jungle beside the river. Although the sun had risen, it was cool and moist in the forest, the sun's rays pouring through gaps in the trees in bright shafts that illuminated the flecks in the air. The river was running high with monsoon rain and thundered ominously below. Lorraine was enthralled by the spectacle.

"This is the greatest adventure of my life," she shouted to Justin. "What a wonderful idea it was to come here." She reached for his hand and squeezed it.

The group followed the guide along the slippery pathway. He warned them to be very careful, saying there were often landslides after the rain. He explained to Justin that soon they would come across antelope on the banks of the river. This was the best time of day to see them. Lorraine lagged behind the group, absorbed by the magnificent view. She had taken plenty of pictures already and suddenly remembered that she had left her camera in the Land Rover. She called to Martha on the path ahead of her,

"I'm going back for my camera. I'll catch up with you in a moment."

"Would you like me to come with you?" asked Martha.

"No, there's no need. I'll be back in a wee minute."

She ran to where the vehicles were parked, anxious not to hold up the group. Sure enough, her camera was on her seat where she'd left it. She snatched it up, slung it over her shoulder and hurried back along the pathway, taking the camera out of its case as she ran. Unseen by anyone, she skidded, lost her footing

121

and found herself catapulted down the khud. She grabbed at the undergrowth and screamed as she saw the waters coming up to meet her. She felt a shock as the cold river enfolded her and swallowed her up in its turbulence. She rose up again and again, gasping and calling Justin's name, desperate with fear. But the churning waters claimed her frail body, and she was swept away, a tiny, white figure in the gray river.

On the pathway above, Justin had allowed people to pass him, so he could rejoin Lorraine.

"Are you looking for your wife?" asked Martha, to whom Lorraine had spoken her last words. "She went back for her camera. She probably stopped to take pictures."

Just then they heard a scream, a tiny, high-pitched scream of terror. Justin ran towards the sound. The group turned to follow him, making way for the guide who caught up with Justin just as he came across the camera lying on the path. They looked down the steep khudside and could see the trail of trampled undergrowth leading down to the river. There was no sign of Lorraine.

"Lorraine," screamed Justin, "Lorraine, where are you?"

They called her name, running frantically in all directions, unable to acknowledge the terrifying possibility that she could be in the river. Justin wanted to dive in and find her and had to be physically restrained by Tom and the guide.

"Let me go," he pleaded. "Let me go with her."

They dragged him unwillingly toward the Land Rovers.

"We need to get help," Peter Phillips, one of the local planters, said to Tom. "We have to make a report to the police and organize search parties. They need to check the river banks downstream."

No one wanted to accept the futility of the situation, but there was little else to be done. The police were swift to dispatch dozens of men to comb the area and search the banks. They telegraphed districts farther south to check the river for the Memsahib's body.

"Let me go find her," Justin pleaded. "I need to do something."

In the end, Peter, understanding Justin's need to be physically involved, drove him to where there they were able to walk beside the river in safety. The water was at its highest point. In the dry season, it receded, exposing the jagged rocks that lined the river bed. Peter knew that the chances of her body ever being found were slim. The undercurrents would have sucked her down into the Brahmaputra's murky depths.

He could not have been kinder to Justin. He insisted upon Justin spending the night at his bungalow. His wife Anne had the guest room, which had just been vacated by a couple attending the Annual General Meeting, made up for him. That evening Justin couldn't eat but accepted a scotch and soda which somewhat calmed him.

"What am I going to do?" he moaned. "How will I live without her? And how do I explain this to her family? I have been remiss. I should have taken better care of her."

He was beset with guilt. He blamed himself for allowing her out of his sight, his fragile, precious wife who had always been so plucky and accepting of every circumstance. He paced up and down the verandah until he was exhausted and collapsed into bed where he slept sporadically. When he awoke, he reached instinctively for Lorraine's body and not finding it, moaned in despair as the memory of recent events bore down on him.

He left a note for Peter and Anne, who were still asleep, and jumped into his car which was filled with Lorraine's things. He knew what he must do. He could not possibly telegraph the news of her death. That would be too terrible and too shocking for her parents. There was nothing else for it. He had to get home as soon as possible. He had to get himself on a plane, drive to the McIlroy's home in Belfast and personally deliver the news to them that their beloved daughter was dead.

Chapter 15
Dooars, 1978

Charles was home for lunch from the factory. Jetha padded down the verandah with a glass of chilled nimboo pani for him on a tray. He gulped it down and went to join Ramona and Samira who were sitting under the whirring ceiling fan, a welcome oasis in the blistering heat. He was flushed and damp from the sun. It was June and people were longing for the rains. The tea bushes were smothered in a layer of dust. Spiked with brittle yellow shoots, the paddy fields were so parched that cows roamed through them, their coats caked with dried clay.

Time seemed to stand still for Samira. The days passed, and nothing happened. She was hot and constantly tired, waiting for some great crisis to enfold her and change her life forever. A feeling of lethargy took hold of her, an inertia that prevented her from moving forward. She had waited to be done with college, so her life could begin. And here she was, almost a year later, her fabulous life still not begun.

She constantly made excuses to postpone making decisions. It was summertime in England. All she had to do was book that flight. Inwardly, she denied that she was waiting for Ravi, unable to fathom what was going on in his mind. He alternated from being frighteningly remote and maddeningly unavailable to being his old charming self. She couldn't bear the uncertainty of it. She knew there was no one else in his life. It would not have been possible for him to carry on another relationship in this small community. They were young, free and single. Her parents had no objection to her seeing him, going out of their way to make him feel welcome and giving them every opportunity for privacy. When exactly had things changed between them? What had she said or done to drive him away? Was it her reserve? Had she been too eager? She felt like an instrument that he could pick up and drop at will, always at the ready if he should happen to feel like playing.

The bearer announced tiffin, and they went to the dining room for lunch.

"Anything new going on at the factory?" Ramona asked Charles.

"For once, everything seems to be running smoothly. Nothing to report, really," he replied. "Oh, yes, I nearly forgot. Dilip Gupta, the VA, was here this morning. Nice chap. I invited him to lunch, but he had to dash."

"So what's the gossip?" asked Ramona. Dilip was notorious for gleaning information about everyone and then spreading it, something he was well-positioned to do in his travels as visiting agent.

"Nothing that I can recall," said Charles. "Well, actually, yes, he did give me some news. There's a new manager at Simling, Justin Laird, a Scot apparently, quite young. He was transferred from Assam."

"Assam?" asked Samira, surprised. "That's a little unusual, isn't it?

"Yes, it is, rather. It's something to do with his wife dying three years ago. She drowned in the Brahmaputra River, I think he said."

"How awful! Did they have children?" asked Ramona.

"I'm not sure. I didn't ask."

"It's a wonder he didn't go back home," Samira said.

"Yes, it is. The few British planters who choose to remain tend to be the old-timers who've been here forever. Like me," said Charles, rising from the table. "Well, excuse me, ladies. This old-timer is going to take his nap."

The following club day, Samira was on library duty when a man who could only have been Justin walked in.

"Good afternoon, young lady. Are you in charge of the library?" he spoke with a brogue.

"Hello! You must be Justin," said Samira, extending her hand. "And, yes, I'm on library duty today. I'm Samira Clarke," she continued. "My father is the manager at Ranikot."

"I'm very pleased to meet you, Samira. I was just introduced to your father. He told me you were here."

He was of medium height, with dark, slightly graying hair. He was not particularly handsome or remarkable-looking in any way, except for the lines beside his eyes that creased in an attractive way when he smiled. He was dressed for golf in khaki shorts and a light blue bush shirt. Samira guessed he was in his early thirties.

"Please feel free to borrow some books. You're allowed six. Shall I add your name to the register?"

"Aye, please. The name is Justin Laird. This is a nice library. Won't take me long to get through this lot."

The library consisted of thirty or forty shelves of well-worn books.

"So you like to read, obviously?" Samira asked.

"Yes, I do," he said. "I read a lot more...now, that is." There was an awkward silence. Samira took the opportunity to express sympathy for his loss.

"I heard about your wife's accident, and I'm very sorry," she said. "If there's anything I can do to help you settle in, please don't hesitate to ask."

"Everyone's been more than kind," Justin said. "Thank you."

"Where in Scotland are you from?" she asked, changing the subject.

"Everyone assumes I'm Scottish, but I'm actually an Ulster man from Northern Ireland. Our brogue sounds very similar to most people. Not that it is, of course."

"Oh. I'm sorry," Samira exclaimed. "I naturally assumed...."

"Not to worry. I fully understand. There are many more Scottish than Irish people in tea. In fact, I think I must be the only Irish person here. But people from Northern Ireland are in fact British, as it's part of the United Kingdom."

Charles appeared on his way to freshen up after his game of golf.

"Good. I see you've met Samira," he said to Justin.

"Yes, she's been more than kind."

"And what did you think of our little golf course?" asked Samira.

"It's not a bad," said Justin. "I lost a couple of balls, but if it's anything like Assam, I'll know I'll get them back one way or another."

They all smiled knowing what he meant. The villagers' children scoured the course and river for lost balls to sell to the caddies, many of them little more than children themselves. The caddies would sell them to the golfers at what they considered an astronomical profit. But the planters were grateful just to get them back, given the frequent disappearance of balls into the river, the jungle and even into the mouths of passing crows.

After Justin had selected his books, Samira put the register away and went outside to join the others for tea.

"Have you seen Ravi?" she asked Ramona.

"No, I haven't, actually. He wasn't playing golf. Wasn't he at tennis, either?" asked Ramona in surprise.

"No, there was hardly anyone there," said Samira, a little disappointed at not getting a good game. "Maybe I should have played golf."

Ravi did not arrive till much later, just as people were settling into their seats for the movie. Samira saw him enter the clubhouse and head towards the bar. She found herself seated between Ramona and Justin. The feature was "Goldfinger," a James Bond movie she had already seen in Darjeeling.

As soon as the lights came on during the interval, she excused herself and wandered toward the bar hoping to find Ravi. She was no longer confident of her relationship with him and was almost beginning to wonder if she had imagined the whole thing. She saw him seated at the bar with a pint of beer in front of him, staring into the distance. He seemed unhappy about something. She was contemplating creeping away when Dilip Gupta saw her and said,

"Hi, Samira. Let me buy you a drink."

Ravi heard him and moved over to Samira.

"Thanks, man, but I already ordered something for this young lady." He put his arm around Samira and guided her towards his bar stool.

"Thanks, Dilip. Some other time," she said over her shoulder.

She looked at Ravi questioningly, unsure of what to say.

"I'd forgotten how beautiful you were," Ravi said, reinforcing how long it had been since they'd met.

"Thanks, Ravi, it's nice of you to say that," she said, though what she really wanted to say was, "No wonder you've forgotten. You never want to see me anymore. Then when we do meet, you act as though there's something preventing us from seeing each other, when there isn't."

"It's been a while," she continued, conscious of his intense gaze.

He put his hand over hers and stroked the inside of her arm, sending shivers down her spine.

"Follow me outside in a few minutes," he said. "I'll wait for you in the gazebo."

Obviously, he didn't want them to be seen walking out of the clubhouse together. And it was true that tongues would wag if they were. She stared into her glass of wine and said nothing.

"Promise me," he said. "Please."

She couldn't refuse. She missed his eyes looking into hers and his soft kisses.

"I promise," she said. But Charles and Ramona walked over just after Ravi left, with Justin beside them.

"Can I buy you a drink?" he asked her. "Ramona, Charles, what are you having?"

"Thanks, I already have one," she said.

They ordered drinks, and she excused herself saying she'd be back in a few minutes. She ran along the lawn to the path that led to the gazebo. Ravi stepped out of the shadows startling her.

"Ravi, you scared me."

"Sorry, sweetheart. I didn't mean to." He grabbed her hand and led her along the pathway beside the honeysuckle hedge that bordered the tennis courts.

"Where are we going?" she whispered. "What do you want?"

"This," he whispered back, pulling her to him, "I want you!"

His lips found hers and he held her against him passionately.

"Oh my god, I have missed you," he said. "You feel so good." His hand was on her breast, as it had been the very first time they had met under the jasmine bushes. He held her close, kissing her all over until she quivered. She clung to him, savoring the closeness of their bodies, the sensation of his touch and the rapid beating of his heart. The air was still, and the deep velvet sky was a panorama of stars.

"Why?" she finally had to ask him, needing to know. "Why haven't you wanted to see me? What's wrong?"

"Please, Sammy," he groaned. "Believe me when I say I love you. And I will explain but not now. Let me just hold you."

Eventually, Ravi said,

"I should take you home. I have the jeep tonight. I'll inform your father."

It was a reasonable suggestion. She could not imagine walking back into the clubhouse in her disheveled state. She would just have to deal with Ramona's questions later. She was an adult, after all, and old enough to make her own decisions.

But apparently Ramona didn't see things the same way. She stormed into Samira's room the next day as she was sipping her morning tea.

"And where did you disappear to last night with Ravi?" she said.

"Mother, he gave me a lift home." Samira was all innocence.

"I'm aware of that. But you left without saying anything."

"I thought Ravi told Dad that he was bringing me home."

"We were in the middle of the movie, and you'd just met that nice Scottish man."

"Irish."

"Scottish, Irish, what's the difference? You just took off with no explanation, right after meeting him."

"So that's what this is about. You think Ravi's not good enough for me now that Justin's on the scene."

"That's not true. And what is your situation with Ravi, by the way? He hasn't been to see you in ages. Is he really interested in you?"

Well, she wanted to say that he certainly seemed to be last night. She was tingling with the memory of his touch. But the truth was that she didn't know, even though he'd said he loved and missed her. She hadn't been able to sleep all night, remembering his caresses. He'd deprived her of his company for so long.

"Well?" She'd held back from questioning Samira long enough and now wanted to know exactly what was going on.

Samira felt the weight in her chest bear down on her again, the pain that had begun to ease as she gained in maturity and her relationship with her mother strengthened. She grew defensive again.

"She's treating me like a child," she thought, "Which is guaranteed to make me behave like one."

"I don't want to talk about it. I'm an adult now. I can make my own decisions." The words sounded childish, even to her.

"I only want what's best for you," Ramona softened, sensing her withdrawal. "Just remember, I'm on your side."

But Samira couldn't hear what she was saying any longer. She was too upset. And because her mother had struck a nerve, she no longer felt she could confide in her, as much as she needed a guide and confidante.

"I'm sorry if I did something to displease you, Mother," she said. "But I have a lot to think about."

Chapter 16
Dooars, 1978

At breakfast, Ramona announced that Justin was coming to dinner that night.

"We all need to make him feel welcome," she said. She didn't look her daughter in the eye.

Charles sliced up his eggs and placed the dripping pieces on his toast.

"That's nice, dear." He was reading the paper, his mind elsewhere.

"Sure," thought Samira, seeing through her mother's subterfuge. It was obviously an effort at matchmaking, getting her together with Justin so that she would forget Ravi. She had nothing against Justin. Actually, he seemed very likeable. Besides, Ravi hadn't called and as the day wore on, she realized that he probably wouldn't.

"Would you like me to make a chocolate soufflé?" she asked Ramona, trying to placate her mother.

"That would be lovely," said Ramona. "Would you like to arrange some flowers, too?"

"Okay," said Samira. "I'll ask Ramchand if he can spare some. I know he's been hoarding stuff for the Flower Show next month. Isn't it wonderful that he finally had a son?"

"Yes, very nice," agreed Ramona. "I'm so happy for him and Usha."

She put her arm around her daughter, appreciative of the effort.

Samira went to the pantry to pick out the ingredients for the chocolate soufflé and reflected that while she and her mother made copious efforts with their relationship, Charles and Mark just seemed to muddle through somehow.

Justin arrived in the evening with a bouquet of flowers, which he handed to Ramona. When he saw the array of flowers Samira had arranged, he laughed.

"Oops, maybe I should have brought something else!"

"Not at all, it's the thought that counts," Ramona said. She pushed the electric bell to summon Jetha to put the flowers in water.

He's actually quite handsome, thought Samira, watching him from the corner of her eye. When she invited Ravi over, he was her guest, for her to entertain, but she didn't feel responsible for Justin because her mother had invited him. She was curious about his wife and his life in Northern Ireland, but was sure he didn't want a barrage of questions.

Just then the phone rang, and Samira's heart leapt. But it was the assistant manager for Charles.

"Excuse me, Justin. We've been having labor issues. This could take a while," he grumbled.

"I need to go to the kitchen and see to the food." Ramona jumped up. "Why don't you show Justin the garden, Sammy?"

"If you're interested?" Samira looked at him, questioningly.

"Yes, surely. I'd love to see your garden. I've heard it's quite spectacular."

He followed Samira down the steps and into the rose garden. She showed him the famous Ena Harkness roses that had won Ramchand one of his rosettes last year. They were purest yellow, fragrant and perfect in every way. They strolled over to the shrubbery to examine the jasmine bushes, laden with waxy, full-scented blossoms.

Justin saw Samira shudder.

"Are you okay?" he asked, taking her arm.

"Yes, I'm fine, thanks," she said, memories of her first encounter with Ravi flooding back. "How are you settling in?"

"I really like it here."

"If ever you need a friendly ear, I'm here for you."

Suddenly, he found himself telling her how he had been through the worst three years of his life, how he had had to endure the loss of his dear wife, and tell her parents that their daughter was dead, she had fallen down a cliff and been swallowed up by a monstrous river. And that, no, he had not beside her at the time. He had wandered ahead of the group and was talking to the guide. She was with the other ladies and back went to fetch her camera, something he would have gladly done for her. If only she had asked him! She must have been momentarily distracted as she ran back. The lens cover was open, as though she'd been taking a picture. And when they later developed the film, there was a snapshot of the scene of the tragedy.

"The worst of it is that I felt I was just beginning to fall in love with her. She had been the best possible wife to me. She came with me to this country at a time when…I really needed her. She was so fragile, yet so strong. She made the most of every situation. Her love for me, well, it was truer than mine was for her. I wasn't worthy of her."

"But she wouldn't have come with you if she didn't want to," Samira said. "You picked her to accompany you on your big adventure. And if she loved you more than you loved her, then she was the lucky one. She got to be with the person she loved. If you didn't love her back the same way, it was your loss. She was the one experiencing the love."

"I never thought of it like that before," said Justin. "I just felt guilty that I wasn't more in love with her sooner, no matter how much I admired and appreciated her."

"How many women get to be admired and appreciated by their husbands?" asked Samira.

"Thank you, Sammy." Justin took her hand and held it. "I didn't intend to open up to you like this today. And the fact that I did was probably because I sensed you'd understand."

He couldn't confess that the attraction he'd felt on meeting her in the library was confirmation that at last he could move on. Or that he had fallen overwhelmingly in love with her, in a way that, despite everything, he never had with Lorraine.

During dinner, Justin and Charles exchanged anecdotes about their lives in Northern Ireland and Hertfordshire, and about how they ended up in tea. Samira was always fascinated by stories of her father's life in England, as he was so disinclined to discuss his early days.

"And how about you, Ramona?" Justin asked. "I'd love to know more about your past."

Ramona told him about her mother, Prava, about her father who'd died and how she'd grown up in Kalimpong. She told him about teaching at St. Jude's, the boarding school where she later sent Samira and Mark.

"And now my mother lives very happily in her little cottage in Darjeeling," she concluded, "where we can visit her very often."

"That's somewhere I've always wanted to go," Justin said. "In Assam, we used to visit Shillong, a wonderful place to retreat to during the summer."

"Darjeeling used to be a sanatorium for soldiers who needed to recuperate from various illnesses," said Samira. "It also became an escape for officers' wives who couldn't endure the heat of Calcutta. The site where Darjeeling now stands was originally purchased by a Lord Bentick from the Maharaja of Sikkim."

"Fascinating. I'll definitely go there very soon," said Justin. "And this chocolate soufflé is delicious. You have a great cook."

"You can thank Sammy for that," said Charles. "It's her specialty."

Samira found herself liking Justin more and more. She went to her room after he left and read in bed all night, trying not to admit to herself that she was already regretting the events of the night before.

She moped around the house after breakfast the next day. While Ramona didn't know the full story, she suspected that Ravi was behind her daughter's dejection. She had discussed the issue with Charles the night before, wondering if it might cheer Sammy up to escape to Darjeeling for a few days. Charles was only too willing to agree to anything his wife suggested.

"I had an idea last night while we were speaking to Justin," she said to Samira over lunch. "Your grandmother isn't doing too well with her diabetes, and your father and I wondered if you would like to go and spend a few days with her. I'd go except we have the superintendent arriving next week, and I have to be here to entertain him. It might be a good time for you to get away, too. Not that we want to get rid of you."

She and Charles looked at Samira to gauge her reaction.

Samira's initial response was that she didn't want to leave because of Ravi. Then suddenly, she thought that maybe she did and that it was a great idea for her to get away at this time. She realized that she'd underestimated her mother's perceptiveness, offering a solution to her predicament without even alluding to it.

"I'm happy to go if Gran needs me," she said. "I'd love to visit her, and it would be a relief to get away from this heat."

"Then it's settled," said Charles. "I'll book a taxi, if that's okay, darling. We don't want poor Kala to have to make two separate trips."

"Of course," said Samira. "I understand."

The phone rang. Jetha said it was Justin Sahib.

"It must be for you," Ramona said to Samira. "Would you answer?"

"No, I think he must want Dad. Please, Mum," she begged. "He didn't ask for me."

Her confidence in herself had totally eroded. Men didn't call her any more these days.

"I'll go," said Ramona, jumping up and going into the drawing room.

She returned a few minutes later looking pleased.

"He called to thank us for dinner. Such a polite man! Anyway, I told him that you're going to visit your grandmother. He said that as he was planning to go to Darjeeling soon and would be happy to drive you there. Isn't that nice of him? He'll stay at the club, of course."

Samira tried to digest the implications of what her mother was saying. Was Justin's phone call mere coincidence, or had her mother hatched the whole plot in an effort to bring them together?

"I promise it was not my idea," she said, as though reading Samira's mind. "Though it would have been a rather good one."

Samira laughed. She had to admit she liked Justin, and going to Darjeeling together would be fun. It was a whole lot better than travelling in an old taxi.

"I have to say you are the most interfering, maddening mother I've ever known!"

Ramona smiled mischievously, and they looked across the table at each other, closer than they'd been in a long time.

Chapter 17
Darjeeling, 1978

"What a stupendous view!" said Justin. They had pulled into a viewpoint off the road to Darjeeling for a rest and a cup of coffee. In the distance, six-thousand feet beneath them, the purple plain shimmered. The ravines and crevasses below were smothered by a low-creeping fog, though the sky above them was blue and clear.

"Wait till you see the snow-capped Kanchenjunga Mountains," Samira said, pleased at his response. "You can see them from the Dooars on a clear day, but they're considerably closer from Darjeeling, providing they're not obscured by clouds, of course. Sometimes, you can't see them for days on end, especially now during the monsoon."

"You were educated in Darjeeling, weren't you?" he asked. "Did you like it?"

"I did eventually as I got older. Father didn't see any point in sending us all the way to England to be educated."

"Isn't it strange," she continued, "How when we look up at the mountains from the plains, they appear purple and when we look down, the plains are purple, too? I wonder why that is?"

"It's one of life's mysteries," laughed Justin. "Do you know what you remind me of?"

"No. What?" she asked, in pleasant anticipation.

"You're like a D.H. Lawrence heroine, full of questions and perplexities, if that's even a word."

"I love Lawrence," said Samira. "I've read all his books."

"What, even *Lady Chatterley's Lover*?" he teased.

"No, not that one," said Samira, blushing, "but only because I haven't been able to get hold of a copy."

They were soon on the approach to Darjeeling. The weather stayed clear, but to Samira's disappointment, clouds had built up over the Kanchenjunga Range. They drove past rosy-cheeked, slit-eyed children, who called and waved to them, playing on the roadsides with homemade go-karts and metal hoops. The town was spread over two mountaintops with palaces crowned with blue domes built on each one of them. Most of the buildings were constructed in colonial-style, gray stone. The town was inhabited predominantly by hill people, Nepalese and Tibetans. The Nepalese were short and wiry with slanted eyes and smiling faces. By comparison, the Tibetans were tall, powerful and solemn.

There was a nip in the air, a respite from the heat of the plains. Already Samira felt better. She had barely given Ravi a thought all day. Justin asked if she would join him for lunch before he took her to her grandmother's house. Samira accepted, unsure whether Prava would have a meal ready. She didn't have a telephone, but Ramona had sent her a message via one of the neighbors to let her know that Samira would be arriving.

Prava was sunning herself on her verandah when they arrived. Her graying hair was plaited into a long braid that was rolled up into a bun on the nape of her neck. She was gaunt, her face creased from years of exposure to the sun. She had long ago professed to having lost interest in her appearance, claiming not to have time for such trivial things.

"Welcome, Justin! Samira, my girl, how thin you look. Come, come. Make yourselves at home. My, what a handsome man! As you can see, my house is so small. Let me make you some tea." She was happy to have company.

"Why don't we take you out for some tea later on?" asked Justin solicitously, thinking that she might appreciate an outing, which, of course, she did.

"I'm going to freshen up. Why don't you change into something warmer, Gran?" suggested Samira, noticing that Prava was wearing a cardigan with holes at the elbows. Her clothes were a source of mortification to the family. When buttons went missing, she never replaced them, using huge safety pins instead. Sometimes, to Ramona's extreme embarrassment, she would appear in a pair of Charles' old socks she had sworn that she would only wear in bed at night. Her drawers were stuffed full of clothes given to her by Ramona, English lamb's wool sweaters, cashmere shawls and woolen socks that she said she was saving for special occasions. Ramona always would exclaim,

"But today is special! We are here. Look how we dressed for you!"

Today, she gave in by putting on a decent sweater and a cashmere shawl for Justin's benefit. She enjoyed the drive in his car, which was a rare experience for her, and strolling up Chowrasta for tea and cakes at Glenarys.

"So, you're from Northern Ireland," she said, sipping her tea. "That's close to Scotland, no? I once had a good friend from Scotland."

"Really, Gran? Who was it? I didn't know you had a Scottish friend."

"My poor girl, you think you know everything about your old grandmother. You must allow me a few secrets." She fluttered her eyelashes at Justin, flirting with him and spilling cake crumbs over herself.

"Put this in a box," she instructed the waiter in Nepalese, giving him her half-eaten macaroon. "Are you going to eat that, Sammy?"

"No, Gran. You can have it." Samira was mortified. "But why don't we go into the bakery and buy some cakes and patties to take home?"

Prava's miserliness was legendary. Although she never quite starved herself, she deprived herself of good things to eat to such an extent that when she did eat well, her weakened digestion would cause her to suffer. She saved scraps for her next meal that most people would have thrown away.

"If you insist on eating stale food, you must expect to be ill," Ramona would scold her. But Prava couldn't help herself. She was so much in the habit of thrift it was painful for her to waste anything. A penny saved was a personal triumph she derived more pleasure from than she did from spending it.

"Wasting money!" grumbled Prava now, nevertheless allowing Justin to escort her into the bakery. They picked out an

141

assortment of cakes and patties. Justin insisted on paying for them. The shop assistant remembered Samira and raised her eyebrows appreciatively over Justin.

"Your husband?" she asked, to Samira's extreme embarrassment.

"Come on, Josie. I just left college a year ago. Justin is a friend of mine."

"Sorry, madam," Josie said, not wanting to overstep the mark. "It's good to see you again!"

Samira was cross. Why did everyone want to marry her off? As if that was a woman's only goal. After seeing Prava into the house, Samira walked outside with Justin, and he asked if she would like to have dinner with him that night.

"I'd love you to come," he said, but she demurred on account of her grandmother. "I understand. How about a walk in the morning?"

"That would be lovely," said Samira, thinking how nice it was to be pursued for a change.

"All right, I'll see you tomorrow." He bent down and kissed her cheek.

Samira ran into the house to find her grandmother.

"So, you have a new boyfriend already?" Prava said. "What happened to the other boyfriend, the Punjabi? Your mother kept that very quiet. Always trying to keep things from me! But you can't fool me. As soon as I saw the way Justin looked at you, I knew-romance!"

"Don't be ridiculous," said Samira. "No one's trying to keep anything from you. I've only know Justin a short time. You always think everyone's in love with me! Oh, Gran." She put her head in her grandmother's lap. "It's been awful, you have no idea! I think it's all over with Ravi. I haven't been able to talk about it to anyone. That's the real reason I wanted to see you." Her voice broke. It was sheer bliss to be able to unburden herself.

"My poor child," said Prava. "What went wrong?"

"That's just it, I have no idea," she said, sobbing. "He stopped coming to see me, with no explanation. And I know there's no one else."

142

"He needs to have his head examined," said Prava. "But if I were you, I would have nothing more to do with him. Look at that nice Sahib Justin. So handsome and so polite! What manners! I tell you these Indian men don't know the meaning of the word."

"Oh, Gran, you're like a tonic, not always easy to take but very good for the system." Samira smiled through the tears. "I should have come here sooner. I feel better already. But you mustn't be too hard on Ravi."

"Ravi. Pah! I tell you, forget about him. You know nothing about his family even."

"I know even less about Justin's," smiled Samira. "And I seem to remember that you were opposed to mother seeing father at the start. You said Sahibs were not to be trusted."

"Now, who told you about that? Anyway, things are different for you. You're a Memsahib."

"I'm not, Gran, as well you know. I could end up like Sandra Williams, with no one wanting me."

She had heard the story about how Geoffrey Peters had stood up her mother's friend at the altar many years ago. After courting her and proposing marriage, he lost his nerve at the last minute, unable to stomach the comments people were making about him marrying an Anglo-Indian. Sandra had been humiliated in front of the entire school. For weeks, the choir had been practicing "The King of Love My Shepherd is" for her wedding. Sandra had already handed in her resignation and was ready to move to the gardens, and her replacement had arrived.

Being St. Jude's, though, they kept Sandra on and offered her replacement another position at the school. Eventually, she joined her mother who had retired and moved to a flat in Bangalore.

"Your situation is very different from Sandra's. And times have changed. You have more options now. I'm telling you, if I were you, I would have both of them! A girl like you should have twenty men running after her."

"Anyway, Justin is too old for me. He's in his thirties."

"The older the better, my girl," said Prava. "The older ones have more money and more sense. I can't believe Ramona didn't tell me about him."

She couldn't let go of the idea that there was some form of conspiracy against her. "Now, let's see what Ramchand sent me, and we can decide what to have for dinner." She was excited about the basket of produce.

Charles always joked that Prava had more growing in her tiny patch than they did in their entire mali-bari. Prava always had something in her garden to compliment her meals, coriander, mint, green chilies or tree tomatoes whose piquancy would fill the kitchen. Mark loved her orange tree, which was dotted with dozens of tiny Clementine during the winter. He would sit in its branches, popping them whole in his mouth, then spitting out the pips as far as he could into the street below.

"Then you'll be happy to know that I'm meeting Justin tomorrow before he leaves," Samira told her, as they washed and peeled vegetables. "We're going for a walk. I thought I'd show him the view from the top of the hill, if it's not too cloudy."

"Yes, that does make me happy," said her grandmother. "And I'm also very happy to have you here with me."

Chapter 18
Darjeeling, India, 1978

Ramona was in the kitchen supervising dinner and trying to explain to the cook that she needed a pilaf dish to take to the club the following day when she heard the sound of a motorcycle outside. Sure enough, Jetha came in to tell her that Ravi Sahib had arrived.

"Typical," she thought to herself. "Just when Samira leaves, he decides to visit her."

"Why, hello, Ravi," she called out. "It's been a while since we had the pleasure of your company. Would you like something to drink?"

"Please," he said, seating himself in one of the wicker chairs. "It's very hot."

"Yes, it is. Especially on a motorcycle, I'm sure. Samira's not here, I'm afraid. She just left for Darjeeling to visit her grandmother. You should have telephoned first."

"Oh, no," he groaned. "I need to see her urgently."

Ramona regarded him coldly and wondered what could be so important after he had neglected her for so long.

"I'm sorry, Ravi. I'm not sure when she'll be back. I'll let you know when she returns."

"No. No. That will be too late. Could I telephone her perhaps? Would you give me her number?"

"Sorry, my mother doesn't have a telephone."

"In that case I'll have to go and see her," he said. "Please, Mrs. Clarke, may I trouble you for her address? It's really important. I need to see her urgently."

"I can't think what could be so urgent after all these weeks," said Ramona, conveying her displeasure.

"But here is the address." She scribbled Prava's address on a piece of paper and handed it to him.

"Thank you," said Ravi. "And I'm sorry to have upset you. I'll go and see her first thing tomorrow." He looked disconsolate. "Good-bye."

"How odd," thought Ramona, watching him drive away. "I've never know him to be so nervous and unsure of himself. What's got into him, I wonder?"

Samira awoke the following morning and flung her little window open, breathing in the sweet mountain air with a sense of anticipation. Being away from home was already renewing her sense of perspective, and she decided that she would start making arrangements to visit Aunt Pauline. She bathed in Prava's dilapidated bathroom and put on an old white dress and her black sandals.

Prava was on the verandah drinking tea in the morning sunshine.

"Morning, Gran. How are you today?" Samira bent to kiss her.

"Fine, thank you, my girl. You know how I am. As long as the sun shines, I'm right as rain." She chuckled at her own wit.

"Here's your tea," she said, pouring a cup for Samira.

"Thanks. You know, I feel much better already," said Samira. "I think I'll go and check if the snows are out before breakfast, if you don't mind. I won't be long."

She gulped her tea and ran up the path to the Mall. The air was fresh and the street deserted at this early hour. Fine morning mists in the valleys below were dissipating as the sun gained strength. She took in the familiar view of the white mountain ranges and could see that it was going to be a gorgeous day.

Prava was finishing her second cup of tea when she heard the sound of a motorcycle on the street below her lane. It roared past, stopped and then roared back again as though unsure of where it was going. Dogs barked at the sound and were loudly berated by their owners.

"What a commotion," Prava thought. She was cross. She hated these noisy plainspeople who descended on her town in increasing numbers, cluttering up the streets and filling the shops and restaurants. She was even more cross to find the owner of the motorcycle opening her gate and entering her property.

"No parking!" she shouted, although his vehicle was not even within view. He was a plainsman, just as she suspected, and had black hair and olive eyes.

"Excuse me, madam," he addressed her politely from the path below. "I am looking for Samira Clarke. Is she here, please?"

"And who are you?" Prava demanded, although she already had a good idea who he was.

"I'm Ravi Anand," he said. "A friend of Samira's."

"Samira's not here." She wasn't going to make it easy for him. "She went for a walk."

"Which way did she go, madam?" he pleaded.

Samira was right, thought Prava. He was handsome, though she herself could never trust a man with eyes that color. No wonder the girl was breaking her heart over him! Well, she might as well put him out of his misery. He'd obviously driven a long way to see her.

"She went up that way," she pointed. "Turn left when you get to the Mall and make a right at Government House."

"Thank you very much, madam," said Ravi, making his way quickly up the hill.

She wondered what could have been so urgent for him to drive so far when Samira had only just arrived. He must have left at the crack of dawn. Maybe he was going to propose? Perhaps he'd heard she'd come with Justin? If she were Samira, which man would she choose? That was a tough one, now that she'd seen Ravi.

Samira was enjoying the Sunday morning solitude. She hoped Justin would be up in time to see the snow-capped mountains, although they did not appear to be in any danger of being obscured by clouds today. She had formulated plans for her future during the night, deciding to travel around Europe for a year before returning to India and looking for a job in publishing.

She was so engrossed in her thoughts that she almost jumped out of her skin when she saw Ravi, of all people, walking towards her. He looked upset.

147

"Ravi," she said, surprised. "What are you doing here? How did you know where to find me?"

"Sammy, it's so good to see you." He put his arms around her and held her close. "With a little help from your mother and your grandmother who pointed me in the right direction, not very happily, I have to say."

"What is it? What's wrong?" she asked.

"I have something to tell you, I felt I should tell you personally," he said. "I'm going to Delhi for a few weeks. My parents have made, well, certain plans for me that I feel obligated to follow. It's not what I want for myself. It's for the sake of the family. I need you to understand that."

"You're not telling me they've arranged a marriage for you?" Samira asked, horrified. "You, of all people? I thought you said your family was very open- minded and wanted you to make your own choice."

"I know what I said, and I was telling you the truth. It's not that I don't...care for you." He looked uncomfortable. "But for a marriage to work, people must share similar backgrounds and beliefs."

"That's poppycock! Are you saying that my background is so different from yours?"

"Sammy, please don't. Two months ago, I told my father of my intention to ask you to marry me."

"And what made you change your mind?"

"What he and my mother said to me. Marriage is not about two individuals coming together, it's about two families."

"I understand that, Ravi. I'm Indian, too, remember? I've lived here all my life."

"That's just it, Sammy," he said. "If you were Indian, there would be no problem."

"So, it's because my father's a Sahib?"

"It goes deeper than that. You would never belong in Delhi with my relatives."

"Relatives!" scoffed Samira. "You live here, not in Delhi. And what does it matter what they think?"

148

"Sammy, please believe me when I say I made all these exact arguments to my father. What my family thinks matters very much, and that's maybe where we differ. I have a large family, large and closely knit. My relatives are all very dear to me, and I would never do anything to upset them."

"Not even marry the woman you love!"

"It's different for you. If I were to prick this little finger of yours," he kissed it gently, "I know what I would find running through your veins, not blood but tea! You've known no other life. It's different for me. I'm still trying to adjust to things here. And I like it well enough. But I can't base my decision on the assumption that I'll stay in tea forever."

"You've been brainwashed," she said, accusingly. "This doesn't sound like you at all. I'd go the ends of the earth for you, Ravi. You know that."

"Think about it," he said. "Would you really be happy living among my Punjabi relatives? Would you, now? Can you see yourself wearing a sari and being one of the womenfolk?"

"No, I can't," she said, tossing her head. "And nor would I have to. Delhi is full of modern girls, who wear trousers and dresses and who have jobs and careers."

"Try not to delude yourself," he said. "You would not be happy in Delhi. Let me finish." He held up his hand to stop her as she opened her mouth to speak. "Okay, we may be blissfully happy for a little while. What then? You would miss your own family, friends and way of life. You'd be miserable, and eventually you'd come to blame me."

"So you're marrying someone you don't love? Are you leaving tea, too?"

"No, I'm not leaving tea. I haven't made up my mind about that yet. Please try to understand how upsetting this has been for me. And I'm not getting married yet. I'm going away to get engaged – maybe."

"Tell me this is not happening," she said, her eyes filling with tears. "I can't believe we're having this conversation. Tell me I'm dreaming, Ravi. Everything you just said undermines my parents' marriage and their entire lives together. They had far less in common than you and I have."

"I've observed your parents," he admitted. "And you're right, they are happy. But they live in isolation on a lonely tea estate with no family to consider. Charles would never have been happy adapting to a Sikkimese lifestyle or Ramona to a British one. I'm not saying it doesn't happen, but it involves sacrifice on both sides, sacrifice and a lot of compromise."

All the beauty of the day was gone. Ravi had made up his mind. His protestations added up to one thing, something he would not admit. His relatives were opposed to his marrying an Anglo-Indian. They felt the stigma and did not want her offspring to be part of their family. The same thing that happened to Sandra Williams all those years ago was now happening to her. But in her case, she was being rejected by an Indian, not a British, Sahib!

She could now understand his long silences and prolonged absences. She was hurt that he hadn't considered confiding in her or even consulting her until the entire matter was a fait accompli. She thought their relationship had been very special, and she personally would have overcome any obstacle to be with him. Obviously, her feelings were not reciprocated. He preferred to marry a complete stranger, rather than her. What was the point in arguing? She couldn't make him love her.

So summoning up all her pride and dignity, she held out her hand and said,

"Well, it seems there's nothing more to be said. I can see your mind is made up. Thank you for having the decency to come and tell me face-to-face. I know this hasn't been easy for you, either." Her voice broke.

"Good-bye, Ravi. Remember, I will always love you."

"Please don't," he pleaded. "I am desperately sorry to have hurt you, and it doesn't mean I don't love you." His eyes gazed down into hers.

"Please go," she said. "I need to be left alone to think."

He walked away with a hollow feeling in the pit of his stomach. He hadn't expected to feel such a heel about the whole business. His father had been so persuasive and convincing.

"The days of mixed marriages are over, son," he had said. "These are the seventies. Marriage is complicated enough as it is. We all have these flings, but in the end we marry women of our own kind and class. I can guarantee that you'll be glad you did in the long run."

So he'd broken the heart of the woman he loved and would now have to wonder for the rest of his life if he'd done the right thing. He walked disconsolately back to his bike, spun it around and headed for the plains and the loneliness of his Chota Bungalow nestled amid the tea.

Chapter 19
Darjeeling, 1978

After taking Samira and Prava home after tea at Glenarys, Justin drove to the Planters Club and checked in at the front desk. He was shown into his room by an ancient Nepalese bearer who had joined the establishment as a chokra more than fifty years ago. He had witnessed many changes in the club and in the town. One thing he was sure of, though, was that the Sahibs knew how to do things in style. It was not just that their tips were larger or that they were more polite, they had a respect for the order of things, which made serving them so much more satisfying.

Dali had been trained to wait at table, serving dishes from one side and removing them from the other, setting the table with mysterious implements that had to be arranged in the correct sequence and keeping the impression of being invisible so as not to intrude upon the Sahibs and Memsahibs. It was all a mystery to the uncouth lad from a village near Sonada, but he mastered the intricacies of serving at table, pouring drinks at the bar and carrying tea and breakfast trays to guests' rooms with an air of total anonymity.

It upset his sense of propriety, therefore, when people swept aside the old niceties with no knowledge or respect for established conventions. New staff members were impossible to train, not understanding why they should do things a certain way when guests did not expect it of them. Dali would be confused and unsure. He was too old to adapt to change.

But this was a real Sahib today, and there weren't many of them left. It would be a pleasure to serve him at dinner tonight. The older Indian Sahibs were also a pleasure to wait on. Some were even more British in their ways than the British themselves. It never once occurred to Dali that his opinions were disloyal in any way. He was Nepalese, though he had never once been to his country, and the club seldom had Nepalese guests, so everyone seemed foreign to him.

From the balcony outside his room, Justin admired the view. Below were the shops and restaurants on Chowrasta. He could see a blue-domed building between the trees in the direction of Prava's house that she said was the residence of the governor of West Bengal. He wondered what she and Samira would be talking about. Samira seemed a trifle pensive, he thought to himself, but perhaps she was just apprehensive about her grandmother. He couldn't stop thinking about her. In many ways, this was a relief after all the years he'd mourned and thought of Lorraine. Getting rid of the guilt had been the worst part. He'd felt responsible for her death. It was something he couldn't shake off. And certainly her parents had done their share to make him feel responsible, too.

"Why weren't you walking beside her if the river was that dangerous?"

"Why even take her to a place like that, we can't understand."

"We knew no good would come of this. We should never have allowed her to go to that heathen country."

It went on and on, one family member after another expressing shock at his presumed negligence. Finally, the day of the memorial service came and went, and he flew back to India, relieved to get away from the intensity of it all. He could sense his own parents' disappointment seeping out of them, first having been deprived of a grandchild, and now this. Then, as if things weren't bad enough, he insisted on staying on in that god-forsaken country, instead of taking over the bakery as Edward had asked him to do.

"I just can't think about it right now. Please allow me some time," he had begged. He almost felt obliged to return and mourn for Lorraine in the place where they'd lived so happily together. He needed to regain his equilibrium, get his bearings.

The tragedy of losing her had weighed down on him for the longest time. He missed her body beside him in bed, her company at mealtimes, her presence beside him on social occasions where she had been the center of attention. He felt a nonentity without her. She was the more social of the pair, the one people had warmed to and wanted to invite to parties.

There was the matter of dealing with her possessions and her clothes. In his distraught state, he hadn't thought to take anything home to her parents. Who would even fit into those dresses she loved? Martha took them away one day and sent them to an orphanage in Shillong. The poor in these parts had no use for such elegance. He discovered the typewriter they'd bought from the planter who was retiring and the pages she had spent afternoons typing. She had written children's stories about India, dedicating them:

"To our unborn children, and to Justin, my love, who I know would have done anything to give me the children I yearned for."

She'd put on a brave face about not being able to have children but the stories demonstrated that she'd wanted children above all else. He showed them to Tom. Martha reckoned they were good enough to be published, so he sent them to a publishing house in Belfast. One day out of the blue, a hard-bound volume arrived in the mail. The book of short stories was entitled *Tea Time Tales*. He had copies sent to Toby and Bernadette and instructed the publishing house to forward any royalties from the book to them.

He went through years of heartache, craving sympathy and human company. He devised ways to avoid being alone, which was not easy in tea. He worked long hours at the factory, supervising shift after shift until he went home and fell asleep from exhaustion. He played golf with anyone he could persuade to join him, and he often played alone. He exhausted Tom and Martha, arriving at their house unannounced for drinks and lingering for invitations to dinner.

Suddenly one day, he found he could feel nothing at all. He became numb and impassive, struggling to even remember her face. He wasn't sure which was better, the heartache or the indifference. At least he knew he was alive when his heart ached. He craved solitude, becoming reclusive and taking long walks by himself. He grew a beard. His hair became wild and unkempt. He wanted to get away from everything familiar. Impulsively, he asked for a transfer out of Assam, which his manager gladly recommended to head office, unable to deal with the new, unapproachable Justin. He was long overdue a promotion, which they had postponed when his wife died, not wishing to burden him with added responsibilities. After six months, a position came up, and the company named him manager of the Simling Tea Estate in the Dooars.

He shaved off his beard, cut his hair and went to Calcutta to buy much-needed new clothes. His new life began in a place where nobody knew him and where there were no memories of Lorraine. Shortly afterwards, he met Samira and found himself coming alive again. He had thought he would never be interested in another woman. Samira was much younger, so earnest and innocent. But when she smiled her whole face lit up, and he found himself waiting for her smiles and wanting to be the one who made her smile. At long last, he felt that he had regained his equilibrium and could start living again. He missed being married for the companionship it brought. He craved a woman in his bed, more for the company and closeness than the sex. He yearned to have someone to come home to in the evenings and to whisper to deep into the night.

This trip to Darjeeling with Samira was another milestone in his process of recovery. It felt good to be involved in the lives of others, to travel someplace new and to look forward, rather than backward.

He decided to take a stroll through Chowrasta before dinner and went inside to unpack his overnight bag. He put on a jacket and tie, so he could go straight to the dining room after the walk. But when he stepped onto the balcony, it had started to drizzle. He abandoned the idea and went to the bar instead. He ordered himself a scotch and soda and watched teenage boys play billiards. They told him they were students at St. John's, an all-boys boarding school up the hill and were having dinner with their parents who were in town for a few days.

Dinner was an interminable affair, with the old bearer, Dali, waiting on him and a number of other tables. He was served a mediocre meal in great style. The kitchens must have been some distance away judging by how much time it took for his food to get to him and how cold it had become. It didn't help that the old man walked slowly and stiffly and kept forgetting the most basic items.

The following morning, he slept late and decided to check out of the club before breakfast, to the intense disappointment of Dali. He ate at Keventers, a café opposite the club, where he feasted on scrambled eggs, bacon, sausages and black pudding.

"As good as an Ulster fry," he thought, remembering his mother's huge breakfasts, with soda farls and potato bread from the shop.

"I'm a devil with the frying pan," Irene liked to say. No one in the world could produce meals like she did. He remembered the roast beef on Sundays with both mashed and roast potatoes, York-shire pudding and delicious gravy. Thinking about her made him nostalgic for home. He hadn't been back since that awful trip after Lorraine died three years ago, the lowest point of his life. He was due home leave. In fact, he was due six months' leave. It was some-thing to think about, though at the moment he was preoccupied with developing his relationship with Samira.

It was beautiful day and he decided to walk to Prava's house. It was pleasant to gaze in the windows of the little curio shops. He was fascinated by the Tibetan and Nepalese handicrafts, jew-elry and artifacts and by the distinctive hill people he saw on the streets, dressed in their ethnic costumes.

Prava was glad to see him and called out loudly as he drew near,

"Good morning, Justin, how are you, my boy?"

"Good morning, Prava. Don't you look pretty today?" He climbed the dozen or so steps to the verandah to join her.

"What rubbish!" she tittered, susceptible as any other woman to compliments.

"Sammy has gone for a walk. You can either wait here or try to find her. She usually turns left on the Mall."

Prava had observed, as she observed everything that hap-pened on her street, a grim-faced Ravi return to his motorcycle.

157

Whatever it was that went on between them had not gone well. And judging by the time that had elapsed since, Sammy was not rushing home with joyful tidings. She was certain, in the circumstances, that her granddaughter would be pleased to see Justin. She'd known all along that that Ravi was no good, just like all plainspeople. Hadn't she told Sammy yesterday to go for the British Sahib?

After Ravi left, Sammy took refuge in the woods behind the Gymkhana Club. Few people knew about the narrow dirt path that cut through the undergrowth beneath the trees. Steep and slippery, it didn't lead anywhere except to the top of the hill. She and Mark had stumbled across searching for a lost tennis ball years ago. It was a good place to cry. No one would see or hear her. But she had already shed all her tears over Ravi. And what was the point of crying when he'd made things patently clear? In some ways, it was a relief to have the uncertainly taken away. She now knew the reason for his withdrawal and didn't have to agonize over it.

Ravi had chosen a stranger over her. The thought hurt like crazy. But, since he didn't want her, she would just have to get on with her life. At least she wouldn't have to wait in the wings any longer.

Feeling slightly cheered, she made her way down the hill, past the tennis courts and the Gymkhana Club. With all the drama over Ravi, she'd completely forgotten about her date with Justin and was taken aback when she saw him walking toward her, smiling until he saw her tear-stained face.

"What is it, Samira? Is something wrong? Are you hurt?" he asked.

She had no idea what to say. She didn't want to tell him about Ravi. It was too long a story, and in any case, it was over. Better to forget about it and move on. Some things were better kept in the family. She knew she'd be telling the story to her grandmother later and to her mother when she got home.

So she smiled at him and lied, saying the walk had brought back memories of her time in Darjeeling and made her realize that she had some decisions she needed to make.

"What can I do to make you feel better? Where would you like to go?"

"Well, first I would like to go home and wash my face." She was conscious of her swollen eyes and red nose. "And after that? Actually, I know exactly what I would like to do, if you don't mind!" She suddenly remembered one of the reasons she had wanted to come here, "I'd like to go shopping!"

Justin laughed. How like a woman! When men were upset, they wanted to hit someone or something, or sweat it out in some way. What did women want to do? They wanted to shop.

"Excellent idea! I had to resist going into all those wonderful shops on my way here. I'm more than happy to go shopping."

Back at the house, she could see that Prava was all agog, though she realized that Samira was not going to say anything in front of Justin.

"Would you like some breakfast, Justin? Sammy?"

"Oh, no thank you," Justin said. "I had a huge breakfast at Keventers. I couldn't eat a thing."

"How about you, Sam?"

"I'm fine, thanks, not really hungry."

Which was worrying, thought Prava. Sammy wasn't easily put off her food, especially breakfast.

"Are you ready?" Justin asked Samira. She had washed her face, put on some of her new makeup and changed out of her old white dress into something more respectable.

"Yes, I am. I'll just grab my purse."

Prava watched them leave; happy that Samira had Justin to distract her during what she was certain was a difficult time. She could not imagine what Ravi had to say that required him to drive all that distance, but she had a few scenarios in her mind.

She noticed that someone was coming to her gate. It was Tashi Dorjee, the woman who collected her rent each month. Strange, the rent wasn't due, and she didn't recall telling her there was anything that needed fixing.

"Good day, Tashi," she said. "What brings you here on a Sunday morning? Can I offer you some tea or coffee?"

'No, thank you," Tashi said. "No need. I have relatives visiting and need to get back to them. But I have news for you that I wanted to tell you personally."

"I paid my rent on time. I know I did. What is it?" Prava said, beginning to get nervous.

"I have a message for you from your landlord, who is my uncle. You've never met him. But it seems he's going to need this house back. I'm so sorry. I know how much you love it and how long you've lived here. You've been a perfect tenant, and I promise to find you something else. But rents have gone up considerably. Houses are hard to find these days, so it may have to be a flat somewhere or a house in Ghoom."

Prava was speechless. Ghoom! A flat! She could think of nothing worse. Leave this house where she had lived for almost twenty-five years? Impossible! What about her lease, she asked. Apparently, it was coming up for renewal in a couple of months, the period of notice the landlord was willing to allow her. He was really a kind person. He was a big businessman in town and wanted the house for his old aunt who was moving to Darjeeling from Sik-kim. He wanted to come and see the cottage and would be stopping by next week. Tashi said she was truly sorry and promised to do everything she could to find something suitable for Prava.

She went on her way, leaving Prava shocked and stunned. This was something she'd never envisioned. She could not bear to think of leaving her cottage. It had been her home for so long. It was small, but it suited her perfectly. What was she going to do? She couldn't conceive of living anywhere else.

Meanwhile, Justin and Samira were shopping on Chowrasta. First, they visited some of the old curiosity shops that so captivated him. He picked out a silver pendant to take back to his mother and when he saw that Samira liked a topaz bracelet, he went surrepti-tiously back to the shop and bought it. He found a cap of yak's wool he knew his father would like and asked Samira to pick out some ornaments for his bungalow. Everyone seemed to know her. She spoke to them in Nepalese, haggling for the best possible price.

Next, she took him to a fabric store and said she needed to order some clothes.

"Probably not today but I just need to start planning what to buy. I've decided to visit my Aunt Pauline in Ireland," she told him. "She lives in Bray with her husband, Sean. I also want to go to Europe."

"When are you going?" he asked, surprised.

"As soon as I can arrange it, Justin."

"Is this a sudden decision?"

"It is and it isn't. I've always known I'd be going. I was just waiting for the time to be right."

He looked thoughtful. Things were not going as planned, or were they? He didn't want their relationship to lose momentum. He'd thought he had more time to allow it to develop, not that he needed it for himself. His mind was made up. He knew that he wanted her in his life and could not bear the thought of losing her.

"And what makes it right now?" he asked, needing to know.

"It's… summertime. I graduated from college over a year ago. I need to make some concrete plans for my future." She couldn't tell him her heart had just been broken, and she needed to escape as far away as she could to avoid running into the person who'd caused her so much pain.

"Yes, I'm sure it is," he agreed. This was hardly the time to extract any kind of promise from her. But later, as he delivered her back to her grandmother's front gate in the afternoon, he took her hand and said,

"Sammy, I need you to know that I'm crazy about you. I'd like you to think about whether we might have a future together. I don't want to rush things, but the fact that you're going away soon means that we don't have much time. I never…I thought I would never feel for anyone again, but I know I couldn't bear to lose you."

Samira looked at him, surprised and flattered. As usual, she didn't know what to say and struggled for the right words. It had been an emotional roller coaster of a day.

"Thanks, Justin. I will. I'm a little surprised but very flattered. I've had a lovely time. You're sure you won't come in?"

"Unfortunately, I need to get going. But I've had a wonderful weekend. Please say good-bye to your grandmother for me."

❧❦❧

Chapter 20
Darjeeling, India, 1978

It seemed odd that Prava was not at her usual post on the verandah. Samira called to her as she entered the house and found her in the kitchen vigorously stirring things in a pot. She wore a length of cloth around her waist like an apron and a bandana over her hair. She looked like she'd been crying. Samira had never seen her grandmother cry.

"What's wrong, Gran? Why are you crying?"

It had been a day of tears.

"I have terrible news," said Prava. "I had a visitor while you were out, the woman who collects my rent. She told me that I have to move out of my cottage because the new owner wants it back. I have two months to find another place."

"You mean it doesn't belong to you?" It was also a day of surprises. "But you've lived here ever since I was born and before that, too."

"We've lived here ever since we moved from Kalimpong when your mother was twenty- one, a little younger than you are now. I've always loved this house. It never occurred to me that they would ever want it back. I realize I should have at least considered it might happen."

"Maybe you can reason with them?"

"No, the owner wants it for a relative. I don't even know him. Tashi has taken care of everything during the last few years. She's his granddaughter or niece, I think she said. What am I going to do?"

Samira lit the stove and put the kettle on. "I'm so sorry Gran, but we'll find another house. I'll help you."

"It's not that easy. Tashi said rents have gone up a lot, and I might have to move into a flat or even to Ghoom."

Ghoom was like its name, a gloomy town just outside Darjeeling, perpetually smothered in fog.

"But listen to me going on as if I'm the only one with problems! What about your news? I'm sorry, my girl, I should have asked you sooner. I saw Ravi on his way back to his motorcycle. He didn't look at all happy."

"Gran, it's finally over between us. He's going to have an arranged marriage." Samira started to cry, as she'd known she would. "His family doesn't want him to marry me because they think I won't fit in with their customs. They don't approve of mixed marriages."

"Yes, I thought that might be the case with those Punjabis." Prava spoke scathingly. This just reaffirmed her bigotry against plainspeople. She added two spoons of sugar to her tea. But there was no point going into that now.

"So when's he getting married? Have they found a girl? Or do they just want him to not marry you?"

"Oh, they've found someone. It seems he'd rather have a stranger than me," she said. "He's going to Delhi for the engagement. Maybe, he said, if he likes her. There's no wedding date yet. So that's what's been going on all these months, while I've been breaking my heart over him."

"I'm so sorry, Sammy. But at least now you know and can get on with your life. Tell me what happened with Justin? Did you have a nice time with him?"

"Actually, I did. The whole Ravi fiasco has made me appreciate him even more. The reality is that I've seen very little of Ravi for quite a while, except for one night at the club last week. What he said to me today was just a confirmation of what I already suspected, except about his getting engaged. I'd never have suspected that. So, now I feel I'm in a better position to appreciate someone like Justin, someone older, more stable, and...well, someone who doesn't have Ravi's prejudice."

They moved to Prava's drawing room and made themselves comfortable.

"How did you leave it with him, with Justin, I mean?" Prava asked.

"He asked me to think about having a relationship with him. He told me he's crazy about me. But Gran, I've only just decided to go to England. I kept putting it off because of Ravi. If I don't go soon, it will be wintertime, and I don't want to postpone it to next year."

"Listen to the girl!" Prava mocked, looking heavenward. "Try to live your life one day at a time, child. You always want to rush things. It will all work out. Listen to your old grandmother. Now how about pouring me some brandy? And help yourself to some wine before we have dinner."

The next morning, Samira went to Chowrasta to buy a newspaper. She wanted to check the classified advertisements for a house to rent. She hadn't been able to sleep, her mind filled with the events of the day. She wore the topaz bracelet Justin had given her as he was leaving the day before. The yellow stones were set in a silver filigree design. He'd asked her to think things over. Obviously, he didn't want her to set off on her travels without giving him some form of commitment. Was she really ready to do that? And why would she want to just as she was about to embark on her big adventure? She bought the newspaper and decided to take the long route home to stretch her legs and clear her mind.

Back at the house, Prava was picking chilies and coriander in her garden. She'd planted them among the marigolds and dahlias. The shadows under her eyes revealed that she hadn't been able to sleep, either. She wondered if she should have gone back to her family in Gangtok when Ramona got married. Her sisters and cousins were still living in the houses they'd grown up in. They had always urged her to come home. But events in her life had taken her away, from one place to the next, almost as though she'd had no say in the matter. Somehow, it never seemed to be the right time to go home. And now she felt she would be imposing on her siblings by moving in with them.

She was so engrossed in her thoughts that she didn't see someone open her gate and walk over to where she was crouched among the flowers. She looked up startled, unable to see who it

165

was because of the sunlight behind him. She rose unsteadily. He held out his arm to help her.

"I'm sorry to disturb you, madam," he said politely. "Why don't I come back another time?"

She looked up at him, a faint glimmer of recognition in her mind. She could see that he, too, was looking at her incredulously.

Memories of times together and of friendship, companionship and vulnerable young love flooded back into her mind, memories of how he had loved and waited for her, patiently and uncomplaining, and how she had belittled that love with her betrayal. Prem! It was Prem Dorjee, the man she had known and loved in her youth.

"Prava?" he asked, uncertainly. "Is it really you?"

"P...Prem?" she stammered. "I can't believe it...after all these years!"

His body had filled out and his hair was almost white. He wore a brown business suit and carried himself with an unmistakable air of prosperity.

"It's been so long, and yet I knew you instantly!" He took a handkerchief out of his pocket and wiped the sweat off his face.

"Please, come inside. Have some tea." She pushed a stray hair out of her eyes and smoothed her clothes, aware that she must look a sight, in addition to being more than forty years older than when he last saw her. He followed her up the steps into the cottage.

"Please don't go to any trouble," he said.

"Oh, it's no trouble at all. The pot is still hot. Please sit down."

She went into the kitchen and seeing her maid, Tiki, asked her to bring a tea tray into the drawing room.

They sat facing each other, a trifle awkwardly. It had been so long. There was so much unsaid between them. Where would they even begin?

"How did you find me?" she asked, finally. "What brought you here?"

"I have to be honest. I wasn't looking for you. I came to look at my house."

So he was her landlord!

"It's inconceivable we never met," she said. "I've lived here for twenty-five years."

"I inherited it only four years ago," he said. "But I've lived in this town ever since…ever since after I last saw you."

She now remembered Tashi telling her that the house had a new owner, and that it would not affect her in any way. She wanted to know all about Prem and the kind of life he'd led.

"So, you came here? After you left Gangtok?"

"Yes, I had family in the town. I started a business. My son runs it now."

"You have a son? And a wife?"

"I have two sons and five grandchildren. But sadly, I no longer have a wife. She died six years ago."

"I'm very sorry," said Prava, trying to take it all in.

"Thank you." He took the cup of tea she handed him and placed it carefully on one of the rosewood side tables. "And you? Where is your husband?"

"I never had a husband," she said. She had paid for her indiscretion her whole life. "He… we didn't marry. But I had a beautiful child. Her name is Ramona."

The child who was a manifestation of her infidelity, he thought, bitterly. So it now emerged that he had left his home and had given her up for a man who hadn't even married her. It happened long ago when he was young and filled with idealistic notions. But he could still remember the pain and the heartache. And now, she had come into his life exactly when he was beginning to feel vulnerable again, and still with that aura he'd found so irresistible.

"And how is Ramona?" he asked. "Does she live here with you?"

She told him about Ramona and Charles and was just starting to tell him about Samira and Mark, when Samira walked in, flushed and rosy from her walk.

"Oh," she said. She was taken aback to see Prem. "I'm sorry. Am I interrupting?"

"No, Sammy. Please stay. Meet a very old friend, Prem Dorjee. It turns out that he's also my landlord."

"Pleased to meet you, Prem. I'm Samira." She shot a quick, hopeful look at her grandmother. Did the fact that he was a friend mean that he might reconsider and let them stay in the house? There was a long silence, and she felt that she was intruding on something more than a chance encounter between two old friends.

"Please excuse me a moment. I need to speak to Tiki," she lied, going to the kitchen where she could hear Tiki singing as she cooked lunch.

Prem looked at Prava and cleared his throat. Tashi had told him that his tenant did not want to vacate the cottage. But he'd already promised it to his aunt. He needed to think things over. This wasn't going to be easy.

"I'm delighted to have come across you again," he said to Prava. "I realize that you want to stay here. I can't promise you anything just yet, but rest assured I'll do my best to find a solution."

"Thank you. I can't ask for more than that. In fact, I've no right to ask you for anything. Also, I know it was a long time ago, and maybe you forgot all about me and about what happened, but I want you to know how sorry I am about what I did to you and to us. I tried to find you, but your family wouldn't help me, which is understandable. And I was pregnant with someone else's child. Why would you have wanted me? I don't want to make excuses, but I was very young. I missed you desperately for many years."

She gazed at him, determined to grasp the opportunity to say all the things she'd always wanted to say to him while she could, in case she never saw him again. She might never have another opportunity to beg his forgiveness and explain her behavior in some way.

"I've never forgotten you." He spoke clearly and deliberately. "I left because I couldn't bear the pain. If I'd known you still cared, I would have stayed, but I assumed you'd marry the child's father. And I would gladly have asked for your hand if I'd known you hadn't. I would have helped you bring up the child."

The thought of what might have been swept over them. Prava's head bowed in sadness at the loss to her life. It was almost too

168

much to bear. The years had passed and could not be re-lived. Prem stood up, and she went to him and took his hand.

"Once again, I'm truly sorry. I realize I can't expect you to help me. I'm just happy to have had this opportunity to talk to you and to explain things from my perspective."

Days passed. Prava and Samira were in limbo not knowing whether to start hunting for another house or to hope that Prem might reconsider.

"If he was truly in love with you, Gran, he won't let you down now."

"But I let him down in the past. Why should he help me now? And what about the situation between you and Justin? Have you thought about it, as he asked?"

"Gran, don't change the subject! I think Prem's still in love with you."

"Oh, stop it, child."

"Are you in love with him?"

"Have some respect and stop asking questions! I'm much too old to think about such nonsense."

"Sixty-five is not old. And you're still beautiful."

"Darling, you're too sweet. And before I forget, my neighbor said you're to call your mother."

"Oh, all right. I'll go call her now."

She went next door to telephone her mother. She got her mother on the line, and Ramona told her she had a message from Justin offering to bring her home next Sunday. He was arriving in Darjeeling on Saturday afternoon and wanted to take her out to dinner, such a nice man! Samira laughed and said that as she'd already been considering leaving at the weekend, she'd be happy to accept Justin's kind offer.

As she returned, she saw a delivery man at the gate carrying a bouquet of flowers. How kind and romantic of Justin, she thought. But the man needed a signature from Mrs. Roy, he said, as the flowers were for her. Samira ran into the house and hugged her grandmother in glee. Prem had sent her a bouquet of red roses with a note inviting them both to tea at his house the following day. He would send a car to pick them up at four o'clock. There was a number for her to call.

The next day, Sammy made sure her grandmother dressed appropriately for the occasion. For once, Prava didn't protest too much. Consequently, she looked wonderful in gray silk Sikkimese robes, a white sweater and pearls that complimented the gray and white tones of her hair.

Prem's house was a colonial structure with a stone façade on the other side of town, above the main thoroughfare into Darjeeling. It was built into a hillside and overlooked the town's twin blue domes and the Kanchenjunga Mountains beyond. Prava gasped in awe when she walked in and saw the view through the Georgian window panes. Prem explained that the house had belonged to his grandfather and that he had moved in four years ago after he died. His son now occupied the large family home where he had lived with his wife. Prava noted that the house was furnished with great magnificence, although it looked badly in need of updating. There were fine pieces of antique mahogany furniture, including a dining table and sideboard, grandfather clock and desk.

"I know this place needs work," he said, ruefully. "But being a typical man, I keep putting it off." He pushed a call button beside his armchair and ordered tea.

"I love it!" cried Samira. "These old houses are beautiful. And better to do nothing than to modernize unsympathetically."

"Very true," he agreed. The servant wheeled in a tea trolley laden with cakes and sandwiches. "Prava, will you be mother?"

Once they were settled with cups of tea and plates of food, he said, "Ladies, I have some good news for you, nothing conclusive as yet, I'm afraid, but you can, at least, stay in the house for a further three months. My aunt can't move in till November."

"That is good news," said Prava. "Thank you so much. That gives me a little more time to find something. And it's always easier to find places in the wintertime."

It confirmed her belief that things were not to be "over-thought" because in the end fate would intervene for good or ill.

"What a relief. Gran, this gives you more time to de-clutter," Samira teased. Prava threw nothing away, and her little cottage was bursting at the seams with her possessions.

They walked in the garden after tea, Samira lagging behind to give Prem and Prava some privacy.

"It's very kind of you to do all this," said Prava. "I wonder if you would allow me to cook dinner for you Saturday night? Samira is going out to dinner with a young man."

Prem accepted, and the ladies returned home very happy at the recent turn of events.

Saturday came round and there was much shopping for meat, vegetables and wines by Prava and for shoes, sweaters and accessories by Samira. She had already cajoled her tailor into sewing three pairs of trousers and a dress. He grumbled and shook his head as though she was asking for the moon, only relenting when she said, fine, she would to go to the tailor at Fancy Fabrics.

"What a waste of money, all these clothes. Men don't notice such nonsense," said Prava, who was planning to impress Prem via his stomach.

"Well, maybe not, but no holey sweaters or socks for you tonight!" Samira said, going into her grandmother's room. She picked out a navy gown and a red shawl and laid them out on the bed. The colors would look good on Prava. She wore beige trousers and an ivory -colored blouse with a cream cardigan. Her hair gleamed, and she put on some coral lipstick that emphasized her brown eyes. She'd been thinking about her relationship with Justin, not allowing herself to think about Ravi. Fortunately, everything that had happened in the last week helped divert her thoughts away from him. Hard to think that only two weeks ago they'd held each other in the starlight. She pushed the memory of it firmly out of her mind.

Justin arrived right on time, suntanned from forgetting to wear his topee the previous day. He kissed Samira warmly and told her how wonderful she looked. She was very happy to see him

171

and held on to his hand, not wanting to let him go. She left final instructions for Prava, whom she hadn't been able to persuade to change yet.

"Now, make sure you wear what I laid out for you!" she threatened, before departing with Justin.

It was exciting to be on a real date. They drove to the Planters Club for dinner. Dali's maddening slowness didn't seem quite so bad to Justin with Samira there to distract him. She was excited and a little unsure of herself, which endeared her to him even more. After they'd eaten, they went upstairs for coffee and brandy beside the fire in his suite. The fire was lit even though it was July, and the warmth was comforting in the draughty, old building. The room glowed with the light from the fire, the deep red curtains that hung in the tall windows and the scarlet Tibetan rugs on the floor.

Samira sank into one of the armchairs. Her hair shone in the lamplight.

Finally, Justin spoke, "Would you hear me out on a plan I've devised? It may seem a little farfetched, but I'm excited about it and hope you will be too."

Samira nodded and waited for him to tell her what it was.

"When you told me of your plans to go to England and Ireland this summer, it made me start thinking because I, too, have been planning to go to those places. I have leave due to me, and the Tea Company would like me to go now before they transfer the existing manager somewhere else. So I thought to myself, why don't we go together? It will make travelling far more enjoyable. We could visit my parents and your Aunt Pauline, and we could take trips to Paris, Rome and Venice or anywhere else you might want to visit."

He studied her face for a response he hoped would be positive. Her eyes sparkled, and she seemed intrigued by what he was saying. He wasted no time and before she could speak, he went down on one knee before her and held out a little velvet box which he opened to reveal a diamond ring.

"Nothing in the world would make me happier than for you to agree to marry me. I love you, Samira, and want you to be my wife."

Samira looked into his handsome, tanned face, stunned beyond words. She was warmed by the fire and the brandy and felt completely overwhelmed. She stared at the ring catching the firelight in its little silken cushion. In a haze, she saw him take the ring from the box and put it on her finger. Then he tilted her face up to his and kissed her till her senses swam.

"Say yes, my darling. Say yes, and the world will be ours."

"Yes. Yes, of course, I will marry you," Samira whispered, unable to resist. They were made for each other. It made perfect sense. He was a tried and trusted tea planter, just like her father. He loved her without question, which felt extremely good, and helped to heal her self- confidence which had been so badly shaken.

He kissed her face and neck, and his hands stroked her body.

"I love you, Samira. I want you."

"I love you and want you, too, Justin." She whispered at last, her body craving the sensation it had so recently been awakened to. Holding her close, he took her by the hand and gently led her into his room.

Chapter 21
Dooars, Delhi &
Darjeeling, India, 1978

Samira returned to Ranikot with her ring and her new fiancé, her life transformed from when she left only a week ago. She ran up the steps hand-in-hand with Justin and found Ramona and Charles on the veranda, waiting for their arrival. Samira kissed them both and took Justin's arm possessively.

"We have great news to announce! Mum, Dad, I'd like to present my fiancé! Justin and I are engaged!" she held out her left hand, proudly showing them her ring.

"Good lord!" exclaimed Charles. "This is a surprise! I say!"

"Sammy?" Ramona was stunned, to say the least. Only a week ago, Sammy had left home nursing a broken heart over Ravi. She'd gone to her grandmother's to get over him, but Ramona didn't think it would happen quite so quickly. She didn't want to cast a dampener on proceedings or imply that she had reservations about Justin, but it was all so sudden.

She suspected that her daughter was on the rebound and not thinking clearly. Still, she was elated, and who was she to talk when she and Charles had known from their very first meeting that they would marry? She scrutinized her daughter. There was something different about her. But there was no denying that she looked happy.

"Mum?" She saw that Samira was waiting for a response. She put her arms around them both, exclaiming loudly how delighted she was and congratulated them warmly. Seeing that Ramona was happy, Charles decided that all must be in order and that the Ravi fellow was a thing of the past. He preferred Justin in any case, a nice, steady lad who had been married before and knew what it was all about. He was a little old for Sammy, but maybe that was what she needed, someone able to take care of her, give her a little leeway. This would mean that she would not be going away. That reminded him that he had news to announce, too. Was this the time, though? He glanced at Ramona, questioningly. She was the one who knew how and when to say things. But when Samira said,

"And isn't it wonderful that we'll be so close to you?" he cleared his throat nervously and said,

"Actually, Mum and I have some news for you, too. Tell them, darling."

"Yes, we have an announcement of our own. As you all know, Charles has had to deal with endless labor problems and lack of cooperation from the company. I wish they were more like your employers, Justin. Anyway, to cut a long story short, he has resigned and is taking early retirement."

"I'm not planning to just sit around, however," he interjected. "I have been offered some consultancy work by a firm that owns a number of plantations in and around Darjeeling."

"So we will be leaving for Darjeeling," Ramona continued, "in a month's time."

It was Samira's turn to be stunned. "So soon! How long have you been planning this?" She was more than a little peeved at not having been consulted.

"Actually, it all came about quite suddenly," said Charles. "I submitted my resignation to the superintendent while he was here last week, and he put my case forward to our head office in London by telephone. They're always ready to agree to anything that will save them money, and it's obviously going to be a whole lot cheaper for them to hire someone local than to continue paying me."

"And you've been busy, too, darling," Ramona reminded her. She wasn't sure if Justin knew of Samira's relationship with Ravi, although it had ended by the time Justin met her.

"Where will you live in Darjeeling?"

"We plan to buy a house when we find one. And my mother will be welcome to live with us, of course. It's one of the reasons we want to go there."

So, it had all worked out for Prava. She may have lost her beloved cottage, but now she would live with her daughter and Charles.

"That's wonderful," said Samira, happy for her grandmother. What had she said about things always working out? And they had worked out for both her and her grandmother. Not only was she getting married, she was getting to travel to all the places she wanted, which reminded her of the other half of their news.

"Justin and I have other news for you, too," she said. Would the announcements ever stop on this momentous day?

"Yes, we do." He told them about his plans for his vacation that coincided with Samira's travel plans. "We will be leaving just as soon as we can make the arrangements."

"And have you set a wedding date?" asked Ramona, a little confused by how quickly things were moving.

"That's something we need to discuss," said Samira. "Exactly here and when the wedding is to be. Justin thinks his mother will want it to be in Ireland, and I would like it to be here when we get back. Naturally, there hasn't been time to discuss all the details."

"I understand that you would want your daughter to be married here," said Justin. "And as it is my second wedding, I'm pretty sure my mother won't mind too much."

"So, you're going away for six months and will get married when you return?" asked Ramona, a little uncomfortable about the idea of her daughter travelling with someone she was not married to.

"It's seems that's the plan," said Samira, looking to Justin for confirmation. "There's so much to be done."

"But all of it good," said Charles. "I'm very happy for you both. And we'll be only a few hours away from you. Justin, would you like to stay to dinner? We already set a place for you."

In his bungalow at Baghrapur, Ravi was packing his bags. July in Delhi would be even hotter than in the Dooars, but at least his parents had air conditioning. Some of the tea bungalows had air conditioning, but not his. He packed a few pairs of trousers, shirts and ties knowing that there would be a number of formal occasions to attend. He needed to have his trousers taken in. His lifestyle here was far more active than it had ever been in the city. And there was nothing like good, home cooking. His cook was mediocre to say the least.

His flight left at nine the next morning. It took less than three hours to fly from Baghdogra to Delhi. His parents were at the airport to meet him, delighted that he was complying with their wishes.

"Look how thin you are!" his mother said. "And the sun has made you darker, but it suits you. It's okay for a man to be dark." She surveyed him dubiously as they walked out of the airport terminal. "What do you think, Sunil? Doesn't he look thin? Never mind, we will fatten him up."

Ravi smiled at his father who seldom got a word in edgeways and had become reconciled to his wife's interminable chatter.

"You will really like Radhika. She's a very sweet girl," she continued in the same breath.

"Yes, Ma, I'm sure I will," said Ravi. His throat was dry. This was not a scenario he had envisioned for himself. Why had he agreed to it? It was ridiculous. He should just have agreed not to marry Samira and left it at that. How had they talked him into this? He felt that he had been manipulated into agreeing to their plan to compensate for the indiscretion he had committed by even thinking about marrying someone like her.

Driving home, he looked disconsolately out the window at the helter-skelter of urban life he had been so overjoyed to escape. Everyone tore around in frenzy with horns honking, brakes slamming and a nerve-racking attitude of one-upmanship. Cars sped towards each other on the narrow pot-holed streets, with one driver finally giving way to the one who stood his ground. It was a miracle more people weren't killed. In wintertime, the dust lay thick on every surface. Now in the monsoon, mold and mildew blackened the sides of buildings and turned the footpaths slick and treacherous.

"If you don't like her, just tell us," said his father, Sunil. "There are other girls."

"Don't talk like that, Sunil. Of course, he will like her. Remember how pretty she is."

Yes, there were thousands of prospects in Delhi, each one of them described as "tall, fair and convent-educated" in the matrimonial columns. So, where were all these fabulous women, he wondered? He knew of only one who truly fit the description, he thought wryly to himself. She was the tallest, fairest and most beautiful girl in the land, and he had broken her heart and couldn't get her out of his mind. He was still smarting from causing so much hurt, and was about to perhaps create more pain. Could he even contemplate saying,

"She won't do. This girl's not tall, fair or educated enough. Next please."

After all, there were plenty more for him to choose from.

But what was the difference? His heart wasn't in it. They would all seem the same to him in his current frame of mind. He might as well go for the first one. Obviously, his parents and family thought highly of her. She must be pretty special. Why make things more complicated?

His father maneuvered the car up the driveway, and they entered the house, going up the marble staircase. The living room was furnished with low couches upholstered in purple brocade, brass side and coffee tables and white drum lampshades. There were large pictures on the walls depicting medieval scenes of crossed-legged men playing lutes, women balancing earthenware pots on their heads and half-clad dancing maidens surrounded by deer. Cool and uncluttered, it could have been any middle-class home in Delhi, with no personal stamp on it except for a small number of sepia picture frames of the family in front of the Taj Mahal, one of him with his sister Deepa, and Sunil and Poonam's wedding portrait.

His bags had been taken to his room. He discarded his sweaty travelling clothes and went to the bathroom. The water smelled strongly of chlorine. He had grown accustomed to the pure, unsullied water of the Dooars. As he poured tepid water over his body, he felt himself grow tepid and indifferent. He had presented every argument to his father, who had refuted all of them and won. Ravi was defeated. Like a Christian before the lions, he would go forward and meet his fate.

After a cup of tea and some of his favorite sweetmeats, they climbed into the car for the short ride to Radhika's house. The houses were all flat-roofed and faintly Art Deco, if a particular architectural style could be attributed to the buildings that cowered behind protective cement walls, with concrete paths and driveways constructed to defy the intrusion of any wayward weed or wildflower. The odor of disinfectant used for cleaning the floors combined with the scent of incense that burned in an alcove in homage to the deity Krishna.

They were ushered in by the girl's parents, the stress of the occasion evident on their faces. Their beloved daughter was about to be assessed by a highly eligible bachelor. The right of refusal on her part was purely academic. The likelihood of her making a better match was highly unlikely. In any case, this bridegroom was so handsome that she would have to be out of her mind, or blind, to turn him down.

"Please come, come in. Be seated. Have some tea. We will fetch Radhika." Pushpa fussed, passing plates of food, while Ashok, went to summon their daughter. She rejected their protests that they had already had tea.

"No, no. I insist," said Pushpa, who had gone to great lengths to select the very best sandesh and samosas for this auspicious occasion.

Radhika was in her room, anxious and flustered by the ordeal ahead of her. She had been told that Ravi was a great match, besides being extremely handsome and intelligent. But she didn't want to leave her friends in Delhi and to go to the tea plantations or to be separated from Santosh, whom she pined for every minute they were apart and who loved her desperately, but would never be anything but an office clerk, whom she knew her parents would never agree as to as a suitable match for her.

Should she try to look as pretty as possible? She wasn't quite sure what the better course of action was. While she ached to be with Santosh, she did not want to be rejected by Ravi. And if she couldn't have Santosh, then surely it was better to be with someone she didn't love who had good looks and a good job, than someone who had neither? So she wore her prettiest salwar and dutifully followed her mother downstairs, jasmine- scented, silks rustling, bangles and anklets jangling.

Ravi had to acknowledge that she was exceptionally pretty as she entered the room, her large, frightened eyes darkened with kohl. He didn't think it polite to examine her too openly and looking down, he saw her slim feet resting in gold thong sandals with toenails painted red. She saw that he wore leather tasseled moccasins, gray socks and dark trousers. She had been instructed to cast her eyes down and look demure, but in truth she scarcely dared to raise her eyes and look at him, fearful of what she might see, as though that first glance would seal her fate forever.

"See how shy she is!" her father said, proudly. "Don't be shy, Radhika. Come and meet Ravi."

He had stood as she entered the room and waited to sit until she had been ushered into a seat beside him. She sat with eyes lowered until finally her father intervened,

"I think we should show Poonam and Sunil the view from the terrace and leave you young people alone."

After the older couples left the room, they looked at each other for the first time. Finally, Ravi said,

"You are very pretty Radhika. Please don't be nervous."

"Thank you. I am a little nervous," she finally spoke.

"Where did you go to college?"

"I went to the Lady's Academy," she said, fiddling uneasily with her gold bangles.

"I would like to get to know you better," he said.

They both knew each other's histories, and she realized he was trying to make conversation. At least he was not rejecting her outright if he wanted to get to know her.

"Then, I would like to get to know you, too," she replied.

"Would you like to go to a movie with me, perhaps?" he suggested. "You can choose which one."

That seemed like a good idea. It took the pressure off having to talk and finding things to say to each other.

"That sounds fine," she said. "When?"

"How about tomorrow evening? I'll come and pick you up."

"Okay. Do you like English or Hindi movies?"

"Either one, you can choose."

The parents decided to return as it was hot out on the terrace. They were pleased that the couple had arranged to meet again the following day. After that, they would know if they had a match.

In the balmy air of Darjeeling, Prava and Prem's romance was being rapidly rekindled. The two previously solitary individuals were suddenly discovering that they couldn't function without each other. Prem could see no reason to return to his lonely villa after he left the office each day when Prava was waiting eagerly for him at her home with a glass of rum and a hot meal. He couldn't remember what he had done and how he had passed his days before he met her. They enjoyed animated conversations, long walks or just pottering about the house. Prem found many projects that needed to be done in her little home, which hadn't had a man living in it for almost twenty-five years.

When they were at his house, she arranged flowers, rearranged furniture and supervised the cleaning and polishing till the house gleamed and started to smell of mansion polish and pine just like hers. Eventually, it made no sense for him to go back to his house after an evening at hers or for her to return all the way back to her cottage when it was so much more convenient, not to mention pleasurable, for them to just stay together.

Charles and Ramona would soon be arriving and had spent a weekend looking at properties, helped by Tashi. It was understood that Prava would move in with them, and Prem found that he was contemplating their arrival with more than a little dismay. Prava realized that it would put an end to their intimate evenings by the fire, cuddling and giggling on the sofa and eating breakfast in their pajamas.

"What are we going to do," he asked her, as they cleared the dinner things one evening in her kitchen, "when Charles and Ramona arrive?"

"I was wondering the same thing," she said, stacking plates in the sink ready for Tiki to wash in the morning.

"Could you in your wildest dreams consider moving in with me?" he asked. "Or would that be too unconventional?"

It was something she had already considered. It would be unconventional, but it wasn't as if it didn't happen all the time.

"Or we could get married," he said, "If you prefer." He passed her some glasses to put in the sink.

"We could," she agreed. "If we really had to. But do we really need a piece of paper at our age?"

"It's your decision, my darling. Please think about it. I would be very happy to marry you."

"I will," she agreed, pragmatically. "But the real issue is which house we would live in."

"You really like this place, don't you?"

"It's just that I've lived here so long, and we can walk to shops and restaurants or just take pleasant strolls, which we can't do from your place. It's the only permanent home our family has had and, yes, I think it's because I just love it, almost as much as I love you."

It was the first time she'd said the words. He came over to her and took her in his arms. His voice shook.

"I can't believe my incredible good luck finding you again and being given a second chance to have you in my life. I love you and adore you and would do anything to make you happy. And if it means spending the rest of my days with you in this little cottage, then nothing would bring me more joy."

Prava rested her head on his shoulder and felt a great sense of contentment. They would be able to grow old together. It was a comforting and reassuring thought.

The next day, he instructed Tashi to have Prava's name added to the deed and to tell his aunt that the house was no longer available, as he was moving into it himself. His third instruction to her was to put the villa up for sale.

In Ranikot, the manager's bungalow was in complete chaos. There were piles of newspapers in every room. Kala had picked up dozens of plywood tea chests from the factory storage go-down and taken them to the bungalow in the pickup truck. China, silver, linen and the all the accumulation of thirty years had to be wrapped and carefully packed in the chests. There was also a growing pile of items they no longer needed, to be distributed among the servants.

Charles came home one afternoon and said that the baboos and office staff would be arriving at three o'clock for the farewell party.

"Oh, how nice of them," said Ramona, preoccupied with packing. It seemed everyone was throwing farewell parties for them. Charles instructed Ram and Jetha to set up tables and chairs for sixteen people under the Poinciana tree. Kala was dispatched to pick up the ladies.

By two-thirty, the first people started to arrive, excited about having the afternoon off and being at the manager's bungalow. Some came on bicycles, others on foot. Kala returned with a jeep-load of women, and Ramona started to get concerned when she saw that no one had brought any food.

"So, who is doing the catering?" she asked Charles.

"What d'you mean?" he said.

"No food has arrived yet, darling. Who is bringing it?"

"No one is bringing it. We're providing it!"

Ramona looked at him with horror. "But no one said anything to me about a party! The first I heard of it was when you came home for lunch today!"

Charles flushed. "Bloody hell! Did I forget to tell you? You mean to tell me we have sixteen people coming and no food!"

"Honestly Charlie, you're the limit! What are we going to do?"

"Tell Ram to go and fetch Mohammed, and tell Kala to come back."

Ram left hastily on Jetha's bicycle to summon them. Ramona buttered bread and sliced cucumbers for sandwiches, and Jetha sliced onions. Charles went outside to greet guests and keep them talking as long as possible.

When Kala arrived, Ramona instructed him to take the jeep to a sweet stall at the market and buy four dozen assorted sweetmeats. Mohammed arrived looking sleepy and disgruntled and was not at all pleased to hear that he was to fry up a huge batch of pakoras as quickly as possible. Ramona smiled wryly to herself. She would deal with Charles later. Men were impossible beings!

Outside, Charles tried to persuade Lakshmi, one of the female staff members known to be musically inclined, to sing for them.

"No, no," she tittered, lifting her plump hand to her mouth in embarrassment, delighted at being asked.

"Oh, come on. We know you're a great singer," the others urged.

"Come on Lakshmi!"

"Yar, just sing."

Finally with much feigned reluctance, she was cajoled into performing. Rising to her feet and rearranging her fluffy yellow sari, she gave a loud rendering of "Dum Maro Dum." Suddenly, one of the older baboos leapt up and started to dance wildly on spindly legs, clapping his hands to the music, his dhoti flapping wildly around him. Soon they were all on their feet, dancing and singing as she belted out one song after another. Giggling coquettishly, she pulled Charles up to join them.

He allowed himself to be persuaded to dance and mimicked them by holding out his arms and jerking his shoulders up and down. This caused great mirth among the dancers, who pushed him into the centre and formed a circle around him. Next, he was gyrating and shaking his hips suggestively like an Indian movie star, which had everyone convulsed with laughter. When Ramona went down to join them, he grabbed her hand and spun her round and round till the tears rolled down her cheeks.

"Look at the Burra Sahib!"

"Look at the Memsahib!" they all pointed and laughed, having a wonderful time.

Tea was served all too soon, and a very good tea it was, too, with excellent food prepared by the Sahib's cook. When it was time to go home, they all agreed that it was the best party they had ever attended and that Charles was the best Burra Sahib ever.

Their last club day was a poignant occasion with long speeches and the presentation of a silver tray to Charles and Ramona. Everyone promised to visit them in Darjeeling. After all, it was only a three-hour drive.

But on the day of departure, with their furniture and belongings gone ahead in a delivery van, Charles and Ramona stepped out of the bungalow for the last time to bid farewell to the household staff. It was one of the hardest things they had ever done. They lined up beside the car, Mohammed, Ram, Jetha, Ramchand and the gardeners, tears streaming down their cheeks. They had devoted their lives to the Sahib and Memsahib, Mark and Missy Baba, watching the children grow from babies to adults. In all probability, they would never see the Sahib and Memsahib ever again. Samira was with her new Sahib Justin, and Mark was in college in Calcutta. Samira was the only one among them not moving away, though she would be gone for six months.

Ramchand had prepared a tribute for the Memsahib, a massive bouquet of flowers artistically arranged in a flat wicker rice tray that she could easily transport to Darjeeling. He handed it solemnly to Ramona, his head bent low, so she couldn't see his tears. She accepted it with her heart breaking. Their relationship went back thirty years to when he was an obstinate lad of fifteen who treated the garden of the Chota Bungalow as if he owned it.

Charles shook them all by the hand, and Ramona handed out envelopes with baksheesh in acknowledgement of their years of service. They drove away for the last time, with everyone waving forlornly.

186

It was early evening when they arrived in Darjeeling. They pulled off the main thoroughfare and up the hill to the home they had bought. Prem and Prava were eagerly waiting for them, with fires lit, the tea trolley ready and plenty of hot water for baths. It was a gray colonial villa with a strip of lawn in front and Georgian windows that overlooked the town and the Kanchenjunga Mountains.

Chapter 22
England, Northern Ireland, 1978

"I'm just going to have to re-read absolutely everything I've ever read," declared English Literature graduate and bookworm Samira to her fiancé.

"I've read all the classics, Chaucer, Shakespeare, Hardy, Dickens, without knowing what England was really like. I'll have to read everything all over again now."

They were on a double-decker London bus that went from Victoria Station past Buckingham Palace, St. James' Park, Trafalgar Square and Piccadilly Circus up the curved colonnades of Regent Street to Oxford Street. It was like reliving a dream, being able to see many of the places she'd read about in books. It was thrilling to experience the city that was the setting for numerous literary works.

"Baker Street!" she cried, as the bus turned off Oxford Street, "Where Sherlock Holmes and Watson solved their crimes, only there's no smog now. And there's Regents' Park! Can we get off? I have to see the pond." They alighted from the bus to explore the park and wander up Primrose Hill with its sweeping views of the city. Justin shared her enthusiasm, never having spent much time in London. They went to the theater, to Agatha Christie's "Mousetrap," billed as the longest running show in London, to the musical "Jesus Christ Superstar" and to a concert by the London Symphony Orchestra at the Royal Albert Hall. They danced at the elegant Café de Paris and had tea at the Ritz. Anita Dutt had not exaggerated when she described the stores as being "bigger than your bungalow and more than four stories high." They explored the food halls at Selfridges, Harrods and Fortnum and Mason where they saw miniscule packets of tea being sold for astronomical sums. They held the tiny packages up to each other in total disbelief. In the Dooars, they distributed tea to friends and relations in pillowcases.

"Darjeeling tea in teabags!" laughed Samira. "What sacrilege!"

She was amazed by the fashion and the sophistication of the women with their immaculately styled hair and perfect makeup, striding through the streets in high heels. Her new outfits made by her tailor in Darjeeling now looked homemade and provincial.

"I have so much to learn," she sighed. "I'm a total country bumpkin. I daren't visit Rachel looking like this. And what will your mother think of me? Added to that, I'm getting fat eating all this wonderful food."

"You're more beautiful than all these Londoners," said Justin. "And perfect just the way you are."

She felt shabby and unkempt in the glossy city, but the price of everything was exorbitant, especially when converted to rupees.

"You can't think like that," said Justin. "If you do, you'll never buy anything."

So she bought some high-heeled sandals, a black pencil skirt and a beige jacket that fitted her form perfectly. For sightseeing, she bought a pair of Gloria Vanderbilt jeans, a white tee-shirt and a pair of comfortable loafers.

"Darling, you're a Londoner now," said Justin, as they boarded a British Rail train in Victoria to visit the Moorheads who now lived in Surrey, after finding the climate of Aberdeen impossible to adapt to. She acquired a new sophistication in her London clothes, although she was nervous and excited about visiting Rachel.

"It's been so long. I wonder if we'll have anything to talk about."

Greg was at the station to meet them, grinning broadly and even burlier than of old.

"Sammy, you're all grown up! Justin, nice to meet you, old chap!"

190

They drove through streets of identical, manicured houses, and he pulled up outside one of them. Samira wondered how he recognized it as his. Lorna was at the door, her hair in a blue rinse, immaculate as ever. She hugged Samira and shook Justin's hand.

"I can't believe you're here. It's just wonderful to see you. We miss India so much, you've no idea. Come on in. This is our own not-so-Burra Bungalow."

They crowded into the hallway. Suddenly, and Samira said to Lorna,

"Could you excuse me for a second? Where's the bathroom?"

She emerged a few minutes later looking pale.

"Are you okay, darling? Is it your motion sickness again?" asked Justin.

He turned to Lorna and said, "Poor Sammy is having a difficult time travelling on planes, buses and trains. London is quite a change from Ranikot."

"Let me get you some water," said Lorna. "Or would you rather have tea? We'll be having lunch as soon as Rachel gets here. She lives in Brighton. She should be here any minute."

The house was small and confined and couldn't have been more different from the Burra Bungalow at Ranikot. It had wall-to-wall carpeting, an ornate fireplace and a bay window that overlooked the street. Relics of their time in India were in evidence throughout the house, framed prints of leopards and tigers, photographs of Greg on safari with his beaters beside him, Rachel in a topee on her horse and the family in front of the bungalow. There was a stool made of an elephant foot, silver and brass ornaments and a faded Kashmir wool rug.

"Those were the happiest days of our lives," said Greg. "I wish we could have stayed longer. How are Charles and Ramona?"

Samira started to explain how they had left tea and moved to Darjeeling when the door burst open and suddenly Rachel was there, and she and Samira were hugging, jumping up and down with tears in their eyes. Rachel had grown plump, her blonde hair cut short. She wore baggy jeans and a sweatshirt and was still the tomboy she'd always been.

"Rachel, meet Justin, my fiancé," Samira said. "I've told him all about you."

"Congratulations, Sammy! How d'you do, Justin? You're a lucky man. Now, tell me all your news. How are things back in dear, old Ranikot?"

Presently Lorna announced lunch,

"It's chicken curry and rice with dhal and poppadums," she said. "Our favorite meal. We thought you might be ready for some Indian food."

"Wonderful!" said Justin. "Just as I'd hoped!"

"I can't believe how much weight I've put on in the two weeks we've been here," said Samira, surveying her waistline. "With a bulging midriff, I'm going to look like Anita Dutt soon."

"How is the old gal, anyway?" asked Lorna. "She and Shiv came to visit us last year."

"Apparently, she's taking over from my mother at the club. She'll do a great job, I'm sure."

The time passed quickly, filled with reminiscences. All too soon, it was time to catch the train back to London. Samira gave Rachel their address in Newcastle and made her promise to visit.

Justin and Samira spent their remaining days in England taking trips to Oxford, Stratford-upon-Avon, Cambridge, Windsor Castle and Bath. It couldn't have been more different from India. Samira marveled at her father's initiative, travelling so far to seek his fortune back in the forties. Justin had done the same thing many years later with his new wife Lorraine, gone to India and become a Sahib.

She wondered what Ravi was doing and whether he was now engaged to the girl his parents had chosen for him. She pushed the thought out of her mind, as though even thinking of Ravi was unfaithful to Justin. Justin was kind, generous and thoughtful, and they got along so well. She looked forward to going to Ireland and meeting his parents. They were going to stay with them for a few days, separate rooms, Justin warned her, before renting a house of their own, as it was such a long visit.

⚜

Irene was more than a little apprehensive about the "foreigner" Justin was marrying. She was glad he'd found happiness again, though slightly concerned at the speed with which he proposed to her. They'd known each other such a short time. But Justin had always been impetuous. As soon as he set his heart on something, he had to have it right there and then. She remembered how he'd proposed to Lorraine out of the blue, when he was offered the job in the tea garden. But she knew they'd been happy and had some idea of the desolation he must have experienced mourning Lorraine the past three years.

Some of her apprehensions about Samira were allayed when she saw her walk down the airport ramp. Her coloring was like any Irish girl's, her foreignness only slightly discernable in her exotic eyes. Justin looked his old happy self, so unlike the haunted figure that arrived at their door three years ago. They never saw Lorraine's parents, Bernadette and Toby anymore. There was nothing left to connect them. Furthermore, she was disconcerted by the insinuation they conveyed that somehow Justin had fallen short in his responsibilities to Lorraine. That Justin had now found someone else would further fuel their disapproval.

There was a distinct chill in the air, even though it was the middle of summer. They all piled into Edward's Ford Cortina, and Samira surveyed the dreary landscape that rolled past her. It was bleak, despite the domesticity of the patchwork of fields, the trimmed hedges and cozy cottages with smoke rising from their chimneys. They sped through the outskirts of Belfast, with its great battalions of high-rise tenements plastered with grim slogans and streets of crumbling brick houses huddled together.

No wonder Justin felt a need to get away from this, Samira thought to herself, shuddering a little. Sensing her disquiet, he reassured her,

"Newcastle is nothing like this, darling. It's a lovely wee town, and although our Mourne Mountains are nothing like the Himalayas, they're the highest mountains in the North. They plunge right down to the sea, which is a pretty spectacular sight."

She noticed that his inflections and his vocabulary had already changed, becoming more regional after only a few minutes with his family.

He was right. The view became more scenic as they approached Newcastle, although the mountains and the sea were a landscape of gray. Edward promised that when the sun shone the sea would be blue as the sky on a summer's day.

"But this is a summer's day," Samira thought to herself. "It's the middle of August." Justin had warned her it could get as cold as Darjeeling in the autumn, so she came prepared with thick sweaters to wear with her jeans.

As they drove through the quaint town, Irene pointed out their little home bakery with the sign that Justin had installed. He noticed that it already needed repainting and inwardly groaned, realizing how he would be spending much of his time. Finally, they arrived at their home which was built on a cliff in the eastern lea of the mountains.

Samira was exhausted. After a tour of the house, she asked to be excused so she could take a nap.

"Are you okay?" asked Justin, slightly concerned. It was not like her to be tired.

"I'll be fine in a few minutes. I'm worn out from the flight and the journey. Please don't worry. You can catch up on all the news with your folks while I rest."

She'd been given her own room, just as Justin predicted. Irene would not have people cohabiting "in sin" under her roof. Samira discovered that it felt actually rather pleasant to be on her own. She was more untidy than Justin and seemed to have a lot more possessions. The room was spotlessly clean and very feminine. There were yellow curtains in the window overlooking the sea. On the bed was a yellow candlewick coverlet and flowered sheets that matched the daisy wallpaper. She hoped she wouldn't spill or break anything.

She fell into a deep sleep. The next thing she knew, Justin was sitting on her bed feeling her forehead. She smiled, feeling better, and drew him down to kiss her.

"Steady now," he warned. "Don't be starting something we can't finish."

"Maybe you could sneak into my bed in the middle of the night," she suggested, slyly. "I'll make it worth your while."

"I might just do that," he said. "You temptress! Now, how about joining us all in the living room? We're about to have a drink before dinner."

The next morning, they visited the bakery after a huge breakfast. Justin had driven Edward there earlier, so they would have use of the car. Edward didn't bake anymore and bought everything in. It had become too arduous for them to mind the shop in addition to baking. They hired someone to help in the afternoons, which made it a whole lot easier, though not as profitable.

"This place has been the bane of my life," Edward grumbled. "I can't sell it or let it. I wish to god I'd never set eyes on it."

Justin knew what he was hinting at. Edward lived in hope that he would leave tea and take over the shop. His older brother had made it clear that he would never return. He now spoke with an English accent and boasted of the money he made, though he never parted with a penny of it or raised a finger to help his parents.

Irene was unsure what to make of Samira. It was clear that she was much younger than Justin, something that concerned her more than she would have thought. She believed that the best relationships were among couples of equal age and attractiveness. And Justin was certainly handsome, especially in his mother's eyes. It was just that Samira had such a glow and an air of class about her. From what Justin said, her father came of fairly humble beginnings. Perhaps her Indian mother was a princess or whatever they called them in that part of the world. She wouldn't admit it to anyone, not even Edward, but she would have been more comfortable if Justin had fallen in love with an Irish woman, or even an English girl, as long as she wasn't Catholic, of course. The awful thought struck her that perhaps Samira was Catholic or maybe a Hindi or whatever that Indian religion was called. She wasn't sure which would be worse. She would have to ask Justin later.

Samira toyed with her food at lunch.

"I need to get some exercise and walk some of this off. Or perhaps play some tennis. The food here is much richer than what I'm used to."

"Maybe you could take a walk this afternoon," suggested Justin, "while Dad and I pick up the rental car."

"You're slim as a reed," said Irene, looking at Samira's figure. "I don't know what you're blethering on about."

"Mother!" said Justin. "Speak English! She doesn't know what that means."

"But I have a good idea," interjected Samira. "Don't listen to him, Ma."

Irene was charmed, softening towards her. If she couldn't persuade Justin to have the wedding here, she would be sure to throw a big party to show everyone how well her son had done. She always thought they were all peasants in India, but obviously there were sophisticated people there, too, perhaps even more sophisticated than here.

Justin drove off to pick up Edward, while Samira went for her walk. She was disappointed thinking they could have picked up the rental car together and maybe grabbed a drink in one of the little pubs. It was another gray day with a brisk breeze that blew down the mountains and whipped up the seas below. She hadn't gone far before it started to rain. She made her way back indoors and watched television with Irene, then excused herself and read a book in her room. She didn't know any of the British programs and was not in the habit of watching television. The time seemed interminable. She wondered what was keeping the men so long. At eight o'clock, Irene said that they may as well eat, she wasn't going to wait any longer. When they finally rolled home, Samira realized with a shock that the men were both drunk.

"Hello, wee girl!" cried Justin, merrily. "Och, come on, don't give me that sour face. We were just having a drink together. Father and son. Right, Da? Father and son!" He stumbled, and Irene caught him before he could fall. Edward, who knew better than to rile his wife, went into their room and passed out on the bed.

196

Samira said goodnight to Irene, leaving her to deal with her son. This was something outside her realm of experience. She had not realized that Justin could be like this. But perhaps he and his father were just happy to see each other and were celebrating his return. She tried to be reasonable going down to breakfast the next morning. Needless to say, Justin didn't sneak into her room during the night. He'd collapsed on top of the bed and woke with a splitting headache.

Edward went to the shop as usual at eight, and they realized that they'd left the rental car at the pub the night before. So Samira and Justin missed the appointment Irene had made to look at the house she'd picked out for them to rent. Just before lunch, the landlady called to say she'd let the house to people who bothered to show up. She said she had another house available and didn't have time to show it, but they could have it if they wanted. The rent was lower than that of the original house.

"And it's in a better location. Sometimes, your miss is your mercy," said Irene. "What d'you think? Do you want it? She needs to know now."

Samira was angry and upset and didn't care anymore. Justin had a splitting head and just wanted to go back to bed.

"We'll take it," he said, so Irene told the landlady that they would rent it for five months from the first of September. It was a two-story house on Tullybrannigan Road close to the center of town. They drove by that afternoon, and it was charming and full of rustic character.

Samira couldn't wait to move in and to have some privacy with Justin. He seemed different when he was with his parents. He sulked and was moody, not at all like the Justin she was used to. Irene was charming but obviously accustomed to having the house to herself. Samira felt she was an intrusion. Irene was forever fussing and cleaning behind them.

The following morning, she discovered at breakfast that the men had left to go fishing at the crack of dawn when she was still asleep.

"Justin didn't say anything to me about it," she said to Irene. "I would have liked to go, too."

"Oh, you wouldn't want to sit out in the cold in a wee boat all day long," said Irene. "You can come with me for coffee at my friend Alana's instead."

The smell of the eggs Irene was frying suddenly made Samira nauseous. She jumped up and ran to the bathroom to throw up. Irene knocked on the door, concerned.

"Samira, I think you should see a doctor. It's not right that you should be sick like this. Maybe you have some sort of bug."

She scarcely dared to hope that it might be for another reason, not minding the fact that they weren't yet married in the least.

She made an appointment with Dr. Gibbons, and Justin drove Samira to his surgery the next day. It took the old doctor no longer than five minutes to examine her and pronounce her pregnant.

"I'll need a urine sample and will run some blood tests just to make sure everything's okay, though I see no cause for concern. Congratulations, my dear!"

Chapter 23
Northern Ireland, 1978

Samira was stunned by what Dr. Gibson told her. She was pregnant, nearly two months pregnant! She'd failed to recognize the symptoms because she'd never even considered such a thing or even known anyone who'd been pregnant. She always used protection except for, well, there were a few times when they hadn't, including their first time at the Planters Club two months ago. In the waiting room, Justin was reading a magazine.

"Did he give you a prescription?" he started to ask her, till he saw her face.

"What is it? What's wrong? Are you ill?"

"No, not ill," she said, not knowing whether to be happy or dismayed. "I'm pregnant, Justin. We're going to have a baby!"

He went pale with shock, jumped up and grabbed her with both hands. Samira was surprised by the intensity of his reaction.

"You're sure? Is that really what he said? Are you sure?"

"Well, he said he would run some tests to make sure the baby and I are both okay, but he seemed very sure." They got into the car and Justin drove back to his parents' house full of uncertainty. He never said a word. It seemed clear to her that he was not happy about the baby. Maybe it was because they weren't married, but surely that didn't matter these days? They were going to be married soon, in any case, and maybe they could bring the date forward. Irene would understand, thought Samira. She must have known that they had been intimate, even though she didn't want them sleeping together under her roof.

Irene was anxiously awaiting their return. Justin asked Samira if she wanted to go and rest in her room, rather than join them.

"Well, of course I want to join you!" she said. "I'm not sick. And I want to be there when we tell her our news."

"Samira, how are you? How did it go?" asked Irene, as they walked into the room. "Is it your stomach?"

"Yes, I guess it is, in a funny sort of way," Samira said. "We have great news. But I think Justin should be the one to tell you."

"Ma, she's pregnant," said Justin, white-faced. "We're going to have a baby."

"What is the matter with you?" cried Samira, seeing his distress. "Aren't you happy? Don't you want us to have a baby?" She ran to her room in tears, still in shock herself and deeply upset that he didn't seem to want their child.

"I knew it!" Irene cried triumphantly to Justin, after Samira left. "I knew it wasn't your fault that you could never have children. I knew it was Lorraine all along! And now you have found a beautiful young woman who will give me grandchildren at last." Beside herself with joy, she hugged and kissed her son.

"Ma," said Justin. "Please listen to me. I never informed Sammy that I couldn't have children. I didn't mean to deceive her. It just never came up. It was irresponsible of me. I realize that now. If she finds out...she'll be furious. I wanted her so much, I wasn't thinking straight."

"Well, then she doesn't ever need to know," said Irene, wanting things to go smoothly. "There's no reason to tell her now. I'll speak to Ed. It will be our little secret. There's no harm done. Obviously, the doctors were wrong in their diagnosis, so it's just as well you never told her. It all worked out for the best! Now go you and tell her how happy you are. Don't you understand? You're going to have a child at last!"

He couldn't take it in. He and Lorraine had tried so hard to have children. He hadn't even contemplated having a child with Samira. He realized it had been very wrong of him not to tell her about his infertility. She was a young woman, and she would obviously want a family. This had happened a lot sooner than either of them had expected, but for all he knew, it was their one and only chance. Perhaps it was a miracle that they had proved the doctors wrong. And his mother was right. There was no point in confessing to Sammy at this point, when evidently there was nothing to confess.

So he went into her room and kissed her and told her how happy he was. He was just a foolish man who hadn't known what to say and needed his mother to tell him. He rubbed her back and then her front and made her giggle and was finally able to coax her back to the living room. Edward had come home, congratulated them both warmly and went to pour gin and tonics for everyone, except for Samira who could now only have tonic or lemonade.

Justin and Samira's landlady went to the bakery shop just before five the next day, the last day of August, to pick up Justin's check for the first and last months' rent. In exchange, she gave Edward the keys to the house. They'd already paid a deposit to secure the rental agreement. When Edward arrived home, Justin was at the pub with some school friends, and he didn't get home till dinner time, despite promising Samira that they would look at the house that evening.

"Well, it's no use going now," said Edward after dinner. "The power won't be turned on till tomorrow."

"I'm sorry, darling, but I ran into some fellows I hadn't seen in years, and one drink led to another," Justin explained to Samira. She was sulking in an armchair in the corner of the room, pretending to read. It felt to her like she was always pouting over one thing or another these days, a new feeling for her, and something she didn't relish.

So it wasn't till the following morning that they finally went to see the house that was going to be their home for the next five months. They loaded up the car with their clothes and a few odds and ends that Irene said they might need.

"Ma, it's furnished, and she said there were plenty of linens," Justin said, handing back the towels she said they should bring.

It was only a short drive to the house on Tullybrannigan Road. Samira ran up the mossy pathway and waited for Justin to unlock the front door.

"Just think, our first home!" she said. "Much as I love your parents, it will be so nice to have our own space."

"Absolutely," said Justin, opening the door. "Ohhh."

A smell of damp hung in the air. All the curtains were drawn, and it was so dark they could barely distinguish the staircase in the hallway. Justin went into the front room and flicked the light switch, but the power hadn't been turned on yet. He went to the window and pulled the drapes which felt cold and clammy. The room looked and smelled like someone had died in it. The sofas were old and dingy, the rug was threadbare and the furniture could have been picked up from the side of the road.

"Oh, my god!" said Justin. "What a dump."

The dining room was just as bad, and the kitchen was deplorable. The burners on the electric range were rusted through, the sink was an original from the thirties, and the cupboards were dank and smelled of wet plywood.

"No wonder she didn't want to show us the place," said Samira. "What are we going to do?"

"We're going to her house and getting our money back, that's what we're going to do." said Justin. "Let's go."

They jumped into the car and went to the address on the lease. Justin went to the front door and pushed the doorbell. No one came to the door, and the house had an abandoned feel. There was no car in the driveway. Finally one of the neighbors who was passing said,

"Oh if you're looking for Maxine she's gone to England. I doubt she'll be back before Christmas. Is there anything I can help you with?"

Justin told him they had just rented a house from her and needed to see her.

"You mean the house on the Tullybrannigan Road, no doubt. Ach, well." The man stopped, obviously not liking to say more.

"Yes, and it's a disgrace!" said Samira.

"So I've heard," he said. "One time, there were tenants who kept a cow in the backyard. It was in the newspaper and all. But I guess you didn't know if you're not from round here. Well, I'm sorry I can't help you. Cheerio."

"Thank you, sir," said Justin, getting back into the car. "Looks like we've been conned."

"And she has all our checks. Even if we give her notice in writing, she has two months' rent and our deposit," said Samira.

They told Irene their story. Samira was furious with Justin. If he hadn't been so busy with his friends and his fishing trips, this would not have happened. But because she didn't want to castigate him in front of his mother, she kept her feelings to herself.

"It seems there's nothing for it but to give the place a good clean," Irene said, going to her cupboards and filling up a basket with cleaning products, brushes and dusters. "Grab the vacuum cleaner, son, and let's see what we can do."

Irene was just as horrified by the house as they'd been. But no one could clean like her, Irene proclaimed, and went about trying to prove it with gusto. Samira had never cleaned anything in her life. She'd been excited at the prospect of keeping house without a single servant to help her. She hadn't cooked much, either. Her experience of cooking was limited to helping Prava and baking the occasional dessert or cake at home.

But she helped as much as she could. Irene laughed at her clumsy efforts.

"Here, let me do that, you little princess! You're pregnant. You should be sitting with your feet up not scrubbing floors."

They spent the rest of the morning cleaning and returned to Irene's house for lunch and to pick up the towels Justin had rejected, as well as fresh sheets, blankets, crockery and cutlery. In the afternoon, they shook out the rugs, vacuumed, polished and dusted. Edward joined them at five and proceeded to wash the windows. Samira was amazed by his skill.

"That's his thing," laughed Irene. "No one can wash windows like Da."

By the end of the day, the place was unrecognizable. The floors shone, the sofas were draped with a pair of blue bedspreads, and the kitchen cupboards were lined with fresh paper. All the chipped cups and plates were put away and replaced with some of Irene's blue, willow-patterned china. Samira had found some flowers in the garden and arranged them in a vase on the dining table, which was spread with a blue-and-white checkered tablecloth.

Upstairs, the bedroom had been aired, the mattress turned and the bed made with fresh sheets and blankets. The bathroom gleamed and smelled of pine, and there were fluffy towels in place of the indescribable ones that had hung there earlier.

"Holy Jesus, I'm done out," gasped Irene. Finally, she could find nothing else to clean.

"I just can't thank you enough," said Samira. "We could never have done this on our own. The place is totally transformed."

"We'll come back another day and tackle the yard," said Edward. "After all Justin's help with our shop, it's the least we can do for you."

"How about we all clean up and meet at the Northern Star for dinner around seven?" suggested Justin. "My treat."

"We'll be there," said Irene, enthusiastically. "I couldn't do another thing today!"

Samira felt no compunction about her ignorance when it came to washing machines or vacuum cleaners, or not knowing how to cook, wash up and clean but Justin hated to admit that he had limited experience in those departments. He had become a Pukka Sahib accustomed to issuing orders, not doing things himself. Their little experiment with housekeeping was not going well.

"Everything seems to burn," cried Samira. "I just turned my back for one second, and the bacon burned to a crisp."

They were cooking a late breakfast the next morning, after stocking up on groceries at the supermarket. Samira was amazed by the abundance and variety in the shops.

"My god, Justin, I could go mad in here, and I am eating for two, after all."

"Well, just put whatever you want in the trolley."

"But it's all so expensive! That chicken is two hundred rupees!"

"I told you to stop doing that!"

"I know, but I can't help it. Well, okay. I need that apple pie, whatever the price!"

Justin, washing the breakfast dishes, said,

"There's no hot water. I thought you said you had turned the water heater on."

"You mean that's not the switch?" asked Samira. "I'm so sorry, darling."

"Oh, by the way, my parents are coming to help with the yard this afternoon."

"I wish they wouldn't. They've done so much for us already. And do we really need to worry about the yard?"

"They enjoy helping us. They have all this pent-up energy."

Sure enough, Edward and Irene arrived in the afternoon equipped for some serious gardening. Irene's hair was tied back in a bandana, and Edward was wearing wellington boots. Samira felt obligated to join in, but Irene told her to go and put her feet up, which she gladly did. How was she ever going to cope without servants? It felt like their needs were unending. Justin was instructed to trim the hedge, while Edward cut the grass and Irene weeded and hoed the flower beds.

Samira made tea a little later and invited them in.

"Ach, we can't come in and filthy your clean house after all the work we did. We'll have tea on the lawn," protested Irene.

Tea on the lawn was a lot less glamorous than it sounded. There was no garden furniture, and they had to stand around sipping their tea and eating ginger snaps out of the packet.

"We've always wanted to try Indian food," Irene said, as they were leaving. Food was her passion. She could remember what she ate on any given day many years later. She produced fabulous meals and loved to eat. It was an obvious hint.

"It's the best food in the world!" said Samira. "Come and have dinner with us on Saturday. I'll cook you an Indian meal!"

She was subdued after they left.

"What's wrong? Are you okay?" asked Justin. "Put your feet up. Or would you like me to rub them?"

"I'm worried about cooking the Indian meal. I've no idea how."

"Yes, I wondered about that. Well, maybe we can do it together. Let's get a recipe book from the library."

But there were none to be found in the Newcastle library or in the book store, either. So they drove to Belfast to find an Indian recipe book and hunted out a supermarket where they could buy spices. They were told there was an Asian market near Queen's University. The spices were wildly expensive when converted into rupees, and Samira groaned.

"Oh, why did I ever suggest this?"

Early on Saturday, they started to prepare the meal, chicken korma, dhal and vegetable pulao rice, nothing too hot and spicy. But it just wasn't as easy as it sounded in the recipe book. The onions were impossible to slice, the spices turned into a burned mess twice, and the chicken stuck to the pan.

"It's not me, it's the range. I can't turn the temperature down," protested Samira. "What are we going to do?"

"I have an idea. We can make it to Belfast and back if we're quick," said Justin. "Make sure you turn everything off before we leave."

He drove her to the Taj Tandoor, a new Indian restaurant on the Lisburn Road.

"Let's just order everything we need," he said. "My parents will never know you didn't cook it."

A grateful Samira hugged and kissed him. "You are so devious and so clever. Thank you, darling!"

Irene and Edward arrived on time, excited about the meal. The house was immaculate. Justin was watching television and drinking a bottle of beer, and Samira wore an apron over her expanding bump. There was a faint smell of spices and charring in the air. After a couple of drinks, they moved to the dining room.

"I'm starving," said Irene. "I've been looking forward to this for days."

They had chicken curry, spicy potatoes and lentils served with a colorful vegetable pulao, all of it cooked to perfection. Justin and Samira ate heartily, hungry for Indian food. Edward and Irene started somewhat gingerly, but then dug in, appreciating the spicy flavors. Samira spooned more pulao rice onto their plates, delighted that they were enjoying it.

"This is absolutely delicious," said Edward.

"Yes, well done, Samira," said Irene. "Everything is wonderful. So clever of you. How on earth did you manage to cook the rice in all those different colors?"

The grains were green, yellow and orange with vegetables mixed in.

Samira stared at her, at a loss for words. She'd eaten multicolored pulao all her life without ever wondering or knowing how it was done.

"Er, well, I just used colors, and…and…different spices." It was hopeless. She was not a good liar.

"We cooked the colors separately and then blended them," said Justin "It's not as difficult as it looks."

Samira shot him a grateful look and mouthed, "Thank you."

Irene continued to eat with relish, oblivious to Samira's discomfiture. When she said she'd love the recipes as they took their leave, Samira handed her the Indian recipe book with a flourish.

"Keep it," she said. "It's a gift." She was done with Indian cooking!

✧

The baby was due at the end of April, Dr. Gibbons said. All the tests came back normal, and there was no reason why she shouldn't deliver a healthy child. The doctor recommended gentle exercise and a healthy diet. He suggested the hospital in Downpatrick for the birth and said that she would go there for her checkups when she was further on in her pregnancy.

She booked trunk calls to Prava's neighbor several times but kept getting cut off by the operator. Her parents said they would call as soon as the phone company connected them. Everything moved at a snail's pace in India. So she had to content herself with writing letters. She and Justin decided it would be best for her to have the baby in Ireland and return to India when it was one or two months old. She persuaded Justin that they should marry in Darjeeling a few months after the birth. It would make no difference to the child, and she was not in the right state of mind for a wedding right now.

She walked miles every day, as recommended by Dr. Gibbons, and became a familiar figure in the town. She learned all the streets and ventured farther each day. Sometimes, Justin accompanied her, but it seemed he always had better things to do. Although she was accustomed to a lonely lifestyle, it felt like she was always alone these days. She went to the library several times a week and started to re-read the English classics just as she had promised herself, gaining a new appreciation and insight into the books she'd studied. She was looking forward to visiting her Aunt Pauline in Bray and meeting her father's one remaining relative.

Chapter 24
Northern Ireland, Ireland, 1979

Irene had come to terms from an early age with the fact that she was not, and never would be, a beautiful woman. She realized that there were aspects of her appearance she would never be able to change. Her eyes were set a little too close to each other, her nose was too wide and her lips too narrow. She waged a life-long battle against freckles, which she had to an extent won with the assistance of a particular Elizabeth Arden concealer that she reserved for special occasions. She had long abandoned hope of ever shedding any of her bulk. There were few pleasures left at her stage of life and with Edward's inadequacies in certain quarters, food and drink were one of the few remaining to her. Moreover, over the years, she had acquired an impressive collection of corsets. The support they gave to her lower body helped to emphasize the size of her massive chest. When she emerged in one of her carefully planned ensembles, she stood out from other women, flamboyant, larger than life and supremely confident.

And while there were aspects of her face and her figure she was unable to improve, there was one feature she could absolutely and utterly control and that was her hair. The vicious auburn of her youth had been tempered into a soft, strawberry blonde. Regular visits to her beauty salon ensured that her hair was always permed and set. It developed a life of its own and sat on top of her homely face like a shining Olympic torch.

Part of her psyche was her need to feel superior to certain individuals, particularly women. Whatever measure of superiority she was not able to impose by her appearance or her intellect, which was somewhat limited, she inflicted through sarcasm and innuendo. For some unknown reason, one of her acquaintances that she felt most compelled to impress was the unfortunate Bernadette McIlroy. It might have been because of her extreme thinness, or her large purple eyes, but in all probability, the reason for her resentment towards Bernadette was that Irene could not forgive her for having a daughter who hadn't been able to give her grandchildren.

Three years after Lorraine's death, her irrational resentment of Bernadette persisted. And now that it had come to light that the doctors had been wrong in their diagnosis of Justin's infertility, she wanted to somehow make it known to her that their childlessness could not be attributed to him. Once the thought took root in her mind, she couldn't shake it off, regardless of the fact that Lorraine had passed away. She felt she had to find some means of communicating to Bernadette that her son was capable of fathering a child.

She devised some reason to be in their neighborhood off the Lisburn Road in Belfast the following day and casually suggested to Edward they should visit the McIlroys, as they were so close. Naturally, she had taken pains to present herself faultlessly for the occasion. As luck would have it, Bernadette and Toby were both home. It was three in the afternoon, and they were about to have tea.

Bernadette was dressed in a form-fitting, burgundy velour pantsuit that only someone with her petite figure could carry off. She was oblivious to Irene's efforts to supersede her, which only incited Irene even further.

There was an awkward silence after pleasantries were exchanged. Finally, Edward cleared his throat and said,

"We didn't know if you heard but Justin's home on leave."

No, they hadn't heard, they said, and hoped he was keeping well.

"Actually, he's engaged to be married," Irene said. "We felt we should tell you personally."

"Oh, I see," said Toby. "Is he engaged to someone local?"

"No, not local," said Irene. "She's a British tea planter's daughter, and her mother, well, actually she's an Indian aristocrat from a Himalayan kingdom."

Edward shot her a sharp look. It was the first he'd heard of any such thing.

"Ach, that's lovely," said Bernadette. "We hope he'll be very happy."

"Indeed, she's a lovely wee girl, so she is," said Edward.

"So, she's here with him? You've met her?" Toby asked.

"Aye, we have. And she's expecting a child. It's due in April. *His* child." Irene looked with triumph at Bernadette, who paled as she digested the implications of what Irene had said.

"But, but, didn't the doctors all say," her voice trailed off. "That it was because... because of Justin that they couldn't...."

"That they did," said Edward, beginning at last to understand why his wife had wanted this visit.

Bernadette sat quietly, her knuckles white. Toby reached over and patted her hand.

"But it seems they were wrong," said Irene, unable to resist, "so it must not have been Justin's fault."

The unspoken implication hung in the air, too awful even for Irene to mouth, 'And therefore the fault must have been Lorraine's.'

"Well, there you are now," Toby said, standing up. "It was good of you to come and see us and share your good news. Please give our best to Justin."

Realizing that they were being dismissed, Irene put her tea cup down noisily. She stood up and picked up her handbag. Now that she had made her point, she began to mourn the loss of Lorraine. She put her arms around Bernadette with tears in her eyes.

"Ach, we miss wee Lorraine every day of our lives, every single day."

It seemed her capacity for grief was more intense than anyone else's, and it was she who was seeking consolation from Bernadette.

"Come along, dear." Edward led her away, seeing the look on Bernadette's face.

"Good-bye. Thank you for the tea."

He was silent in the car, a silence learned from years of living with Irene. It was pointless to ever say anything because he would never win.

"Ach, well. I thought they would appreciate a visit from us," Irene said. "Toby needs to learn some manners. But what can you expect from such a family? Justin has found someone of his own level now. Poor wee Bernadette, though, such a frail, unhealthy little thing, just like her daughter."

Samira was finally on the train to Dublin, visiting her Aunt Pauline. It was the end of February, and Samira never dreamed that it would be this long before she saw her. In October, Pauline and Sean went to their timeshare in the Canary Islands. In November, Rachel came to visit and gave Samira the opportunity to see some of Ireland. It was a happy time. Justin and the two ladies had jumped into the car and driven around the province, staying in quaint bed-and-breakfasts. They checked into a pretty cottage outside Ballycastle and were shown their rooms by a dour, bearded farmer. The inside of the house was nothing like the charming pictures they had seen in the bed and breakfast guide. The bedrooms were musty, and cats perched on every available surface.

Samira and Rachel couldn't understand a word the farmer said and didn't dare look at each other for fear of collapsing in giggles. He asked Samira a question, and she had absolutely no idea what he was saying. She looked at Justin helplessly, beseeching him to translate.

He showed them their rooms, and Samira did some quick, lateral thinking, "Can you recommend a restaurant for dinner?" she asked him.

"Aye, surely," he said and proceeded to give Justin long, detailed directions in his unintelligible accent.

"I'm starving, Justin. Let's go eat right away," she said. "Oh, and let's take our bags with us."

"Really?" asked Justin in surprise. He'd only just hauled them in. She gave him a hard look.

"Yes, please. Really."

Helpless with laughter, Rachel and Samira ran to the car.

"What's going on?" said Justin, a little annoyed.

"Did you see the state of those rooms?"

"They were totally disgusting!"

"There's no way on earth we're staying there!"

"Now, you need to call him and tell him we've been called away on an emergency and therefore can't stay on his farm," Samira said.

"Me? Why me?" said Justin.

"Because you're the only one who can understand him," explained Rachel. "That probably means that you're the only one among us he can understand."

They visited Donegal, staying at an inn over a pub. The weather was abysmal, so they visited the pub the moment it opened. Rachel and Justin drank pint after pint and grew quite merry, joined by a group of golfers from Cork. Samira consoled herself with food, digging into lamb stew, apple pie and Black Forest gateau.

Justin's accent altered with every town they visited. He was able to imitate the locals' dialects and would talk just like they did till they arrived at the next town. He'd fill up the car with petrol and came back talking just like the people in the petrol station. Samira and Rachel killed themselves laughing at him.

They headed south to Sligo, where Samira was in raptures over Yeats' countryside. They went to Lough Gill, and she read the words from "Cloths of Heaven" inscribed on a plaque in his memory:

"I have spread my dreams under your feet,
Tread softly for you tread on my dreams."

At the Lake Isle of Innisfree, she recalled her favorite lines from the poem:

"I will arise and go now, and go to Innisfree,
And a small cabin build there, of clay and wattles maybe."
"And I shall have some peace there, for peace comes dropping slow,
Dropping from the veils of morning to where the cricket sings;"

"I feel I understand Yeats so much better after seeing the sights that inspired him," Samira sighed. "How I wish I were a poet! Is there any poetry written by pregnant women?"

All too soon, it was time to return to Newcastle and for Rachel to leave.

"Promise you'll come and see us in India," Samira begged, seeing her old friend off at Aldergrove Airport.

Then it was Christmas and after all the excitement of an Irish Christmas, January was a miserable month. Samira began to wonder why she was here and not at home being pampered by Charles, Ramona and Prava. She missed them all terribly.

"Let's go back," she urged Justin. "I can have the baby in Darjeeling at the Planters Hospital where I was born."

There was also the question of money. They had not planned on staying beyond six months. Things had not turned out the way Samira imagined when she dreamed of her year of travel. Keeping house and becoming pregnant had not been part of the plan. They had to shelve their plans to travel to the Continent.

Since Justin was frequently at the shop with Edward or out with his mates, Samira was left largely to her own resources and made friends with a girl named Siobhan whom she met in the library. They would meet for coffee on Saturday mornings. Siobhan had a job in Belfast. She left Newcastle every morning at seven-thirty when it was still dark for the hour-and-a-half journey by Ulster Bus to her job at the insurance office in Progressive Square. She worked till five in the evening, arriving home in the dark at six-thirty to cook dinner for herself and her husband. It was a lot better in the summertime, she said, because it was bright in the mornings and evenings. She had no other option, as there were simply no jobs to be had in Newcastle. Her husband was a milkman and faced a lot of uncertainty with people buying milk in cartons in the supermarkets, rather than having it delivered to their doorsteps.

Samira was subdued, reflecting on Siobhan's existence.

"How can this type of life be considered better than what our tea laborers have?" she asked Justin. "It's true they work long hours in the heat, but is that really any worse than a humdrum existence in the cold and dark of an Irish winter?"

"I agree completely," said Justin. "And it's partly why I left this place and your father, too, I'm sure. But life isn't perfect in tea by any means."

Alarm bells started to jangle loudly in Samira's mind.

"So, I take it you're not enamored with the lifestyle here?" he continued, confirming her apprehension.

"Why do you ask?" she said, her eyes widening. "Are you considering leaving tea?"

"Not without consulting you first. But my father is getting old, and it's a struggle running the shop. He would be happy to just hand it over to me, if I would agree. We would make a good living and have a lot more than most people. Certainly more than what I make in tea."

Samira was silent. This was a scenario she had never contemplated. How would she feel about living in this country? She missed home terribly. But where was home? Her life in Ranikot was over. She was an adult about to be married and start her own life. Home would be with Justin wherever he might be, in his bungalow at Simling or here in Newcastle, though, she hoped, not in a house like the one they lived in now.

"I would need to give it some thought," she confessed. "I've really never considered moving here permanently. I thought you loved it out there."

"Ach, of course I do. But sooner or later, we all come back, well, most of us, at any rate. It was different for your father. His parents died a long time ago. He doesn't have the family ties I have."

"Yes, I understand. I'll think it over at Aunt Pauline's."

She set a date for visiting her aunt in the middle of January.

Justin left the house on one of his interminable errands, and she realized that she'd forgotten to ask him to fetch coal from the shed. It was in the courtyard behind the kitchen, beside the original outhouse lavatory. If she didn't fetch more coal, the fire would go out. It was a nightmare to re-light, so she picked up the scuttle and opened the back door. The wind blew with such force she could barely stand and had to fight her way across the courtyard. She gathered as much as she could safely carry and headed for the house. Suddenly, she lost her footing and landed heavily on her back, scattering the coal around her. She clasped her arms around her belly in alarm, feeling a jolt of pain. She wasn't sure how long she lay there, gasping for breath with her head spinning. When would Justin be home, she wondered? He hadn't even told her where he was going. She had hurt her ankle, which must have twisted in the fall. She crawled her way to the house, struggling to reach the door handle.

When he returned, Justin found her passed out on the kitchen floor, with the back door swinging in the wind.

"Sammy, are you okay?" He knelt beside her and felt her forehead.

To his intense relief, she opened her eyes. She was confused and disoriented.

"Where am I?"

"In the kitchen," he said. "What happened, darling? How did you fall?"

She struggled to remember.

"I went to the coal shed. I slipped and fell. My ankle hurts. I must have twisted it."

"This one?" he examined her foot. "It looks swollen. Does it hurt? What about…the baby?"

"I seem to be okay. It's just my ankle that hurts."

He guided her upstairs. "I'll get a cold compress. Shall I call the doctor?"

"I'll be fine when I warm up a little. I'm so cold."

Dr. Gibbons examined her the next day and verified that the baby was okay, but she'd sprained her ankle and had to keep her weight off her foot. She hobbled around for two weeks, which was most inconvenient. She had to postpone her visit to Pauline, and it wasn't till the end of February that she was finally ready to travel.

She hoped that their home would be warmer than hers. There was no central heating in the house, not that she'd ever had central heating, but she'd never known cold like this, not even in Darjeeling in winter. There the sun shone brightly all winter long, melting the early morning frost that glistened on the hillsides. In Newcastle, the sleet beat down on the streets and the gray sea churned. Samira waged an endless battle with the fire. The kitchen, bathroom and hallway were glacial, and the electric heater in the bedroom gave off meager warmth.

She was now on the last stretch to Dublin, whizzing past dilapidated houses adjacent to the railway track. Aunt Pauline was meeting her at the station, and they would drive the twelve miles to her home in Bray.

Sean and Pauline scanned the faces of the passengers arriving on the Belfast train. Samira was easy to identify because of her obviously pregnant condition, which momentarily shocked Pauline although she had known of her pregnancy. Samira recognized them from a faded photograph on her father's desk. They approached each other and embraced somewhat awkwardly, strangers linked only by the blood that ran through their veins.

Pauline was small and slight with short, gray hair. She wore an unfashionably long tweed skirt, navy sweater and sensible shoes. Sean was tall and somewhat overweight, wearing faded corduroy pants and a loose sweatshirt with "Luck o' the Irish" in green across the back. He took Samira's bag and guided her toward their car.

"We thought we'd take you straight home, as you'll be tired after the journey, I'm sure," Pauline said. "We'll bring you to Dublin another day. You'd like to see Dublin, wouldn't you?"

"Oh, yes. I want to see as much as possible while I'm here."

"You'll like Bray. It's just a small seaside town, not very different from Newcastle. We're so happy you're here. I can't wait to hear the latest about Charles. He was never a good correspondent."

The air was warmer compared to the severity of the wind and sea in the North. They drove over roads that were narrow and potholed, passing quaint villages that were no more than clusters of white-walled, thatched cottages. It was like going back in time. The town of Bray had been built between the drumlins of the Sugar Loaf Mountain and the gentle sea that lapped against the walls of its promenade. Wooden boats draped with fishing nets lay on the pebbly shore. The bandstand was deserted and ice cream stalls with pictures of popsicles and cotton candy boarded up for the winter.

"It's very different in the summertime," said Pauline, "when tourists from Europe and America, as well as locals from Dublin, descend on the town. Such a shame you couldn't come sooner."

They turned up a laneway between two buildings on the High Street and drove into a gravel courtyard surrounded by brick walls smothered with ivy. They entered a large Georgian mansion, and Samira gasped at the magnificent hallway with its huge sweeping staircase.

"What a beautiful home!" she said, looking around in amazement. Ornate chandeliers hung from the ceilings, and sunlight streamed through the tall curved windows. Elegant Persian rugs, china ornaments and heavy furniture added to the air of opulence.

"We hope you'll be comfortable," said Pauline. "Let me show you your room. We put you on the second floor, so you won't have too many stairs to climb. Our room is in the back, and this one is yours." She opened the door leading into the bedroom decorated in cream and white.

"Thank you," said Samira. "It's lovely."

"Would you like to freshen up and unpack before we have tea?"

"Yes, please. I'm such a mess."

Pauline left her, and Samira went to look out of the window which overlooked the courtyard and a row of beeches that obscured the back of the buildings on the street. Staying in the center of town was a novel experience. It would be interesting to have a street and shops just a few steps away. What a surprise, too, to discover that Aunt Pauline lived in such a fabulous place. Charles had never talked about it, only the meager, terraced house in London he and Pauline grew up in. She wondered if he had any idea of the change in her circumstances.

She washed her face and ran a comb through her hair. The house was warm, as she'd hoped it would be. What a relief to be out of their rented house! She needed a break from Justin and his family. Well, it was natural to want to get away from each other occasionally. It would be good for their relationship. She changed her shoes, put on some lipstick and went downstairs to join Pauline and Sean for tea.

The next few weeks were a happy and memorable time for her. She learned about her father's childhood and how, having had his heart broken by a woman named Sarah, he had decided to go to India. Pauline told her about her time working at the mental asylum and how Sean had arrived to pick her up from work in the Bentley. His limousine business, which started that very day, flourished, and there were now six branches, three of which he opened after moving to Bray to take care of his mother. It was during that time, after he left London, she said, that he realized he loved her and came back to her with a great, old ring. She, who'd been sitting in the house day after day, nursing a broken heart and not saying anything about it to him because they were supposedly only friends.

"What a lovely, romantic story," said Samira. "How fortunate you are to have found such love."

Pauline looked at her. "You say that as if you haven't. And if not, then why are you engaged? And why isn't Justin with you now?"

"Aunt Pauline, I think I am only just beginning to formulate certain things in my mind that I'm not sure I understand myself. Justin and I hadn't known each other very long when he proposed to me. He came along and swept me off my feet at a time when I was rather vulnerable. I'd just broken up with someone else. It was very exciting and flattering, and it helped restore my bruised ego. But please don't think I'm saying that I don't love him. I really feel I do."

"And this other person? Why did you break up with him? Did you stop loving him?"

"Ravi? No, that wasn't the reason. And he broke up with me because his parents didn't approve of our relationship. Things are complicated in India."

"So you accepted Justin's proposal. And what happened to your feelings for Ravi?" Pauline asked. She was annoyingly perceptive.

Samira was uncomfortable with this line of questioning. "I guess I pushed them to the back of my mind. What was I supposed to do? I knew I couldn't have him."

"Sammy, you can't just turn feelings on and off. It's never that simple. I wish it were. But you've agreed to marry Justin, and you're having his child. What I can't understand is what is he doing that's so important he couldn't accompany you on this trip?"

Samira tried to think what it was. "I think he just assumed he wasn't coming. We never really discussed it. He's been very busy helping his father with his business. That and fishing and going to the pub." She started to sob. "This isn't how it's meant to be, is it?"

Pauline patted her back, not wanting to impose any further. She didn't know Justin so couldn't judge him. But she had grown to love Samira and didn't want to see her hurt. It had seemed callous of him to simply put her on the train to Dublin in her condition, in a foreign country where everything was strange and new to her.

"And when he proposed, it wasn't because of the baby, was it?" Pauline asked. "Not that it's any of my business."

"No, we were engaged before I realized I was pregnant. And I'm not sure we would have planned all this travel if we'd known about the baby. I didn't realize I was pregnant until a month after we arrived in Newcastle."

"You know sometimes children help to bring people closer together. Maybe the baby will help," Pauline said. "And it could just be a case of cold feet."

"There's another thing, too," Samira said. "He asked me to give it some thought while I'm here. He's considering taking over his father's bakery in Newcastle. Aunt Pauline, he wants us to leave India and live here."

"Another thing you're not happy about?" asked Pauline.

"I'm not sure. I'm so confused. I just assumed our lives would be there. This is something we never talked about. He always told me how much he loved India."

"And do you have a choice in the matter?"

Samira stared at her aunt, aghast. She hadn't thought of it quite like that. Did she, she wondered, or was it something he was keeping from her?

"Well, he did ask my opinion. Or did he? Do you think he was just trying to break it to me gently?

"Now stop worrying or you'll make yourself sick. It's not good for the baby. I'll go and put the kettle on and get some of that nice shortbread you love."

Determined to show her a good time, Sean and Pauline took her to Dublin, where they walked down Grafton Street, had coffee at Bewley's and visited Trinity College. They drove to Kilruddery House and showed her the seventeenth-century gardens and to Graystones with its view of the Sugar Loaf Mountain. Samira was charmed to discover that James Joyce had been to Bray and that a house in Martello Terrace had been the setting for a scene in his *A Portrait of the Artist as a Young Man.*

She was sorry when it was time to take the train back to Belfast. Pauline made sure Justin was meeting her off the train.

"And don't be late," she warned him on the telephone, unable to shake off her disapproval of him.

"You are more than welcome to come back any time," Sean said, giving her a hug. "We're here for you any time you need us."

"I can't thank you enough for everything," said Samira, tearfully.

"Remember to follow your heart," said Pauline. "And don't be pressured into doing anything you don't want to do."

They waved her off and returned to their Bentley parked outside.

"Something doesn't add up," Pauline said. "I don't know what it is, but I can only hope things work out for her. I wouldn't like to be in her shoes at this time."

Deep in thought, Samira sat in a deserted compartment as the train headed for Belfast. Her year of travelling around the United Kingdom and Europe had turned out very different from what she'd anticipated. She looked at her face reflected in the glass. It was pale and contorted. She felt ugly and ungainly in her maternity smock. Her coat didn't quite close. It belonged to Irene, who said it wasn't worth buying a new coat for her pregnancy.

But she needed to focus. Justin wanted answers from her. She needed to think. He wanted her to live in Newcastle and become like his mother, the wife of a baker. He wanted her to leave home, to leave her familiar, happy life and to live in their house on Tullybrannigan Road. He wanted her to leave Ranikot and move to Tullybrannigan Road. He wanted to leave her and live in Ranikot. Her head was spinning, it was all so confusing. No, that wasn't it. He wanted her to live in Simling while he lived with the baby in the house on Tullybrannigan Road. She felt a sharp pain in her belly. Oh, my god, what had she eaten? The pain was unbearable. She bent over and clasped her stomach till the pain subsided.

Where was she? Justin wanted an answer from her. Or had it ever really been a question?

She was okay. She was on a train. She was on a train to Ravi. No, not Ravi. He didn't love her anymore because his father told him not to. Justin didn't love her. No, she didn't love Justin. That was it. Ravi didn't love her, and she didn't love Justin. The pain overcame her again. It was the baby! But she didn't want a baby anymore. She wasn't ready. She didn't want to live on Tullybrannigan Road with her baby. And Justin didn't want her. He wanted to be like Edward and for her to be like Irene. She didn't fit in with his plans. Suddenly, the pain receded and she wondered if she'd been imagining it.

Think, think, he wanted her to think, but it was too confusing. What was it Prava had always said? She struggled to remember. Not to think too hard about things. That it would all work out. She missed her grandmother. How could she think of leaving her? Where was her mother? It was too hard, and the pain was too sharp. What were all these people saying? She was vaguely aware of people around her as she doubled over in pain.

The conductor saw that her ticket was for Belfast and told her they would be there in a few minutes. He helped her off the train, assisted by one of the passengers.

"My fiancé is coming to pick me up," said Samira. "He'll take care of me."

There was no one on the platform, so he spoke to a guard at the station.

"I have to get back on the train. If no one shows up, send for an ambulance."

"I'm fine. I am really. My baby isn't due for another three weeks," Samira said to him, embarrassed by all the attention. The pain had ebbed. She was between contractions.

"Aye, well, let me tell you that this won't be the first time your baby won't be cooperating with your plans," the guard said.

Finally, Justin appeared, disheveled and looking at his watch.

"Sorry, darling. I think the train was a little early."

"Well, your baby's early and all," said the guard, dryly. "You'd best be taking your missus to the hospital and quick smart. The baby's coming any minute."

"Sammy, are you okay? Sweet Jesus! You're in labor!" He was panic-stricken seeing Samira bent over in agony. "Let me get you in the car and take you to the nearest hospital."

Chapter 25
Northern Ireland, 1979

Justin fought his way through Belfast's afternoon traffic to get to the Royal Victoria Hospital, where he had gone years ago with Lorraine and where he had been diagnosed as infertile.

"Rather ironical that my baby should end up being born here," he thought to himself.

They rushed to the maternity ward, where the receptionist asked for Samira's name and started to look through their files.

"We're not registered here," Justin explained. "My wife started to have contractions on the train from Dublin. We don't have time to get to our hospital in Downpatrick."

"Please wait a moment and we'll have her admitted."

After a long wait, Samira was led into a cubicle and examined by a doctor. The contractions seemed to have subsided. He told her to get dressed and explained that her cervix was not sufficiently dilated for her to be admitted, especially as they didn't have her records in this hospital.

"What do you suggest we do?" asked Justin. "I can't drive her all the way to Downpatrick in her condition."

"I would suggest you go home and let her rest," said the doctor.

"But we live in Newcastle. That's just as far away!"

"I'm really sorry, but we don't have a bed for her. With all the cutbacks, we can barely accommodate our own patients. I imagine you won't want to wait downstairs. Go to a friend's house or to a hotel and come back when her contractions are fifteen minutes apart."

"When will that be?" Justin asked.

"Hard to say, but my best guess is in three to five hours."

Justin racked his brain in panic for the best thing to do. It just didn't make sense to check into a hotel. He had lost track of any friends or acquaintances he may have had in Belfast. The only people he could think of were Toby and Bernadette who lived not too far away. Surely, they wouldn't mind letting Samira rest in their house for a few hours? There was an irony to the scenario that didn't escape Justin, but he knew that Irene had told them about the baby.

"Where are we going?" gasped Samira, in the throes of a contraction now that they had left the hospital.

"I'm taking you to a friend's house. They'll take good care of you. They are my ex-in-laws."

She groaned, clutching her stomach, and he didn't know whether it was because of the pain or because of where they were going. He found the house easily enough, thinking sardonically that it was only in moments of high drama that he seemed to come here. The first time was to ask for their daughter's hand in marriage, the last time was when he knocked on their door to break the news of her sudden death. Now, it was on the occasion of a birth, the birth of his child with another woman.

"Wait here, darling. I'll make sure they're here," he said, parking the car in the street outside the house.

Thankfully, they were home watching television. He explained the situation briefly, wondering if it was a huge mistake to have come here. But Bernadette was filled with compassion and insisted that he bring Samira in and, of course, they could stay as long as they needed. Samira was exhausted, worn out from the bouts of pain, the train journey, getting in and out of the car and the ordeal of the hospital.

"The poor girl needs to rest," Bernadette said. "Come this way, pet, and lie you down. Help her with her shoes, Justin. Now, you be sure and tell me if you need a cup of tea or anything."

Samira collapsed on the bed, and Justin went to ask Toby if he could use the telephone to call his parents.

He told Edward what had happened. "So, I brought her to the McIlroys. Samira's exhausted. I should never have let her travel alone, but I didn't think the baby would come so early."

"Keep us informed, son. We'll be there as soon as the baby's born. Ma sends her love."

226

Justin monitored the contractions, which thankfully, were now coming with some regularity.

"First babies are usually late," said Bernadette. "And they can take their time. She's far better off here than in that miserable hospital. I've made you some tea and sandwiches. Now, make sure Samira eats something. She's going to need her strength."

They went to bed shortly after ten. Justin said they would leave quietly and lock the door behind them when it was time for them to leave. He couldn't thank them enough.

"We'll come and visit Samira in hospital," Bernadette promised. "Be sure and tell her."

He must have dozed off in the bed beside Samira and was woken by her shaking him.

"I think it's time," she said. "I can't bear the pain any longer."

Once again, they got into the car and sped through the now deserted streets to the Royal Victoria Hospital. This time, the porters took one look at Samira and rushed her to the maternity ward in a wheelchair. She was whisked away by the nurses, and Justin waited wearily in the corridor thinking this night would never end. Samira had already said she didn't want him at the birth. The idea was too new and radical to her way of thinking. She preferred the anonymity of the nurses to the thought of his witnessing her pain.

Finally, just after six in the morning, he heard a long, heart-rending scream, and his stomach churned in fear. After what seemed like an endless interval, one of the nurses came out of the room and seemed surprised to see Justin.

"Are you the father?" she asked him. "Please come in."

Through a fog, he entered the delivery room and saw Samira pale and exhausted in her hospital gown. He kissed her forehead.

"Darling, are you okay? I was so worried."

"I'm fine. Just glad it's over. It's a girl, Justin. We have a daughter."

The midwife brought the baby, swaddled in a blue blanket and gave it to Samira with a slightly perplexed look.

"Here's your wee girl. She weighs seven pounds and four ounces," she said.

She walked out of the room leaving Justin and Samira with the sleeping baby. Samira held her in her arms, and saw her for the first time, a tiny, wrinkled baby with black hair and olive skin. She fretted and stirred and opened her eyes to look up at them. They were an unmistakable shade of green.

Through her pain and exhaustion, Samira knew in an instant that this wasn't Justin's child. There was only one person in the world she knew with eyes that color. A night under the stars flooded into her memory, her first and only time with Ravi. She looked questioningly up at Justin and saw the bewilderment in his eyes, looking at the Indian child in her arms.

"Sammy, we are both exhausted," he said, dully. "This is not the time to talk. We both need to rest. I'll be back later."

He walked out of the room without kissing her, his mind racing with thoughts that were almost too painful to contemplate. Could the baby he his? It was quite conceivable that it was. Maybe it was too scon to tell. The baby was only just born, after all. Another thought came to him, something he had pushed to the back of his mind in his eagerness to believe he could father a child, the indisputable diagnosis the doctors had made years ago. He found his car and made the drive back to Newcastle. Traffic was light going out of town, though the inbound lanes were already clogged with early commuters. This was meant to have been one of the happiest days of his life, he thought, tiredly. Instead, his mind was racing with doubts and possible explanations.

As soon as he arrived home, he went upstairs to the frozen bedroom and flopped into bed, forgetting that he had neglected to inform his parents about the baby.

The insistent ring of the telephone woke him just before eleven o'clock. All the events of earlier in the day came flooding back as he ran to answer the phone in the downstairs hallway. He knew it would be his mother.

"We waited all night for you to call. The hospital wouldn't tell us anything. We thought you'd be sleeping, but I couldn't wait any longer." Irene was reproachful.

What was he supposed to say?

"Samira had a daughter, but I don't think it's mine. We have a baby girl, but she doesn't look like I expected her to look."

"She had a girl," he said, finally. "She was born just after six o'clock in the morning. I'm sorry I didn't call you. I was exhausted."

"What's the matter?" she asked. He didn't sound at all excited or overjoyed, as one would expect a new father to be. "Are you okay?"

"Just tired," he said. "It was a long day."

"Ach, of course it was. What time are you going to the hospital?" she asked. "Shall we go together?"

"I'll leave as soon as I'm showered and dressed. Why don't we go separately? I might want to spend a little longer with Samira."

He needed time to reflect and didn't want the enforced intimacy of the long drive to Belfast with his parents. He showered and shaved and, suddenly ravenous, made himself a sandwich. He remembered to call Charles and Ramona. It was a terrible line, but he was able to convey the fact that they had a granddaughter before the line went dead.

He drove back to Belfast. In the maternity ward, the receptionist told him that Samira was no longer in a private room, something they had reserved at the hospital in Downpatrick. She was sitting up, pale and strangely different without her bump. The baby was in a transparent, plastic crib beside her. There were three other cubicles in the room. The smell of babies mingled with the hospital odor and the scent of the flowers beside each bed.

He kissed her and presented the bouquet of roses he'd bought in the booth downstairs.

"Did you sleep?" he asked, noting dark circles under her eyes.

She hadn't been able to sleep, despite her exhaustion, till the nurse insisted on her taking a sleeping pill.

"You need all the rest you can get while you're in here," she said. "When you go home, the baby will keep you up night and day, and there'll be no sleeping pills for you then."

"I did for a few hours," Samira said, "till they woke me up to have lunch. After that, I fed and changed the baby. She only just fell asleep."

"I'm sorry you're not in a private room." He didn't look at the baby asleep beside her.

"I'll be fine. I went to boarding school, remember?"

"My folks will be here soon. I telephoned your parents, and they send their love. It wasn't a clear line, unfortunately."

There was an awkward silence. Samira knew they would have to talk. After her drug-induced sleep, she had woken with a blurred recollection of seeing her baby for the first time and wondered if it had all been a dream, till she saw the nurse's anxious face bending over her and the crib beside her bed.

"May I have my baby, please," she'd begged the nurse, too weak to lean over and lift her out herself. "And please draw the curtains round my bed."

She wanted to examine her daughter in private. The baby stirred and whimpered as she was passed to her, waving plump arms in the air. Her heart melted as she gazed at the perfection of her tiny face and body. She unraveled the blanket and kissed the little feet. Everything about her spelled Ravi. There was absolutely no doubt in her mind that this was not Justin's child, conceived the week before she took the trip to Darjeeling with Justin and two weeks before he proposed so suddenly.

What was she going to do? She couldn't stay here, that was certain. She would have to go home as soon as she and the baby were fit to travel. What was she going to tell Justin? How would he ever understand? Would he believe that she had not been unfaithful to him? Obviously, their relationship was over. He would not want her now. At least this solved the problem of whether or not she would stay on in Newcastle. How would she ever face Irene and Edward? What would they all think of her?

Now, she faced Justin and realized that she needed to explain things to him before his parents arrived and saw the baby.

"We need to talk before your parents arrive," she said to him, finally. "Please tell the nurse to ask them to wait till we're ready."

He did as she asked, and they sat with the curtains around them, the baby asleep in the crib.

"I think it's fairly evident that this is not your child," she said. "And it's only fair to both of us that I explain exactly what happened."

He listened to her story, white-faced and deeply distressed to have his suspicions confirmed. It was an unfortunate sequence of events and hard to take in. She had been impetuous, but then so had he. They had both rushed into making life-changing decisions that they should have taken more time to consider, he with his usual impulsiveness, she on the rebound from Ravi. And while neither of them was willing to admit it at this point, their feelings for each other had dissipated. If the child had been Justin's, she would have been compelled to leave home and live with him in Ireland. There was no doubt in her mind that he wanted to stay. But if they had been deeply in love, would he have turned a blind eye to the fact that this was not his daughter? Would he have been willing to rear another man's child?

"This is *my* problem," concluded Samira. "And I'm the one who's going to have to deal with the consequences. Your life here will continue as if you'd never known me. The baby and I will disappear as soon as we possibly can, and you will run the shop, just as you hoped. All you have to worry about now is how to tell your parents."

They would be devastated, Justin realized, probably even more than he was, their longing for a grandchild thwarted at the very last minute. It was just too cruel. This would bring all their hopes of ever having a grandchild to an end, the hope that had died and then been rekindled when Samira became pregnant with what they thought was his child. How could he explain all this to them in the hospital? There would be a scene, no doubt. Irene would never forgive Samira and would not immediately see reason.

"I think I'd better go and explain everything to them elsewhere," Justin said. "I can't vouch for how Irene might react if I were to tell her here."

"You're right," said Samira, relieved at being spared that ordeal at least. "Please give them my love and convey my sincerest apologies for the way things turned out."

"You rest," said Justin. "I'll come and see you tomorrow. Let me know if there's anything you need."

"Actually there is something," Samira said. "Would you be kind enough to call my Aunt Pauline and ask her if I can spend a few weeks with her before I fly back to India?"

Justin walked miserably out of the room. It all sounded so final. Despite what Samira said, his life would be completely different from what until yesterday he'd imagined it would be. Suddenly, he'd lost both his wife and his child. There would be no wedding and no christening, just a void in his life that had suddenly appeared from out of nowhere. And now, disconsolate as he was, he had to explain everything to his parents and endure their disappointment too.

They were waiting outside the ward, Edward in a suit and tie, and Irene dressed for her new role as grandmother, clutching an enormous bouquet of flowers tied with a pink ribbon.

He took the flowers from her and gave them to a passing nurse.

"Make sure Samira gets these," he said.

"Come with me," he said to his startled mother and father. "I have something to tell you."

This was an occasion that called for a stiff drink. It would be too cruel to send them all the way back to Newcastle without an explanation.

"Meet me at the Red Lion," he said. "I badly need a gin and tonic."

The other mothers had constant streams of visitors, and husbands that sat beside them all the way through visiting hours. The nurses felt sorry for the beautiful English woman with the foreign-looking baby who nobody came to see. Even her husband, who had only visited her briefly on one occasion, had stopped coming.

Samira's body ached after the agony of childbirth, but she knew that pain would soon heal. It was the ache in her heart that was so much worse. She sensed the nurses' sympathy and was grateful beyond words when they would whisk her crying baby out of her sore arms, rocking and singing her to sleep, so she would rest. In her weakened, vulnerable state, they seemed to her like shining angels.

The following morning she was surprised to hear that she had visitors; Toby and Bernadette, who arrived with a teddy bear for the baby and a box of chocolates for her. They'd spoken to Irene, they explained. She had telephoned them right after Justin told her the baby was born. That must have been before Justin had broken the news that the baby was not his, Samira realized. And Irene obviously had not remembered or had not wanted to confess the fact to Bernadette. Now, Samira would have to be the one to enlighten them.

She was holding the baby in her arms when they came in.

"Ach, would you look at the wee dote!" cried Bernadette, gazing down at the little face. "And to think," she continued, "that all the doctors said that Justin was infertile and could never have a child! Well, this wee creature certainly proved them wrong, didn't she, now?"

She smiled happily at Samira, unselfish in her delight for Justin. Then she noticed the look of horror on Samira's face.

"Justin infertile? What do you mean?" Samira exclaimed. "That's the first I heard of it."

Bernadette exchanged glances with her husband. They had no idea that Samira had not been told.

"I'm sorry. I didn't realize you didn't know. But no harm done because, well, obviously there was no need for anyone to tell you with you becoming pregnant so soon."

Samira was aghast, trying to take it in.

"So you mean to tell me that Justin knew he couldn't father a child?"

"Well, yes, he most certainly knew that," said Toby, "Why, he and Lorraine had been trying to have a baby for years, and they had all those tests and everything."

Why hadn't he told her? Samira couldn't understand. First, it had been wrong of him to propose to her without revealing that they would never have a family. Then, when she became pregnant, he had said nothing about his infertility. Had he made a fool of her? Had he known all along? And what about Irene and Edward? They must have known, too.

"Well, I'm very sorry to have to tell you this," she said, grimly, "But it seems the doctors were right. This baby is not Justin's."

There was a stunned silence. Bernadette recalled Edward and Irene's visit last year when they gloated over the fact that Justin had sired a child. But if it wasn't Justin's, then whose child was it?

"I was never unfaithful to Justin, strange as it may seem," Samira felt obliged to explain. "I had very recently broken up with the baby's father when Justin proposed to me. I think I accepted because I was heartbroken and it felt so good to be wanted by someone like Justin. So here I am." She dissolved into tears, wondering how she would ever extricate herself from this mess.

Just then she heard Justin's voice and saw Edward and Irene, and she was suddenly surrounded by people. She saw a look of horror flash over Irene's face when it struck her that Bernadette must now know that Justin was not the father. This was not a skeleton they could hide in the family closet.

"Ach, Bernadette, Toby, how nice to see you," Irene gushed. "Did you just get here?"

"Oh, we've been here a while," said Toby, thinking, though not saying out loud, "long enough to know."

"We just had to come and see you and the wee babby," said Irene. "Sammy, you look ghastly. You need to rest. Can I hold her?"

Irene was torn in all directions, though her delight in the baby was apparent. To have simply ignored Samira would have been callous. They felt an obligation to come and see her. Their conversation in the Red Lion the day before had been painful beyond words. Justin felt a complete heel, and Edward and Irene had been devastated that their desire for a grandchild was foiled yet again.

Justin knew that Samira had told Toby and Bernadette by the look on their faces and was sorry that she had to be the one to do

234

it. He should have telephoned them, but it was just another detail he'd overlooked.

"Yes, Samira is still in shock." Bernadette spoke loudly, so everyone could hear. "It seems that no one thought to tell her that her husband-to-be was not physically capable of fathering a child."

A silence came over the group. That one remark transferred the intense guilt off Samira's shoulders on to those of Justin. He sat with his eyes lowered, confused, disappointed and ashamed. He knew he should have told her. In his frenzy to hold on to her, having believed he would never find love again, he had neglected to divulge the truth about his infertility.

Samira looked gratefully at Bernadette, realizing that Edward and Irene had been part of the conspiracy, not breathing a word about Justin's condition to her despite their certain knowledge of it.

The sooner she could get away from all of this, the better. The pain was too much to bear.

"Did you speak to Aunt Pauline?" she asked Justin.

"Yes, I did. And she said you are welcome to go and stay as long as you want. Though you know you are welcome to stay with me, too."

"Or with us," piped up Bernadette. "Toby, I think we have exhausted poor Samira. It's time for us to go. But I would love to come back tomorrow if I may."

"Of course," said Samira, warming to the little woman who had stood up for her, "though it will have to be in the morning. I will be released in the afternoon."

There was an awkward silence after they left.

"Please stay with me a few more days," said Justin. "It's too soon for you to travel. And I insist on driving you to Pauline's this time."

"We should go," Edward said. He stood up, unable to bear the tension any longer. It seemed like there was nothing left to say.

Chapter 26
Delhi 1979

Ravi could not believe how time had flown. The marriage he had so reluctantly agreed to almost a year ago was only a week away. He found himself in Delhi again, plunged into the endless preparations and expense that were deemed a necessary part of the process of uniting two people in matrimony. He wanted to see his bride-to-be as soon as possible and was encouraged to do so by his mother.

"Yes, yes, you go, Ravi. Radhika is longing to see you. Poor girl, she has been so lonely."

But when he telephoned her, she seemed vague and preoccupied.

"Oh, Ravi? My, how nice. Tonight? No, no, it's not possible. Okay, tomorrow."

"She's too busy with wedding preparations, it seems, to have time to see her bridegroom," he reported to his mother.

"Come on, Ravi, don't be like that. You men just don't understand how much there is to be done."

"But I just got here," he said. "You'd think she'd want to see me."

When he arrived at her house the following evening, he was greeted by her mother Pushpa, who seemed flustered to see him.

"Ravi, how nice to see you. Please come in. Radhika is just sleeping. I will call her. Take a magazine."

He flipped through the pages of a two-year-old Time Magazine, feeling like a patient waiting to be seen by a busy doctor. A servant brought him a nimboo pani, saying that Radhika baba was now taking a bath. He read the magazine from cover to cover, or so it seemed, before Radhika appeared in a cloud of cerise and mauve chiffon and an overpowering aroma of sandalwood.

"Ravi," she trilled. "I am so happy to see you."

They kissed dutifully, perfunctorily. As they drove off in the car, they regarded each other surreptitiously. They hadn't seen each other since their engagement. If not for the picture on his mantelpiece, he would have forgotten her face. He had returned to Baghrapur after their engagement to find everything changed. Not only had Samira left, but she had gone overseas. And she was engaged to Justin, someone she had only just met. Her parents had gone, too, which had seemed extraordinary to Ravi. They had retired to Darjeeling, which meant that not only had he lost Samira; he had lost Mark, too.

The club wasn't the same without the Clarkes. The level of tennis suffered and valiant as Anita Dutt's efforts were, she simply didn't have Ramona's organizational skills. Ravi took up golf, which he could play on his own, if necessary. How could everything have changed so radically in such a short time? He tried not to think about Samira. It was pointless in any case, now that she was engaged to Justin. He also wondered if he'd been right to allow his father to browbeat him into agreeing to marry Radhika.

Nevertheless, when it was time to return to Delhi for his wedding, he grew excited. He looked forward to bringing his prospective bride back to his lonely bungalow, to having a woman waiting for him when he returned home each night. The engagement period had been endless, but they had to wait for an auspicious date, they had no say in the matter.

"Where would you like to go for dinner?" he asked Radhika.

"Oh, the man should decide," she said, emphatically. So he took her to the Ashoka Hotel, where they had a meager and mediocre meal for an atrocious price. He tried to draw her out and learn more about her. She seemed excited about the wedding, about all the jewelry and gifts they were receiving, and worried how they could possibly accommodate three hundred guests in the shamiana.

On the balcony beside the pool, couples were slow dancing to a four-piece band playing "Feelings" and "Somewhere My Love." Chinese lanterns fluttered in the breeze, setting the dappled water alight. But when he asked Radhika to dance, so he could hold her and become part of the magic, she demurred. She said she didn't dance and wanted to go home, seemingly impervious to the romantic setting. When they arrived at her gate, he leaned over to kiss her and tried to hold her breast. She passively submitted to his kiss and pushed his hand off her breast.

"Why, Radhika? Don't you want me to touch you?" he protested, aroused after his prolonged celibacy. "I'm going to be your husband soon."

"Not as yet," she said, prudishly, leading him to wonder if she had any sexual appetite at all or whether perhaps it was being satisfied elsewhere. He drove off in a fit of temper, dissatisfied with the evening. After breakfast the next day, he communicated his dissatisfaction to his father.

"Radhika does not seem at all interested in me and won't allow me to touch her even," he complained.

"That's quite normal, son. If she's going to be your wife, she has to be careful you don't consider her cheap or easy. Sometimes, when a woman allows her prospective husband to go too far, he starts to wonder if she allows other men these privileges and ends up deciding not to marry her. Just be patient, my boy. Your wedding night will soon be here." He laughed and patted Ravi's knee.

All around him was a flurry of activity. There seemed to be plenty for everyone to do except him. People were constantly arriving or leaving. Tea and sweetmeats were served by exhausted servants. It seemed nothing constructive could be achieved because of the endless and well-meaning visitors.

"I'm going to the club to play tennis," he told his mother a little later. She was not pleased, wanting him to get involved in matters where his opinion didn't seem relevant or heeded.

"At least show some interest, Ravi. There is so much to be done."

"Tell me what to do, and I'll do it," he said. "Meanwhile, I'm going to get some exercise."

He had to get out of the house to breathe and sweat out his frustrations. Perhaps it was cold feet, but he had growing reservations about Radhika and her suitability as a partner.

And if things were bad at the bridegroom's, Radhika's house was in a state of pandemonium when he went to see her after lunch.

"Please tell Radhika I'm here," he said to a female relative, one of the brightly-colored, silken butterflies that fluttered about the house. A pouting Radhika finally appeared. Obviously, she was displeased at his presence. Her hands and feet had been painted with henna, and she wore anklets with silver bells on them.

"How is my little lady today?" Ravi asked, in an attempt to make her smile. The women in the room giggled and tittered, but she remained unsmiling.

"Fine, thank you."

"Come for a drive with me," he urged. "Let's go to Connaught Place for a stroll and some snacks."

"Where's the time?" she seemed in a hurry to get away from him.

"So you don't want to come?" he asked, hurt.

She made an annoyed sound and frowned. "Can't you see how busy I am? Just be happy you're marrying me and till then don't pester me."

She flounced out of the room, her anklets jangling. There was a hush among the women, a shocked silence at her outburst in front of her very handsome young husband-to-be with the soft, green eyes.

"Just go and get her," said one of the women to another.

"Where is Pushpa? She should talk to her."

"Please wait, Ravi. We will talk to her for you."

"There's no need. I'm going." He was furious with her for subjecting him to such humiliation in front of the other women.

So, she thought he was a pest, he reflected angrily, traversing down her narrow concrete driveway. All these preparations were supposed to be to celebrate their union. Yet she was so caught up in the tinsel and the glitter that she seemed to have lost sight of the meaning behind it. If there had ever been any meaning. Was there any substance to her at all, he wondered? In that moment, recalling her pouts and frowns, he knew that he couldn't subject himself to a life with such a person. He couldn't commit to someone so

240

superficial, who such lack of respect toward him. The whole thing was a mistake. They should have taken more time to get to know each other. He should never have allowed his parents to coerce him into it.

He drove home and ran up the yellow marble stairs, calling for his father who was alone in his office on the third floor.

"I need to talk to you. It's urgent."

"What is it, son?" He put down the newspaper, behind which he was taking refuge to escape the madness below.

Ravi was not known for his patience at the best of times, and Sunil could see that his son was very angry.

"I can't do this. Please telephone Radhika's father and tell him that there is to be no wedding. I refuse to marry his daughter."

Sunil turned pale with shock. "Wait here one moment. Sit down. Let me find your mother."

Ravi sat down, shaking. He was not going to run the risk of ruining his life for anybody, not even his parents. The look of contempt in her eyes had proved to him that she was not entering their union with any enthusiasm.

His father returned with his mother, and he knew that they would try to appease him and beg him to reconsider. But his mind was made up. He described how he had been humiliated by Radhika in front of her relations. It was not that the incident itself was so outrageous, he said, but that it was the last straw. She had not made a good impression on him. He had made a mistake in agreeing to marry her, but better to be single than spend his life with the wrong woman.

"All the arguments you made to me about family and customs didn't take my feelings into account. It's my life, and I shall choose how to live it. I cannot succumb to your outdated ideals of propriety at the cost of my happiness. I have already sacrificed the woman I love to please you. Please do not insist upon my marrying a woman I feel nothing for and who shows contempt for me before we are even married."

To his surprise, his parents didn't put up any opposition.

"In that case, we will go and tell them personally that the wedding is off. Ravi, believe it or not, your happiness is important

Nina Harkness

to us. I shall telephone Ashok and Pushpa and say we need to see them immediately. Your mother and I have also observed this girl, and we realize that she probably will not make you happy."

Sunil picked up the phone realizing that there was no time to lose.

As he dialed the number, a servant came to the door and told Ravi that his friend Mark had come to see him. He was waiting downstairs in the living room.

"Mark, Samira's brother?" Ravi said. "What could he be doing in Delhi?"

He ran down and greeted Mark. They were delighted to see each other.

"Ravi, my friend!" cried Mark. "It's good to see you, pal."

In the year since they had met, he had matured and grown more striking in appearance.

"So, are you a married man? Should I be congratulating you?" he asked Ravi.

"Actually, no I'm not. And I'm not going to be, either. Long story. And what brings you into town this time of year? Isn't it the middle of term?"

"I'm staying at the house of a friend from college. Hey, man, we can't talk here." Mark lowered his voice, conscious of people moving in and out of the room. "Can you come and meet me this afternoon? I'll write the address down for you. It's not too far away."

"Sure, Mark. I'll be there as soon as I can get away," said Ravi, totally mystified. "How is Sammy, by the way?"

"She's fine, really fine. So I'll see you later? I have a taxi waiting. I have to run."

Ramona had asked Mark to fly to Delhi to take care of Samira and the baby when she arrived in Delhi from London. He had been shocked and amazed by the series of events she described. He had telephoned Anita Dutt for Ravi's address, not altogether sure what he would achieve by coming to see him, but he felt compelled to visit the father of Samira's baby at the very least. Besides, he wanted to see Ravi again. Samira had no idea he was going to see Ravi, and he was certain that she would never have agreed to it.

242

Anita had not known the exact date of the wedding, just that Ravi was in Delhi to get married.

Meanwhile, at Radhika's house, the atmosphere was tense. She had locked herself in her room and wouldn't speak to anyone. Her parents had been told about her treatment of Ravi by one of her aunts. So, they were not altogether surprised when the phone rang and it was Sunil requesting a meeting.

"The sooner the better," he said. "It would be better for all concerned."

They arrived within the hour. The couples greeted each other politely, but not cordially, and entered the living room which had been cleared of all relatives and visitors.

"Well, Ashok," Sunil said, "I am sure you heard about the incident between Radhika and Ravi earlier today."

"Oh, yes," said Ashok, "Merely a lover's tiff, I'm sure. We parents should not interfere in these matters."

"Please do not tell me what I should or should not interfere with," Sunil said, sternly. "The situation is far more serious than that. Your daughter has shown great disrespect to my son. It is not a good sign when someone who is soon to be a wife lacks respect for her husband before they're even married. I have to tell you that my son is very displeased, especially as the incident took place in front of other family members."

"We will ask Radhika to apologize to him at once," her mother said. "No harm done. She is feeling the pressure of all the marriage preparations."

"I'm sorry," Sunil said, forcefully, "but this was not an isolated incident. Her attitude has been consistently negative. My son's mind is made up. I am very sorry to inform you that he has decided that he cannot marry her. And we, as his parents, support his decision."

Pushpa let out a wail of despair, rocking backwards and forwards in her chair. Her eyes flashed with fear, and she wrung her hands.

"This cannot be. This surely cannot be. Ashok, tell them. It's only two days till the wedding. Oh, my god! Oh, my god!" she kept repeating the words as she rocked.

Ashok looked down, shaking his head, not trusting himself to speak, thinking of all the money he'd spent and the months of planning. They would never live down the disgrace.

"Let's go, Poonam," said Sunil. "The matter is over."

They swept out of the house and into the car, leaving behind a hushed silence as the family tried to come to terms with the fact that suddenly there was to be no wedding. Radhika would not be the center of attention in front of three hundred guests. There would be no shamiana, no brass band and no handsome bridegroom.

Sunil's hands trembled on the steering wheel as they drove home.

"I will send them a sum of money to cover half the expenses," he said to his wife. "I feel that part of the responsibility for this situation is mine, and I should take my share of the blame. I should never have pushed Ravi into this marriage. I was wrong to interfere with his life and to cause him to lose the woman he loved. But that part I will just have to live with. I'm sorry we had to cancel the wedding, but it would be worse to continue with it, just for the sake of the occasion."

"I'm happy you feel that way," said Poonam. "I think Radhika will suffer acutely from a loss of face, but it might be a lesson she needed to learn. Ravi is the person I feel most sorry for. I know he was hoping that Radhika would turn out to be the kind of woman we thought she was. Now, he has to go back alone, and I'm afraid he might never want to get married now."

"The best thing for us to do is to stop interfering. Fate will take its course. Ravi has proved to be quite capable of looking after himself," said Sunil.

They drove the rest of the way in silence, full of regret and wishing more than anything for their son's happiness. Ravi was waiting for them anxiously, hoping they'd had the strength to stand up to any opposition from Radhika's family.

"They were not at all happy," Sunil told him. "But it's done. Now, we have a lot of work ahead undoing all our plans."

Ravi breathed a sigh of relief. "Thank you. I know that was not an easy thing for you to do. I acknowledge and appreciate your support."

He asked if he could borrow the car to visit his friend Mark.

"I promise to help with making phone calls and sending messages when I return," he said. "But he's an old friend I really want to visit. He won't be in town for long."

He wondered what had become of Samira and if she was still travelling around Europe with Justin. He could never have offered her that kind of life. If only he had stood up to his parents a year ago, when they first raised their objections! They would not be in the position of extricating themselves from this mess. As for him... he would not allow himself to think about how his life might have turned out.

He found the house where Mark was staying and rang the doorbell. A servant let him in and went to fetch Mark. There was no one around, but he saw that there was a baby in a pink crib in the corner of the room. He bent over the child who was gurgling and kicking her feet in the air. The baby turned her head and her soft, green eyes smiled into those of the man smiling down at her. Ravi was enchanted. He had the strange sensation of having seen the child somewhere before.

He heard someone walk into the room and turned around. Incredibly, it was Samira, looking lovelier than ever, and obviously equally shocked to see him. His heart leapt and he stood, nervous and unsure, unable to take in the fact that it was really her.

"I don't understand," he said, looking around. "What are you doing here? Where is Justin?"

"It's a very long story, but I'm not with Justin any longer. What are you doing here?"

"Mark came to see me earlier today. He said he had something to say to me...you're not?"

"No, we broke up. And what about you? Are you married?"

"No. I couldn't go through with it. I was still in love with someone else."

"Oh?" her voice faltered.

"I never stopped loving you," he whispered, finally allowing the full depth of his feelings to sweep through him after months of self-denial.

"Nor I you," she said. "I only agreed to marry Justin because you...well, didn't want me."

"But now you've left him?"

"I had to leave him."

"Oh?"

Samira gazed down at the baby who chuckled and giggled up at them.

"And who is this cute little lady?"

Samira bent down, picked up the child and presented her to Ravi.

"This cute little lady is Jasmine. She's just one of the many reasons I had to leave Justin. Ravi, this is your daughter."

Ravi looked at the child in total amazement. He turned to Samira who was watching him intently to gauge his reaction.

"I have a daughter?" he gasped. "How is it possible?"

"I seem to remember a night under the stars." Samira smiled, "And the scent of jasmine in the gardens of Ranikot where I met a certain precocious young man."

He took his child and held her in amazement breathing in the scent of her cheek. Then he held out his arm to gather Samira into his embrace and felt her arms around him, and she was kissing him, the way she kissed him every night in his dreams.

EPILOGUE
Darjeeling, 1979

In Darjeeling, Prava and Ramona sat down to lunch in the dining room of the Planters Club, celebrating Ramona's forty-fifth birthday. They were both impatiently counting the days till the arrival of Samira and baby Jasmine.

"It was a good idea to ask Mark to go to Delhi to take care of them," Prava said. "It can't be easy to travel such distances with a baby."

"He said Jasmine is the image of Ravi," said Ramona, who had spoken to her children on the phone when Samira arrived in India. "What an unfortunate series of events for poor Sammy."

"I wish I could wave a magic wand and reunite her with Ravi," said Prava. "I don't think she ever stopped loving him. If only I had such powers."

"Ravi is probably married by now and will never know he has a daughter. We have a lot to discuss when Sammy gets home. My heart breaks for her. I blame myself for encouraging her relationship with Justin, when we really knew nothing about him. I realize I was distracted by Charles' retirement and our move. What a snake he turned out to be!"

She missed her daughter intensely. The prolonged separation had come at a time when she was just beginning to relate to Samira as a woman, and from her letters it was obvious she had been through many new experiences over the past year. She had left home as a child and was now returning with a child of her own.

"Things will work out," said Prava. "You worry too much, darling."

Finishing his lunch at the next table was a distinguished, fine-featured British Sahib who they could tell was Scottish by his accent. He smiled and nodded at the ladies as he paid his bill and prepared to leave.

"Are you an ex-planter?" Prava asked him.

"Aye, that I am. I was in a plantation here in Darjeeling. I used to travel everywhere and go hiking in the mountains in Sikkim, Bhutan, and Kalimpong. Best years of my life, so they were."

"How wonderful that you came back. Are you travelling alone?" Ramona asked.

He looked at her, a beautiful woman with almond eyes, milky skin and a certain delicacy to her features.

"Alas, I'm alone," he said. "I never had a wife or children. It's my biggest regret. All I have are my memories. This is the first time I've been back since I left oh…forty-six years ago."

A faint feeling of recognition stirred in Prava's mind.

"Well, I hope you enjoy your stay Mr.…." she said, although she already knew the answer.

"Sammy Mark Raymond. Delighted, I'm sure." He smiled politely as he walked out of the room.

Prava looked at Ramona to see if she had grasped the significance of the names, her daughter who had never known what it was to have a father. She turned to regard the man walking away, who had yearned for a child yet never knew he had one, who had wanted a wife yet never married and who had cheated *her* of a partner for most of her life.

But Ramona's interest in the Sahib had been fleeting. She was absorbed in the card her mother had given her. She continued to study it while her father walked out of the room and out of her life forever.

Too late, too late, the words reverberated in Prava's mind as she watched him leave. The question of how to react was too suddenly thrust upon her, the implications of revealing the truth too daunting to contemplate. So once again he left them, mother and daughter, fated to be deprived of the love that came so close within his grasp.

The secret Prava had guarded for so long was safe. The secret that had sheltered her daughter from the stigma of her mixed birth would now remain forever in the innermost shadows of her heart and no one would ever know that Ramona was a Sahib's daughter.

THE END

"A well-written romance set in the years after India won independence from Great Britain. The heroine, Samira is totally believable. She is beautiful and educated and her story plays out well against the prejudices of both Indian natives and the English and Scottish expatriates who manage India's thriving tea plantations. Samira's parents, Charles and Ramona, their friends, her brother Mark, her loves Ravi and Justin, and all major and minor characters are true to the times in which this story is set. The plot runs believably, with the twists and turns that are expected in a romance novel. Readers will have no trouble putting "A Sahib's Daughter" on their reading list."
   - Alice D. for "Readers Favorite" Rating: 5 stars

"A well written story in the historical romance genre, set in the last years of the British Raj rule of India, with just enough history to be interesting and even pique the reader's curiosity about earlier events that led up to the story now being told. The author has clearly had first-hand experience of the leisured life of Anglo-Indians in India."
   - Peter Newton (retired tea planter)

"Two generations of British, Indian and mixed-heritage ladies and gentlemen find love and purpose in this story. The author gives us a look at the relatively closed society of expatriate Brits on rural tea plantations, and also the gradually increasing involvement of the Indians who work for and then with them after India gained its freedom. I came to care for most of the characters, each of whom is treated sensitively by the author. The contrast between life in India, surrounded by servants and life back home in lower middle class families for the more junior British managers of the tea plantations was interesting and well developed: an engaging post-colonial look at Brits in backcountry India.

The book had plenty of tension and a satisfying ending. The cultural contrasts were obvious throughout but not the main focus of the work. I look forward to reading more works by the author.
- **Joseph Ellebracht**

"The author skillfully captures the sights, sounds, and smells of India. She has an uncanny ability of bringing her characters to life as she weaves the story of life on the tea farms and the privileged white society. It was full of suspense, intrigue, and romance and I could barely put the book aside until I finished this amazing story. "
- **Barbara Miller, Author of "You Lost Your Marriage, Not your life" and "Dancing in Rhythm with the Universe."**

"A very worthwhile read. You are transported to an ancient country that has fascinating customs..."
- **Jean Brickell, Readers Favorite. Rating: 5.0 stars**

"Nice Read! Passages about Yeats in Sligo..." Under bare Ben Bulben's head.... "brought back fond memories of Ireland, Newry... and the lush, salmon river valleys."
- **John Gillis, Syndicated Columnist, Washington, D.C., Author, Aspen Publishers, Inc.**

About the Author

Nina Harkness draws on childhood memories of growing up in the privileged post-colonial traditions of India's tea plantation society to create the story of "A Sahib's Daughter," her first novel.

She left the Himalayan region to pursue a career in public relations and journalism in London and Northern Ireland, working as a freelance magazine contributor to "Northern Woman," "Ulster Tatler" and "Northern Ireland Homes Interiors & Living".

She married an Irishman and raised their two children, Andrew and Laura in Northern Ireland before the family moved to Florida in the late nineties.

She now lives in Naples, Florida where she is writing her second novel "Marry My Daughters."

Made in the USA
Charleston, SC
11 January 2014